I'll Come Back to Get You

by Jeff C. Stevenson

A HellBound Books Publishing LLC Book
Houston TX

**A HellBound Books LLC
Publication**

www.hellboundbookspublishing.com

Printed in the United States of America

Also by Jeff C. Stevenson

Fortney Road, Death, and Deception in a Christian Cult

The Children of Hydesville

Special thanks to Stevie Nicks for the title,
but not the plot.

Jeff C. Stevenson

I'll Come Back to Get You

I'll Come Back to Get You

**"I and the public know
What all schoolchildren learn,
Those to whom evil is done
Do evil in return."**

–W.H. Auden, *Another Time*

April 5, 1994

Dear Diary,

As I write this, that little girl is outside my window again. I've waved to her, tried to coax a response. She ducked her head, moved behind the shrubs, hid herself from me. I suppose she's shy. But a few moments later, she's there again, looking up at me as I gaze down. This has been going on for several days, maybe a week.

I wonder who she is, and why is she so intent on watching me?

<u>The First Week</u>
Carl

On the day her husband was kidnapped, Adel Daniels woke before the alarm clock buzzed. She felt elated. It was this delighted feeling that had aroused her from sleep. *Ecstatic*, she thought, as she nuzzled in closer to her husband's back. Carl slept on; Adel was gentle in her embrace, not wanting to disturb him.

Joyful. Content. Enthralled. Delighted. The cheerful words danced before her closed eyes like cartoon characters. *Why am I so happy?* she wondered.

She sighed. Smiled lazily. Lots to be happy and thankful for. Her six-year-old son, Scotty—soon to be seven—was at a magical age. He was the light of her and Carl's life. And Carl, of course; married ten years, still in love, the affection and kindness of early attraction had remained. He was her foundation, her rock, and had created the family they relished. Best of all, they still *liked* one another.

His business, the small electronics shop he co-owned, was going well, was turning a profit, a nice one, after almost seven years of hard toil. Most new start-ups in Manhattan failed at the five-year mark, about fifty-percent of marriages eventually collapsed.

"We beat the odds," Adel whispered to herself. "We're *winning*."

She eyed the clock. Still a few minutes before the alarm went off. It was nice to be awake, have the luxury to be still, to not have to move about, to be somewhere; time to think about the past, the present, the future; a few moments to rejoice, be thankful. Once the alarm sounded, Adel would be the first one up. She'd wash her face, brush her teeth, and make herself presentable to the two men in her life, the first she'd encounter that day. They both loved to sleep; it was up to her to start their day.

Adel didn't consider herself a housewife; she was a home engineer, and she kept things running. Without her, Carl and Scotty would continue to snooze until nine or ten. Then they would dally over the paper or the news (Carl) or play games (Scotty) on the iPad. Without her motivating them to get up, get dressed, eat breakfast, get going…well, that's why the alarm was on her side of the bed. If it was near Carl, he'd hit the doze button repeatedly.

And then where would we be? she thought, spinning out the consequences. They'd be unwashed, unfed, the shop would fail, Scotty would never make it to school, and he would be a dropout before starting second grade.

She glanced at the framed glow of light around the edges of the window. Even with the shades pulled, curtains drawn, the mid-September sun was trying to make itself known in the room. The Indian summer persisted; it would be another fiery day, but at least it was Friday. Tomorrow, they could all sleep in, spend some time together without being scattered in three directions. *It's like we're shot out of a circus cannon each morning*, Adel thought, visualizing the long fuse, the three cylinders pointed at the sky, the gleeful clowns lighting the long coils like tails at the base, then each of them shooting off in a different direction.

Boom. Boom. Boom. Scotty to school, Carl to the shop, and she to her part-time job in Brooklyn.

She held on to her husband for the few remaining minutes before the alarm went off and the day would begin.

The day her husband would vanish.

#

"Hurry up, sweetie! Breakfast is ready. The Captain is waiting for you," Adel called out to Scotty. She poured the skim milk over the Cap'n Crunch cereal, set a toasted bagel, cup of coffee down at Carl's place.

"Carl? Breakfast."

"Right here," he said, coming up from behind her, kissing her neck. "Mmmm," he murmured, his hands on her waist. "You feel so good."

She reached behind, patted his freshly shaved face. "You, too." He released her, she turned, they kissed good morning as Scotty climbed into his chair at the table. Carl reached into Scotty's bowl, tried to steal one of the golden corn squares.

"No, Daddy!" Scotty squealed, protecting the bowl with his hands. Carl pecked his son on the top of his head, then stuck his tongue in Scotty's ear. He was rewarded with wild squirms, shrieks, and giggles.

"Okay you two, eat!" Adel said. "Work and school await."

"Daddy tried to steal my cereal!"

"Yes, he tries every morning, champ, but you are just too fast for him."

Fifteen minutes later, Carl and Scotty were finished

with their breakfasts. Carl herded his son into the bathroom to brush his teeth while Adel put their few dishes into the dishwasher. When she turned around, they had returned to the kitchen, both with their arms up like monsters, toothpaste foam running out of their mouths.

"Grrr!" they both growled. "Arrgh!"

"What funny clowns," she said, clapping with delight.

"Mommy! We're not clowns, we're *monsters*!"

"Yeah," Carl said, "scary monsters."

"And we're going to eat you up!"

"But if you eat me up, who's going to make dinner?"

This stopped both monsters in their tracks. They consulted. Carl finally said, "Maybe we shouldn't eat Mommy right now. Maybe we'll just nibble on her so she can still make us dinner? What do you think?"

Scotty nodded as toothpaste foam dribbled down his chin. "Okay, we'll just nibble."

"Don't come any closer to me," Adel warned. "If you get any monster drool on me, things will get *really* scary around here. Now, wipe your faces so we can to leave."

Five minutes later, at twenty to eight, Scotty darted down the hallway of their apartment building so he could push the elevator button. Adel called after him in a loud whisper, "Scotty! Don't run. People might be asleep."

After double-locking the door, Carl caught up with his wife and son. Once they were in the lobby, Scotty called out a cheerful good-bye to the morning doorman, Mel. Carl and Adel nodded at him, smiled, stepped out into the already-tepid September morning. Carl kissed his wife and son goodbye, started down First Avenue to his shop which was within walking distance. It opened at eight-thirty, closed at five. He always arrived by eight in case anyone showed up early. When the day was done and he had cashed out, he was always home by six.

Hand in hand, Adel and Scotty headed west for the four-block walk to his school. When they arrived, she hugged and kissed him goodbye. He fled into the building. She stayed, chatted briefly with the other parents dropping off their kids, then headed to the garage to retrieve the car for her drive to Brooklyn where she worked part-time at the Second-Hand Rose thrift shop.

She had taken the job months earlier after reading a profile about the store in the *Times*.

With Scotty in school all day, she found she was restless for something to do and the store sounded like a good way to occupy her time. Plus, Adel had been impressed that a portion of the income was donated to the Nelson's Most Needy orphan outreach charity. She had a special place in her heart for those who had been abandoned. She had always given money to Feed the Children and other international organizations to assist the needs of the less fortunate.

"Can't you find anything local?" Carl had asked when she told him about the job.

"Not with these hours. I can be home before Scotty finishes school. Besides, I like getting out of the city during the day. It's perfect for me too since I love thrift stores, so I think I'll do great. Plus, we're paying for the garage space but we so rarely use the car that it seems a waste and—"

"Okay, okay!" Carl had said, hands raised in surrender. Smiling, he told her, "You're right, we don't drive the car much, might as well earn some money to at least cover that expense. And if there is anything that gets donated that I could fix, send it my way, right?"

Adel smiled as she recalled the conversation. She

eased the car out of the garage. It really had turned out to be a lot of fun at the store, and she had taken items home for Carl to repair, so it had worked out well for everyone. Waiting for a break in the traffic, she glanced through the windshield up at the sky. At that exact instant, a cloud passed over the sun.

She sighed contently, expectantly. The elated, all-is-right-with-the-world feeling she had awoken with remained.

It was the type of Friday morning in which anything could happen.

# # #

That afternoon, Adel arrived back in the city as she always did just before 3:30. She felt grimy, sticky, was desperate for a cold shower. The car's air conditioning wasn't working very well, didn't seem up to the task of doing its job.

After leaving the car in the garage, she hurried through the thick humidity to Scotty's school. They shared an ice cream cone as they meandered home through the oppressive heat. Adel only half-listened as Scotty chattered on about his adventures at school. For some reason, she felt unfocused, felt exhausted, wanted silence, wondered if she was coming down with a bug. It required a lot of effort to pay attention.

"Mommy!" the sharp rebuke cut through her weary distraction. "You're not listening!"

"Sorry, honey. I'm just tired. It was so busy at the store today," she said, although she couldn't remember much of what had gone on. Some days—most days— were like that, passing so swiftly and uneventfully, they barely registered. Had it only been that morning when she'd actually had ten minutes to herself to just be thankful? It seemed like days ago. "Do you want to go with me while I do my errands?"

Adel knew Scotty would not want to stay with her; he had become addicted to watching the cartoons stored on the DVR. Carl had found the ones he loved as a kid and Scotty was immediately entranced by them. They recorded them off the Cartoon Network, so he now had a steady diet of *Rugrats, Johnny Bravo,* and *Ren and Stimpy.* Before he could howl in protest at the very thought of missing them, she patted him on the back. "Just kidding, champ! We'll go home now so Mommy can get cleaned up. You can stay with Sally and watch cartoons on your iPad, okay?"

Once they were in the apartment, Scotty turned on the TV, Adel quickly showered. It felt better than she had expected, the cold, spikey water rattling against her face, down her breasts, her stomach, between her legs. Cool at last, *thank God*, she was cool at last. She dried off, saw that it was already four-thirty. She needed to go grocery shopping, wanted to be home by six when Carl returned. She called his cell to see what he wanted for dinner, it went to voice mail. She texted, waited. No response. She tried the shop. Neal, his partner, answered.

"He got a call for some big estate sale," he said.

"Where was it?"

"Oh, man, let me think. Queens, maybe? Or Brooklyn? I think it was Brooklyn, but no idea where. Some woman who worked in IT is moving and had a ton of stuff she wanted to sell. Carl left about noon, haven't heard from him since, so he must be happily wheeling and dealing."

"Too busy to answer my calls and texts?" Adel asked.

"Yep," Neal kidded her. "You know how he is with

this kind of thing."

"A kid in a candy store," she agreed. "Okay, thanks, Neal."

Adel took Scotty next door, told Sally she'd be back by six, kissed her son goodbye before he pulled away, settled on the sofa with his iPad and cartoons.

"What did mothers do before television?" Sally asked.

"Imagine what it was like before DVRs and iPads," Adel answered.

# # #

Adel was home before six. She turned on the news and unpacked the groceries while Scotty colored. Her phone rang.

"Hi, Mama. How you doing?"

"I'm fine, my bell. Just called to see how you're handling the heat. Awful, isn't it…?"

For as long as she could remember, Adel's mother had called her, "Adel, my bell." Just after she was born, she had been holding Adel as she fussed, all red, screaming, arms and legs kicking. Mama rocked her gently, listened to her wails, all the while staring into her little face.

And that's when she saw the bell.

Adel's face, flushed with her robust cries, had peaked bright red yet just below her left eye, in the center of her cheek, was a faint, pale spot that looked like a tiny bell. The more she wailed, the deeper her face flushed and, in turn, the more prominent the tiny white bell became. The nurse had explained that a baby's complexion didn't really settle for a few weeks, in the same way an infant's hair color could also vary week to week, shade to shade.

"You'd think they were involved in intense, internal

debates about exactly what they want to look like," the nurse said good-naturedly over the protesting howls of Baby Adel. "Usually, those little blemishes are shapeless, but you're right, this one looks like a tiny, little bell."

"Yes, I can see it. Clear as a bell!" Mama had said, delighted with her discovery. From then on, it was always Adel my bell.

Her mother phoned her from Westchester when she could. Adel knew her mother's memory was fragile, easily broken, and frequently wandered.

"Is Scotty getting excited about his birthday?"

"Oh, yes. I told him that seven is a magic number, so he's looking forward to an extra special birthday and party."

"Seven years old already," Mama marveled. "And you're right, that is a magic age. I remember when you turned seven…"

Adel glanced at the clock, almost dropped the phone.

It was six thirty. Where had the afternoon gone?

And where was Carl?

"Adel? Honey, are you there? I have to go now. I'm being told others are waiting…"

Scotty wandered into the kitchen, whined that he was hungry, asked where his Daddy was.

"I'm going to call now to find out, champ." She hastily said goodbye to her mother. Carl wasn't home yet and she needed to find out where he was. She dialed Carl's cell. It rang and rang and rang. Never went to voice mail. She texted him—*Where are you?*— watched the message confirm that it was delivered, waited for the *Read* indicator to appear to confirm he had seen the text, and waited a few seconds for the composing bubbles to begin, indicating that he was answering her.

Waited. Waited. Waited.

Nothing happened.

She knew the shop would be closed but she tried the number anyway. The answering machine with Carl's voice picked up.

She kept staring at the phone in the palm of her hand, willing it to react to her messages.

"What's wrong, Mommy?"

She was suddenly perspiring in spite of the air-conditioned apartment. Moisture rolled down her back, rivulets of apprehension. Carl had never been late before. *Never.* For anything.

She shuddered. She rubbed her arms. Blood pulsated in her head; hard, fast, a nervous beat. Was she overreacting? Why was she suddenly so nervous, so scared?

"Mommy?

Scotty was standing before her, staring up. He seemed so small and vulnerable; he reminded her of one of those Feed the Children photos. Abandoned, fearful, alone. She hunched down, pulled him to her, hugged him so tightly that after a moment he started to squirm in protest. She released him.

"Mommy, what's wrong?" he demanded.

Without thinking, she asked, "Where's your Daddy?"

"He's at work. Right?"

"No, he should be home by now. See the time? Remember, he's always home by six, when the two hands slice the clock in half..." While Scotty carefully studied the clock, Adel went to the window and looked out, hoping she could see eight floors down and identify Carl from the hundreds of people she saw on the street. He'd be the one hurrying into their building.

She didn't see him or anyone who even resembled him.

Adel buzzed the doorman. No, Carl hadn't come

through the lobby yet. She called the repair shop again, hung up before the answering machine kicked in. Called him again, texted him again.

"Mommy?"

"What!?"

Scotty cringed at her tone.

"What is it, honey?" Softer this time.

"I'm *hungry*. Where's Daddy?"

"I…don't know, champ. But maybe we should get you something to eat, okay?"

She was just spooning the pasta onto Scotty's plate when her phone rang. Adel answered before the second ring.

"Hello?!"

"Hello, my bell. Is Carl home yet?"

"No, Mama, he isn't. I'm worried."

"No one answered at the shop?"

"Mommy? Who's on the phone? Is it Daddy? I want to—"

Adel shooed him away, turned her back to him so she could concentrate on the conversation with her mother. "I called the shop, twice. No answer. Same with his cell. It just rang and rang, he didn't respond to my texts. I'm going to call Neal at home, see if *he* knows anything."

"All right. You do that. You let me know, okay?"

Scotty left the table, started to ask another question, but Adel shook her head, pointed at the table. "Eat!" she instructed. He trudged stubbornly back to the table, plopped down in front of his plate.

"I *hate* you, Mommy" he muttered to himself.

Adel dialed Neal's cell. He lived in New Jersey, took New Jersey Transit, should have been home. She listened as Neal's phone rang, watched her son slowly spoon the pasta into his mouth. He caught her staring at him and glowered hatefully at her. She stuck her tongue out in return which caused him to smile. He turned away so she wouldn't see him giggle.

"Hello, Neal? It's Adel. I was wondering about Carl. Do you know where he is? He isn't home yet. Did you hear from him after that estate sale?" Adel leaned against the kitchen wall, needed something solid to hold her up. She didn't want to overreact, didn't want to scare Scotty, but she couldn't help feeling frightened.

"Mommy? Look!"

"...never did hear from him. What time is it? Almost seven...?"

"Mommy! Look at me!"

"...did you leave a message?"

"Mommy!"

She turned in fury to her son and shouted at him. "Stop it! Scotty, stop it!"

He had been playfully sticking his tongue out at her. Startled at her outburst, he flinched, dropped his fork on the plate with a loud, sharp clatter. He whimpered, "Don't yell at me." The tears filled his eyes, his face crumpled up in despair. "Where's Daddy? I want Daddy..."

"Neal? I'm sorry. Scotty was making some noise. What did you ask?"

"Did you try the shop, leave a message there? You know he sometimes forgets to turn his phone on. Maybe he had a lot of stuff in the truck to unload?"

"I tried the office, just got the machine."

He didn't respond, she couldn't think of what else to say, still felt disoriented. Her mind stalled.

"Adel? Do you want me to come back in? I could meet you at the shop, see if—"

"No, you don't need to do that. Thanks. I'm sure he's...just delayed. Something came up, maybe he lost or broke his phone..." Her voice stopped, she was unable to form any other words.

"Call me back and let me know when he gets home, okay? I'm sure he's fine. But call and let me know, all right?"

"Yes, yes of course. Thank you, Neal. I'll call you when he comes home." She felt like she was just repeating back what he had said, like she was an answering machine. She turned, saw her son was sulking at the table. She had planned to have wine with dinner, went ahead and poured herself a glass. After just one swallow, she dashed to the bathroom, gagged, vomited. It took her several seconds to recover. She gazed at herself in the mirror. Almost didn't recognize the reflection. Her eyes were glassy, unfocused. She blinked several times, tried to make herself appear more…alive. She washed her face, dried herself. It was still too painful to see the woman in the mirror. Whomever she was, she was clearly on the verge of an emotional collapse. She had to be strong for Scotty and whatever was ahead for them. She brushed her teeth to remove the sour taste.

"Maybe it's nothing," she told her reflection. "He'll come home any minute."

Adel returned to the kitchen, looked at the clock.

Seven-thirty.

Carl was now ninety minutes late.

# # #

Adel looked at her phone as she had been every few minutes. No returned calls or texts from Carl. The awful pit in her stomach and fluttering apprehension in her chest seemed to change locations, switch places over and over so she felt dizzy, like she was about to topple over.

What had happened to Carl? Where was he?

Call the police now, or wait? But for how long? If he's not home by eight? Or midnight? Or in the morning? God, she couldn't make it through the night without him! *I can't even make it for more than a couple hours,* she realized. She steadied herself against the wall, made her way to the sofa where she laid down, stared at the ceiling, begged her mind and body to calm themselves down.

"Mommy? What's wrong? Where's Daddy?"

She gathered Scotty in her arms, held him tight, felt the light-headiness pull back a bit. He didn't resist her embrace; he tolerated her need for him. "I don't know where Daddy is, champ," she murmured into his shoulder, her voice catching, then cracking, breaking. She couldn't help it. She was scared, felt so alone. She wept, Scotty patted at her tears.

"Mommy, don't cry. I'm sorry I was loud. Don't cry."

She wasn't able to stop. Something deep inside of her suddenly broke loose like a centuries-old rock formation that pulls free with no warning, crashes into others, causes a cave-in or an avalanche. She could feel the shift inside of her, the dangerous *whoosh!* as the hole—the emptiness—was created, a huge, hollow place. All she could do was cling to Scotty, lock her arms around him, hold on for dear life. That was enough for the moment. He nestled himself deeper into her arms. She pulled him onto the sofa. Together, they gradually slipped into a listless, unsteady slumber.

# # #

Adel woke with a start. Scotty stirred in her arms, his thumb in his mouth, something he had given up a couple years earlier. *Hadn't he?* she thought, then wondered why they were asleep on the couch. She looked over at the kitchen clock.

Ten-thirty.

It all rose up, rushed back at her, knocked her over as it shook her up her new reality: *Carl had been missing for more than four hours.*

She gathered Scotty in her arms, carried him to bed, tucked him in, kissed him goodnight.

He murmured something, then clearly asked if Daddy was home, he wanted a kiss, was Daddy home?

"Soon, champ, soon."

Adel returned to the living room, her heart pounding so hard it was hard to swallow. Terrified at what she was doing, for the first time in her life, she called 911, was transferred to the police.

"Hello, I need to report a missing person," Adel said. "I know I'm supposed to wait 24-hours but it's my husband and—"

"No, ma'am, that's not true," the male voice on the phone said. "That's TV and movie stuff. There is no set amount of time that has to pass before you report someone missing."

Relief swept through Adel, tamping down some of her fear. "Oh, I'm so glad."

"We can do this over the phone or I could send an officer over to your home."

"Oh. By phone is all right."

"Okay, let me open this incident report. Now, you said it's your husband. Is he elderly or suffering from any mental or physical condition?"

Adel shook her head. "No, he's 32, in fine health."

"How long has he been missing?"

"Since six p.m. He's always home by then. I waited only because I thought I needed to wait. I've called and texted, called his business partner, no response."

"Do you have any reason to suspect he's the victim of a crime?"

God, no! she thought, all the panic returning. *Oh, God, no.*

"Ma'am?"

"I'm sorry. No, I don't think so. I mean, maybe, since he hasn't called—"

"You could call the local hospitals, see if they have anyone who matches his description. That's probably a good place to start at this time. And before we proceed, you should know that people over the age of 18 legally do not have to return home."

"But we have a son! A family, we're a *family*. He wouldn't just take off, leave us alone, abandon us," she said, realizing she was babbling.

"I understand. But look, unless we can prove that there was an involuntary disappearance such as the victim of a crime…"

She waited for him to continued.

"What I can do is open a file up, get the paperwork going. How's that?" He began to ask her a series of questions: Carl's full name, a detailed description of his height, weight, hair and eye color, date of birth, any unique identifiers.

"What are those?"

"Things that would set him apart. Does he wear glasses? Any distinguishing marks, scars or tattoos?"

Adel continued telling the officer all she knew, all she could remember: What Carl had been wearing when she last saw him, his last seen or known whereabouts— "an estate sale in Queens or Brooklyn, but I don't know the address. His partner, Neal, didn't either"—a list of places that he frequented, friends or relatives that he may have been in touch with. When the questions were done, he said, "Email me a recent photo."

Adel nodded, logged on to the address he told her, uploaded and sent a picture of Carl, and was given a case file. The officer stayed on the phone with her the entire time.

"How often does this happen?" she asked when the process was finished. She didn't want to hang up, didn't want to be left alone.

"People missing? In New York, we have about 13,000 cases a year. Most come home or are found in a matter of hours, usually within 48 hours."

"What happens now?"

"Like I said, since he's an able-bodied adult that you have no evidence to believe has been involved in a crime or abduction, he'll be added to the system as missing."

"What system?"

"We have a couple. The National Crime Information Center, or NCIC, works as an electronic clearinghouse that every criminal justice agency nationwide has access to. Your husband's file was just included. We also use the National Missing and Unidentified Persons system, or NamUs, and you have access to that too."

Adel wrote down what he said, along with the website addresses, listened closely as he explained about the online databases that were used for missing persons records.

"Families, law enforcement agencies and investigators use it to search nationwide for missing persons," he said.

"So, you'll be using these sites while you're out looking for Carl?"

"He'll be in those data bases. If the police do happen to come across your husband, they are only legally allowed to ask him questions, to make certain he is acting on his own free will, is mentally and emotionally stable. You'll receive a call that they have spoken to him. Most police agencies will tell you where they found the person, but they will not detain them."

"But what do I do?" Adel could only imagine an endless set of computers—the system—all blinking in place, but none of them able to physically move or actually locate Carl.

"Like I mentioned, contact local hospitals and you could hire a private investigator," the man suggested. "He or she will focus all their time and attention on finding your husband. But they can be expensive. I think you should wait a little longer, see what happens."

Adel rubbed her forehead, sensed the conversation was about over, that the man was out of ideas now that Carl was in the system.

"There's no one I can talk to in person?" she asked. "To help move things along?"

The man said, "Your local precinct where the case is reported will handle the logistics first. Give them a couple days. If your husband isn't home by…Sunday, call them. That precinct will hand off the case to the Missing Persons Squad if your husband is not found." He hesitated. "Ms. Daniels, I want you to remember that this is not a special category case, so it's best to give it a few days, then call your local precinct. That would be the 19th Precinct."

Adel nodded.

The voice asked, "Have you and your husband had some disagreements lately, some

financial difficulties, alcohol or spousal abuse, unfaithfulness on either side—"

"No! No, nothing like that. None of that," Adel said, feeling as if she had to choose one of the options but none of them were correct. "We're happily married, have a son, a business that's doing fine. A good life, a family! No problems…like that. I love my husband. He loves me. Everything's fine. Except he's missing…"

"I'm sorry, Ms. Daniels. Be sure to sign up at NamUs. Remember, most of the time missing persons show up, they return home. Goodnight now. I bet your husband will be home soon."

# # #

Carl didn't return that evening. Adel called, texted him a dozen more times, always with the same result. She had finally phoned Neal, told him Carl still hadn't come home, told him about filing the report with the police, all that the officer had said.

Neal told her he'd call the hospitals. An hour later he reported that none of them had admitted anyone matching Carl's description. Adel thanked him, said she'd call him as soon as she knew anything. There was really no one else to contact; Carl had no brothers or sisters, his parents had died years ago, Neal was his closest friend. If anyone they knew had found Carl, they would have called Adel immediately.

After checking on Scotty who was sprawled out in his bed in a tangled mess, Adel went to the NamUs site, registered, filled out all the information about Carl, submitted it, finally fell asleep on the couch after 2 a.m. It didn't seem right to sleep in the bed alone without her husband. That had never happened before. She had never been without Carl in their ten years of marriage. It was something she had insisted on, never spending the night apart.

She woke many times, her stomach always clenched in fear, her chest tight with apprehension, her thoughts a jumble of anxiety and uncertainty.

Where was Carl?

Funny how the day had started out so special, a morning filled, for some reason, with such promise. Everything had been so *right* in the early daylight. Now, in the darkness of night or the misery of pre-dawn—whomever was awake now was only stressing over dire circumstances—a terrible premonition had settled about her, a distress call that was sending out a constant, repeatable beacon: *Carl is injured and close to death, Carl is dying, Carl is dead, Carl is injured and close to death...*

The message was like a drumbeat in her head, a heartbeat that pushed the disturbing thoughts throughout her mind over and over and over again.

# # #

Saturday morning Neal called to say he was at the shop and the van wasn't there. He was going to report it stolen. He asked if he could stop by to see her, if she needed anything, wanted anything.

"No, Neal, but thank you. Thank you. I'm just...waiting for Sunday so I can go to the police station. It's the waiting that's driving me mad; time seems to pass so slowly..."

"Have the police called you or followed up?"

"No. It's in their system. Just sitting there, I guess. If he was a child or older or ill, they'd be all over it, dogs, helicopters, police everywhere."

The morning crept by. Scotty was subdued, watched cartoons but rarely laughed or giggled at the antics. He kept returning to Adel, hugging her, crawling into her lap, something he hadn't done in some time. She spent the morning hours on the NamUs site. Her file had been approved, but there were no updates. She visited other websites for missing persons—The Lost & The Found, The Charley Project, North American Missing Persons Network, the Community United Effort—joined chat rooms and forums, but soon discovered most were for children who had been abducted. She checked Craigslist and similar sites to see if anyone had posted about an IT estate sale in Brooklyn or Queens.

Her reserves of self-control were used up quickly. She had snapped at her mother twice when she had called, told her that *of course* she would call her with any news or as soon as Carl returned home. Adel had no patience for Scotty's behavior; he wanted to know where his father was, when he'd be home. Since she had no idea, he continued to ask, not able to understand the disappearance of his daddy. He clung to his mother, didn't want her to disappear too but also lashed out at Adel when she couldn't answer his simple questions, his hurtful words adding to her grief.

Affection and rejection came and went between them all morning. By 10 a.m., it got to be too much. Adel called Sally to watch Scotty. "I can't just sit here, doing nothing. I'm going to drive around…see if I can find out anything. Maybe I'll spot the van somewhere. I don't know what else to do."

She blasted the air conditioning in the car, felt it dry her eyes as the minutes added up into an hour. Headaches came and went; she ignored them, knew the pounding refrain was due to the stress of having her husband vanish from her life.

Carl, where are you? Where did you go? Why?

Hours passed as she drove around, looking for the van. Time itself and her thoughts were blank slates, a time card she never punched in or out of. Her single-minded desire was to *find him*. Nothing else consciously registered with her. She returned to the apartment for a few hours.

"Anything?" Sally would ask anxiously at the same time Scotty plowed himself into Adel's arms.

"No...I just drove around the streets near the shop, then to Brooklyn. Neal thinks it was Brooklyn where Carl went. I drove up and down the blocks, asking if people had seen the store van. I'd show them pictures of Carl from my phone. No one knew anything."

She then ventured out again late Saturday afternoon, searching for her husband.

# # #

Finally, Sunday arrived. Adel called the police station, gave them her case number, spoke to Assistant Chief Steve Willards, Commander of the Manhattan detectives in her precinct. He told her to come by the station that afternoon. She spent the day driving around again while Sally watched Scotty.

Adel walked the few blocks to the 19th Precinct on 67th Street. It was just after four p.m. and the heat simmered just as it had for the past many days. The street seemed strange to her, too loud, too colorful, too fast moving. There was an end-of-the-weekend atmosphere about the neighborhood; people were oblivious that her husband had been missing since Friday night and showed no concern or compassion for her ordeal. They had all enjoyed their weekend as if nothing out of the ordinary had occurred.

The five-story building loomed in front of her, right next to the fire station built in 1887 of red brick with bluestone copings and terra cotta trimmings. Three police officers were on the elevated front entryway, chatting with one another. Adel took a deep breath then hurried up the steps, pushed hard against the old wooden double doors. Once inside, her attention was first drawn to a Memorial Wall that honored every officer killed in the line of duty while working at that precinct. The faces of the fallen stared intently at her.

She had never been in a police station before but wasn't surprised at what she found. It was just like a TV or movie set. The walls were cream-colored, wire baskets overflowed with paper forms, clipboards were attached to the sides of cubicles, computer terminals glowed serenely on desks that were housed behind the maze of small offices, phones rang and rang and rang; men and women crisscrossed around the area, holding papers, talking on cell phones.

Adel stood at the front counter, waiting for a black couple to finish completing a form. The woman was cursing under her breath while her boyfriend patted her shoulder. The female officer behind the counter was staring impatiently at the upside-down forms as if the words were insects she was eager to stamp out as soon as possible.

Finally, it was Adel's turn. "My husband has been missing since Friday. I have a case number, I called and I'm supposed to meet with Officer Willards." It was as if another woman was speaking. The voice was calm, didn't falter, was firm, decisive. Adel marveled at her own composure; she had been rehearsing the words on the walk over but to actually say them out loud, without bursting into tears or wails of grief…well, she had done well. She felt like an actor in a play who had spoken her line correctly. Now the officer would respond in turn.

"Let me get Willards," she said, reaching for the phone.

Adel nodded, thought about how rude she had been to Mama over the weekend, how short-tempered with Scotty. Even with Neal. Pushing people away, that was all she had done.

"Ms. Daniels?" A handsome, blond-haired man in his late thirties was speaking to her. "I'm Assistant Chief Willards. Why don't you come back here with me where we can talk?"

She followed him down a corridor lined with glassed-in offices. Detective Willards was broad-shouldered, had a slow, easy walk, secure and confident in each step he took. *This is the person who will try to find Carl,* she thought. *My husband's life is in his hands.* She glanced around as she strode past other police officers. Everyone around her was busy, talking on the phone or gesturing to nervous or angry looking people, or speaking in low tones to individuals bent-in close, wanting to hear every last word. Some conversations were gentle, tones of comfort, others were sharp, to the point, scary or bleak with black-and-white facts. One woman was shaking her head, crying. A young man leaned back in his chair, arms crossed, his expression one of sheer boredom.

The officers all looked up and nodded at Willards with respect or friendship or both. *He has a good reputation here,* she thought, calming herself, allowing herself to feel hope. *He'll find Carl.*

"Here we are. Why don't you have a seat. Would you like coffee or water?"

Adel declined with a shake of her head. Her throat felt tight; she was suddenly shaky-nervous. She would have preferred speaking with that woman she had first met up at the front desk. Willards closed the door, sat behind his desk. She looked at him, aware of the strong, experienced sense about him. He was sizing her up too, his kind blue eyes tight and focused on her. He fiddled with his computer. Adel sat up straighter, all at once feeling that she was a target, feeling exposed, suddenly unsure of herself. *Calm down, my bell,* she imagined her mother saying. That helped.

Willards leaned toward her, smiled briskly, took aim at her. "Let's start with some basics, just confirm that the information you filed was all accurate." He typed rapidly with two fingers as she verified what she had said late Friday night or corrected bits that didn't seem right to her. Her voice was dry and tight, her answers short, almost brittle. He asked her again if she'd like some water. "I know this is difficult," he said.

He's on your side, Adel reminded herself. *He wants to help.*

"No, I'm all right. Thank you."

He nodded. "Why don't you tell me again what happened. Don't leave anything out."

"Carl never came home Friday." She stopped. What else was there to say? "He's always home by six. *Always.* Or he would call me." She continued, telling Willards what little she knew. Carl had taken a call about an estate sale, apparently in Brooklyn, a lot of computer equipment. No, he had not told Neal the address, simply taken the van, which was now missing. Yes, Neal had reported it stolen. Willards check; no, it hadn't been found yet. Yes, she had checked the hospitals, no there had been no fights between them lately, no money problems, no, their accounts had not been touched, no unfaithfulness between them...

Willards asked many of the same questions the officer had on the phone. It went on and on and on. He typed in her responses, added a list of items and follow-up inquiries. Sometimes the same question was phrased differently but she gave the same answer. She saw on the wall clock behind him that an hour had passed since she had sat down.

"Let's find out more about you," he said. "Any siblings?"

Adel shook her head. "Only child."

"Parent's living?"

"Just my mother."

"What's her name? Where can she be reached?"

"Olivia Nelson. She…can't. She's been at the Ferncliff Memory Care Facility in Hartsdale for many years. Dementia. When she's alert, they have her call me. On her good days. We speak but…"

Willards nodded, understanding, the computer keys clacking. When he was finished, he looked at her. "I'm sure the officer you spoke with on the phone told you that we now have two paths to go down. Any adult or vulnerable adult age 18 or older who has Alzheimer's, dementia autism or another cognitive disorder, brain injury or mental disability and is at credible risk of harm, they're immediately put into the Missing Vulnerable Adult Alert Program. Was that explained to you?"

Adel leaned closer. "I'm not really sure I understood. I just want to find Carl. I don't care how it's done or what you call it."

"The thing is Ms. Daniels, based on the information you've given me, your husband would not qualify to be part of that program. If he was, information would be distributed electronically throughout New York State to every police agency, all the television, radio stations and newspapers. It would also be sent to the New York State Thruway travel plazas, toll barriers, airports, bus terminals, train stations, border crossings."

"Yes! That's what I want!"

"But Ms. Daniels, that's not the path we're able to go down with your husband. He's a healthy, able-bodied man and we can't devote those resources to him. About 13,000 adults go missing every year in this city and—"

"I know the statistics, but what will you *do*? I don't

understand why I'm here, answering questions when you should be looking for him like I have been looking for him all weekend!"

Calmly he said, "People go missing for a number of reasons, Ms. Daniels. This type of crisis shakes relationships and families. You've done the right thing to file this report. There are some other things you can do. Check your husband's Internet activity. It may provide some clues as to what he was thinking or where he was planning to go."

"He wasn't planning to *go* anywhere," Adel said, furious at the insinuation. "He has a son, a wife, a family! He would never abandon us! Why can't you understand that?"

"I do understand. All I'm saying is to check. Look at his emails, his social media pages, any sites he's looked at lately. It may mean that your husband went missing willingly—"

"Why am I supposed to do *everything*!?" she shouted. "Why won't you help me find my husband? You say he's in your system but nothing is happening!" Her hands were tight, fists had been made. She felt like she wasn't being listened to, as if they were speaking different languages. She tried to calm herself down, ease the rapid breathing, slow her pounding heart.

Willards gave her a moment, then continued. "Look over your bank accounts. If you use a joint account, any unfamiliar purchases should raise red flags. This goes for your husband's business partner too. Hire help if necessary. Private investigators and missing person search firms take on these types of cases." He waited, wanted to be certain she was listening, wasn't going to explode again. "Ms. Daniels, doing everything I've talked about can increase your chances of learning your husband's whereabouts. Most importantly, you must be patient. You must take care of yourself for your own sake and for your son. If you have a church or temple or some type of community of people or friends that can help you emotionally, you need to reach out to them. Let people know what's going on."

Adel let the tears well up, dribble down her face, didn't bother wiping them away. "I'm sorry. I love my husband," she said quietly. "He would never leave me. He would never leave my son."

"Ms. Daniels, people rarely go missing without a reason. You've called the hospitals, he's not been admitted anywhere, so as far as we know, he hasn't been injured. We consider missing people as sort of an indicator of a problem that may exist in someone's life."

"What do you mean?"

"Let's think about this. Allow there to be the possibility that Carl left on his own, all right? Do you have any idea at all why he may have chosen to leave now, at this particular time?"

"No! I've told you—"

"Wait, Ms. Daniels. I'm trying to help. Hear me out."

"No! You don't understand or haven't heard me. Scotty's seventh birthday is coming up in a few weeks. Carl *loves* his son, detective. He would never, ever, *never* leave us!" The tears returned, the shaking, the anger.

Willards handed over a box of tissues, told her the department was going to look into the file she had opened, they *would* follow up, do what they could to find her husband. "If he's not found soon, we'll hand the case off to the Missing Persons Squad, which will continue working on it." He was glad to see his words calmed her a bit. "Listen, I've done this for a long time. I want you to know that they *always* have a reason for leaving, even if you don't want to admit it. And they most always come back. Hold on to that, all right? Most always, they *do* come back."

# # #

Adel left the station clutching a copy of her statement, a print out of the incident report and her case number, along with several phone numbers to call. It was now close to six on a Sunday evening. Nothing had really changed for her since she had left her apartment. She had somehow imagined that the detective would simply type Carl's name into the computer, his location would pop up, they would go and claim him, like something in the lost and found. But Willards admitted he couldn't even track the GPS in Carl's cell phone without a court order.

How did this happen to me? she pondered furiously. *Carl swore that he would never, ever leave me…*

# # #

When Carl had proposed to her ten years earlier, he was twenty-two, Adel was twenty, and he had only been in New York a few months.

Originally from Michigan, he had kidded her by saying, "We're both getting on in years and unless one of us has some dark, nasty secret from their past, I see no reason why we shouldn't spend right now—and the future—together!"

She had laughed off the proposal the first time. They had continued to date. Two months later, he repeated his offer. This time, he slipped a ring on her finger, said he wasn't taking no for an answer. Then he kissed her firmly on the lips. *Sealed with a kiss,* Adel had thought blissfully. Then she had pulled back. "On one condition.

Promise you'll never leave me?"

"Promise."

"Never, ever, *never*?"

"Never, ever, never!"

Adel had been swept up into Carl's focused, orderly life, which so mirrored the concise world of electronics and all things in that universe that needed to be repaired. His plan was to open a repair shop with his best friend from college.

"And you'll be the girl behind the counter whom everyone falls in love with," Carl had declared. "You'll be great for business."

She had only worked with them for a couple years before she discovered she was pregnant with Scotty. "Nobody is going to fall in love with a pregnant lady behind the counter," she had playfully mourned when she told Carl. "Sorry to disappoint you."

"You haven't disappointed me. You've made me the happiest man in New York and I'm more in love with you than ever."

Scotty was born the day after she turned twenty-three. The business prospered, their life together flourished. At last, Adel had a *family*. She felt settled, at home, at rest. Everything had been going so right. Since she was a little girl, she had wanted to be married, have a child, a family. Until last Friday, she had had it all.

She trudged up the street to her apartment. Carl had promised—had sworn—he'd never leave her.

Never, ever, never.

Now, he was gone. How could he be gone?

#

Monday morning, Adel woke with a headache. She hadn't slept much; there was a terrible knot in her stomach, a pain that had kept her curled up in a fetal position, apprehensive throughout the night.

With her eyes closed, she reached out to the other side of the bed. Carl's side. Vacant. Abandoned. Sheets cool to the touch. Unslept in. Absent of any warmth. She sighed with despair, felt as if she had been scratched hollow inside. She didn't know what to do. Go to work? Call in sick? Pull the blinds, snuggle up with Scotty all day or send him to school? Officer Willards had said they most always do come back, so maybe she should stay home, be there when he returned, keep Scotty by her side. Or give in to the tears that were always filling her eyes? Yield to the pain, the panic that was nervously fluttering about her, insects zeroing in for the sting?

She wept until she had exhausted herself, then laid there.

After drying her eyes, she looked at the dresser where she had propped up the three small dolls she had played with as a child. Mementos from long ago. But they were more than that, they were true friends, companions from her childhood. Another life. Not much from her past brought her comfort, but they always did. They were usually kept in the drawer next to her jewelry box, out of sight. She had gladly set them aside when she had married Carl, knew they were a bit childish even though he said he didn't mind.

But now that he was gone…the past was on display again. Last night she had pulled them out of hibernation. There they sat, staring at her, their blank, glass eyes sharing her sorrow, her misery. Silent comfort.

Adel watched them watching her. She thought that if things continued, maybe someday soon she'd rally the courage, dig through the jewelry box, and read again from that painful book, relive—

She closed her eyes. *Shut out the image*, the thought.

Some hidden things should stay that way: locked away in the dark.

Waiting around with her son all day was pointless, did nothing to help locate Carl or bring him back to them. After talking it over with Scotty, he agreed that maybe he would like to go to school and see his friends, but she was to come by to get him the instant his daddy got home. She nodded; that was a good plan. When she dropped him off, she spent time with the teacher and principal, tearfully explaining what had happened, told them to contact her immediately if Scotty needed her.

Her mother had called, asking if Carl was home yet. Adel did the best she could to explain what was happening, what the police had said. She didn't want to alarm her mother, but still wanted her to be kept in the loop and hoped she was able to understand what was being told to her.

Then Adel had gone to work. Just like it was another normal day.

# # #

Monday afternoon at 3:30 when Scotty saw her, he rushed into her arms, immediately started crying, asking about his daddy. Seeing how upset he was brought it all crashing down on her, a tidal wave that had subsided for a few hours. Maybe she shouldn't have left her son at school. Carl was never out of her mind, not for an instant. Obviously, it was same with Scotty, whose miserable face tore the wound open again, fresh and stinging. She did the best she could to calm him down. They walked home hand-in-hand through the ever-oppressive heat, taking comfort in one another's shared anguish. Once they were in the lobby of their building, Adel collected the mail while Scotty ran over to push the elevator button. Tucked in with some bills was a gray envelope addressed to Adel Daniels. There was no return address. *A letter?* she marveled. *Who writes letters anymore?*

Her heartbeat quickened. She didn't know why. She nodded at the other residents on the elevator, yet her eyes returned to the gray envelope. She wouldn't open it until she was back inside her apartment and Scotty was watching television.

Once Scotty was engrossed in his cartoons, she examined the envelope postmark. It was smudged, difficult to read, but it had been sent from the New York area. She could feel something square and stiff inside. When she opened it, she found a Polaroid photograph.

Who takes Polaroids anymore? she wondered before registering what the image was. It took her only seconds to confirm the figure she was seeing.

It was a picture of Carl.

The Polaroid trembled in her shaking hand. She looked carefully, moaned to herself. Her eyes filled with tears. She wiped them away, had to *see.* She backed into the kitchen table, fumbled about as she pulled out a chair, collapsed into it. With both hands, she studied the image again.

The photo was of Carl sitting with his legs tied to a piece of furniture. A chair. His hands were covering his eyes as if he was playing peek-a-boo. Prominently displayed on his chest was the front page of the *New York Times*; it looked to be a recent issue, Adel recognized the cover story, something about children receiving flu shots. At the bottom of the picture there was a white margin. In that space, in heavy block letters, was written:

I'LL COME BACK TO GET YOU.

The phrase was vaguely familiar to her, but she was

unable to concentrate on it because her mind had abruptly become a maze of questions. Why was the front page of the newspaper shown? Why did that matter? It meant something, she knew it did…

She hadn't cleaned the apartment over the weekend. Frantically, she moved aside empty pizza and delivery containers that were still scattered throughout the kitchen, found the unread paper from a few days earlier. She located the page that matched the one in the picture. It was from Friday's edition, the day Carl hadn't returned home.

Kidnapped. The word snapped into her mind, a label, a description. A reality.

Carl had been kidnapped.

"Oh, my God," was all she was able to whisper to herself as she rocked in the chair, staring at the picture, unable to look away. Cartoons played out for Scotty; she didn't want to upset him, didn't want him to hear her, but *oh, my God, oh, my God...*

Billboard thoughts about her husband flashed past her: *Why have they taken you? Who are they? Are you okay? What do they want? Oh, my God, Oh, my God, Oh, my God...*

She turned the Polaroid over. The back was glossy black. There were some indentions lightly marked on it. She was able to decipher some letters as she titled it back and forth in the light. **SCOTTY** was written in simple, barely perceptible block letters.

She flipped the photo over.

I'LL COME BACK TO GET YOU.

Turned it over again to the back.

SCOTTY.

Adel's hands started shaking so violently, she thought she was having a seizure, was about to pass out. She had to see Scotty, confirm he was still in the room with her. She spotted him in the living room, too close to the TV. Of course he was there. Engrossed in what he was watching, paying no mind to her.

Her mind began to skid over thoughts as they cascaded toward her. Whomever had taken the photo of Carl had mailed it to her, so he or she—or they—know where she lived. "Probably where I work too and where Scotty goes to school," she said to herself. "And they knew where Carl worked, they probably called him, led him to that estate sale. It was a trap to kidnap him. They know who we *are*…"

I'LL COME BACK TO GET YOU.

Something about the phrase was familiar, but there also was an implied threat. Would they come after Scotty next? Was that why his name was mentioned? Why were Carl's hands over his eyes? That too was oddly disturbing to her. Her questions stacked up like file folders. Trembling, she had to put the picture on the table so it wouldn't shake loose out of her hand. She focused on controlling her breathing, on calming herself down. She wiped her eyes, exhaled a few times.

Gradually, reason began to assert itself: She'd call the police, they would listen now, do something *now*. They would have to. No one would be able to take Scotty from school; the staff knew they were never to release the children to anyone other than their appointed guardian whom they knew by sight. She and Carl—like every parent—had signed papers to that effect. Adel walked Scotty to and from school. There was no way someone could *ever* take Scotty.

"Never, ever, never," she whispered.

But they had taken Carl, a voice somewhere in her mind slyly whispered.

I'LL COME BACK TO GET YOU. SCOTTY.

Adel examined the picture again: Carl, secured to a

chair, hands over his eyes, the paper in front of him. Carl, alive as of Friday. *Proof of life,* she thought all at once. *That's why they sent the photo with the newspaper in it. To prove Carl was alive, as of Friday. But what do they want, why send me this? What do they want?*

# # #

After calling the police, Adel left Scotty with Sally, telling her she'd be back as soon as she could, that something had come up. She hurried to the police station, almost unaware of the blast of heat the stunned her once she had left her building.

Willards waved her into his office. She handed him the envelope which she had put into a sealed plastic bag. "I don't know if you can get anything off of it," she murmured numbly, her hands tightly clasped. "Fingerprints or fiber or something."

He smiled at her. Everyone watched cop shows. He studied the photo carefully, turning it over several times. "This picture indicates that as of the publication date of the paper, he was alive last Friday and in the possession of whomever abducted him. I know we went through all of this Sunday, but I'll ask again: Do you have any reason to suspect anyone in particular with this kidnapping?"

Adel immediately shook her head miserably.

"What about this phrase 'I'll come back to get you.' Mean anything to you?"

She shrugged. "I…thought it did, just for a moment. Like a song or something, you know? But I really can't place it."

Willards sat back in his chair. "And there is no request for a ransom, and that usually occurs immediately." He paused. "And the way the note reads,

'I'll come back to get you,' with Scotty's name on the back might be an implied threat."

"That's what I thought," Adel said.

"They are trying to frighten you, perhaps stating that your son is either…a ransom? No, that's crazy. Or the target of another abduction? But it's just strange there is no demand for a *cash* ransom…" His voice trailed off as he mused on his own life, his own response if it were to occur to one of his kids. Divorced with two children, he knew he'd fight to the death rather than see one of his kids harmed. He shifted in his seat, wiped perspiration from his forehead, thinking *Crazy from the heat.* Crime increased with the temperature, but nothing this bizarre had ever crossed his desk. *Damn Indian summers or climate change or whatever it was called.*

"There have been no attempted abductions of your husband or son before this, have there? Nothing the school or your son have mentioned? Nothing suspicious at all, no cars or strangers following, nothing like that?"

"No, there hasn't been anything like that at all."

Willards nodded, cutting her off. "I know this seems very repetitive but that's usually what it is, asking the same thing over and over and over; you never know when something might come to mind that you forgot. We have to wonder why the abductors didn't take your son to begin with if that was their goal, right? Or why threaten to come back to get him now that they know we'll be involved. They should be demanding a specific ransom, and soon. Nothing vague or implied, nothing we have to figure it. It doesn't work that way with kidnapping. I'll get a profiler on this case to begin to sort it out, give us an idea of the type of person or persons we're dealing with.

"Also, we'll make arrangements to have all your mail examined before it's delivered to you. I doubt if there are any fingerprints we can use—there usually aren't—but the fewer people that touch your mail, the better chance we have. You've had no unknown callers who hang up or anything like that, right?"

She shook her head.

He jotted down some notes. "We'll contact your phone carrier for access to any calls or texts made to you as soon they occur. We'll operate this under concurrent jurisdiction so the FBI will join us as a shared task force. They can assist us, get involved in the case if warranted—"

"What do you mean, if warranted? Please, I want them involved *now*, I want *everyone* involved to find my husband!"

"We will," Willards quickly assured her. "The FBI *will* handle the K and R aspects—"

Adel's blank expression brought him up sort.

"K and R stands for Kidnap and Ransom; they have a division that focuses solely on that aspect of the case. They will act as your security. They have a seasoned negotiator who will work with you. If the kidnapper contacts you for a ransom, the negotiator will automatically be patched in to the call. This is the best way, Ms. Daniels."

Adel wiped her eyes and nodded. "Do you want to tap my phone?"

Willards smiled again. *Too many cop shows.* "Actually, we don't tap phones, we track them now. Most cellphones have tiny GPS units inside. We know that each call we make is routed through towers that can be used to usually pinpoint a phone's location to areas as small as a city block."

"Can't you track Carl's phone right now to find him? I was told you needed a court order…"

"Not now that he's been kidnapped. We just need

permission from you and your carrier."

She gave him the information and he made the call, waited to be put through to the proper authority, then spoke on the phone for several minutes, wrote something down. He ended the call. "Carl's phone GPS stopped all activity last Friday at 1:37 p.m."

"Where was he?"

"Just a few blocks from the store."

"That doesn't make any sense," Adel said. "He was in Brooklyn somewhere."

"Unless he was finished and on his way back to the shop."

"But the van, it's missing. I don't understand…"

"Maybe whoever took him grabbed his phone, disabled it a few blocks from the store. That would explain why that was the last activity captured by the GPS."

Willards picked up the photo of Carl, held it out to her.

"Is there anything in the environment of this picture that looks familiar? Is your husband being held someplace you recognize in any way? We're going to use biometric scanning to see if we get any hits as to items in the photo, textures and so on, but you may see something we'd never zero in on."

Adel reluctantly held the picture. She hated touching it, knowing that whomever had taken Carl had also touched it. She swallowed, looked closely again at the image. It was a very tight shot, just from Carl's head to his legs tied to the chair. The background was deep shadow black, the lighting was just enough to recognize her husband, the front page of the newspaper. She gazed as long as she could, then shook her head. "No, there's nothing there that I recognize."

Willards typed into the computer, all the while

thinking but not telling her his thoughts. On average, a kidnapping is usually over and done within a week. Nobody wants to risk losing a loved one with any tricky delay tactics, so the money or demand is handed over quickly. But in this case, he assumed they were dealing with an extremely unstable, probably delusional person, or persons. What he couldn't understand and had never encountered was why someone would "keep" an adult— the husband—send a proof of life photo along with a threat of abducting the son but demand no ransom. It made no sense.

"I'll send this report along with a scan of the photo and the words to the profiler so they can start work on this." There was a knock at the door, two detectives squeezed into the room. Willards introduced the officers who would be assisting him on the case. "They'll need to spend time with you, going over the situation once again."

Helplessly, Adel looked at Willards. "Please, can't they read the report. I've told you all I know, all I remember…"

"I understand," he said, "but you may have missed something, they may ask you a question in a different way. Remember? We talked about this."

"What about Scotty?"

"We'll have a police officer to escort you to and from the school each morning and afternoon. And the officers you'll meet with now will interview the school staff tomorrow to see if any of them have any information, and they will talk with Neal to go over his customer list, as well as the people you come in contact with at your job. You never know if there might be an angry parent at the school or a customer, so we're going to interview *everyone* who knows you or Carl or Scotty."

Adel nodded, grateful. She glanced at the clock on

the wall. She had already been there two hours. Exhausted, she followed the two officers into a conference room and called Sally to ask if she could feed and watch Scotty. Once she was done, she took a deep breath, told the officers, "Last Friday, my husband went missing. He's always home by six…"

# # #

On Tuesday morning, Adel called her boss, Nedra Whyler, at Second Hand Rose to say she'd be a little late, had to meet with the police again about a few things. The officer was waiting for her and Scotty in the lobby. Although he was still terribly distraught over his daddy, the boy thought being escorted to and from school by a policeman was fascinating. Adel managed a smile as Scotty chatted nonstop, asking all sorts of questions. He was disappointed when told not to touch the officer's gun.

Adel met Willards at the principal's officer, where two of Scotty's teachers and two FBI agents from the task force listened to her tell her story all over again. Then Willards answered the faculty's questions. Later, he walked Adel from the school to the car garage, cautioned her to stay alert, to be careful.

"Careful of what?" she asked wearily. "This kidnapper doesn't want me, he wants my son."

# # #

It was Friday, early evening, one week since Carl had been abducted. Mama called just as Adel was preparing dinner.

"How are you, my bell? I've been so worried but haven't had the chance to call."

At the sound of her mother's voice, Adel felt like crying, giving over to the tears that were always so close. "I'm tired, scared, Mama. Scotty is too. He has these terrible nightmares …"

"You must be strong for both Carl and Scotty."

"I just don't understand it, Mama. Why would someone take Carl from me? I feel so alone without him…"

"What are the police doing? Any—"

"Not much that I can see, to be honest. They are protecting Scotty but I'm the one that drives around so late at night, looking for the van and for Carl while Sally cares for Scotty. It's like I can't sit still, I have to be *doing* something. I know it's pointless, sounds crazy. Then I get home, collect Scotty, put him to bed, go on the computer, checking sites, sharing information with others. I get to bed so late, get up, start all over again."

Her mother was silent for a moment, then said, "I wish I could do more for you. But I'm here for you, no matter what, I'm always here for you. Remember that."

Adel teared up, grateful again for her mother, wished she'd remember to call her more often.

"Remember, Mama's never left you. No matter what, I'm here for you."

"Yes, Mama," Adel said, feeling better, a warmth seeping in where only cold isolation had been. "Thank you, Mama."

"I love you, my bell but they are saying I need to end the call now."

"I love you, too, Mama."

May 10, 1994

Dear Diary,

My heart is full, overflowing! If only Reggie were alive, I know he would tease me with great affection, saying, "At long last, you have a child of your own!" She's like that to me, and she knows it, the scamp. I find it remarkable that she should seek *me* out, that she could see beyond all the trappings of influence and wealth and manage to worm her way into my life, my heart. After years of sorrow after Reggie's sudden passing, I feel like my life is in bloom again.

For so long I thought she was shy, peeking at me from behind the shrubs, scurrying away when I would wave or gesture at her to come closer. Like a frightened bird. But those days are gone! Now she's here most every afternoon when school is over. Seems her mother is also a widow or perhaps only single, is forced to work. No mention of a father. She's never been clear about either one. And she won't tell me her name, says it's a secret. I offer to guess, but quickly give up, decide to call her my angel. She likes that.

She isn't very clean, needed her hair brushed, her hands and knees washed. I sense she and her mother haven't much money. I offer to help, to meet with her mother, but my little angel refuses. Only wants to be alone with me. She tells me that if I didn't sit in front of the window and write every day in this book, she wouldn't have had the chance to watch me from below. Every day she would spy on me, she says. She tells me that I was always at the window, always there for her when she was looking for me. "I finally found you," she said, then gave me a smile.

"I didn't know you were looking for me," I replied.

She had only nodded, very seriously, then said, "Ever since I was a little girl."

After a few days, she said she wished she was my daughter! It makes me so sad when she tells me that, reminds me of all the children without parents. And the parents without children. How I long to bring them together in love! A love without secrets. A love that has no need to write down in diaries what can never be discussed, something that must be paid for in order to be silenced.

Leaving today for lunch with Deanna in the city. Billy's taking me to the station for the 10:45 train so I must get ready.

The Second Week
Graham

The weekend passed not unlike the previous one. Adel slept fitfully. She would get up to search and update the NamUs site, post in the other forums, chat rooms, and Facebook pages she had visited and the one she had created for Carl. No one posted anything of use, only sad faces and thoughts and prayers. Scotty would awaken her by crying out in his sleep. The result was that in the morning they would both be groggy, quiet. By late afternoon, they'd be spent. Exhausted, she'd take a nap, only to start the same process over again that evening. She lost weight, was nervous, agitated, called Willards too much; she knew she was, but couldn't help herself. He was patient with her. No news. No news. No news.

Sally watched Scotty whenever Adel wanted to drive around, looking for the van or showing pictures of Carl to people on the street. She put up fliers with his photo on lampposts and in store windows.

Sunday was the same as Saturday, a dull blur of anxiety, driving the streets, searching for the van, handing out posters of Carl. There had been no further communication from the kidnappers, no demands for ransom. Adel was so weary from checking the online resources, various websites, printing and passing out missing fliers and driving around that she felt half the time she was in a dream. Was this really happening? Had Carl really been taken from her?

Monday was the same as the previous Friday: Walk Scotty to school with the policeman at their sides, drive to Brooklyn to work, return home in time to meet Scotty and the police officer at the school, then walk home with them. It was like one long train, steel cables connecting each car, a chain that went around and around and around. Then, some type of dinner for she and Scotty, time at the computer, invite Sally over to watch Scotty while she went out, driving, driving, the avenues still dark even with the streetlights. Adel was losing hope, often wept as she navigated the night, wondering what she was doing? *God, what if Carl never comes back?* was the bleak thought that stabbed at her repeatedly.

Tuesday mirrored Monday in every way. Wednesday followed the same fashion.

It wasn't until early afternoon on Thursday that things finally changed.

Adel was at work when her cell phone rang. It was quarter to one.

"Adel? This is Willards."

"Yes?! What's happened?!"

"There's been another kidnapping."

"Another? But—"

"Penny Spencer is here—"

"Who?"

"Her husband, Graham, never came home last Tuesday night. In today's mail, she received two photographs. One was a picture of Carl, the other of her husband."

"Oh, no. Oh, my God…" Adel caught her breath,

waiting. "Did Carl look okay?

"Yes, hands over his face like the photo you have. He doesn't appear to be harmed, looked about the same as he did before."

"What about the back of the picture? Was Scotty's name there like last time?"

"No, but on the back of Graham's photo we made out the name of his son, Ben."

Adel's head was pounding. She didn't care about the other man or his son or wife. *Carl was alive! Proof of life. Life!* She sighed slowly with the relief. The noise in her mind receded like waves pulled back to the ocean.

"—familiar?" Willards was saying.

"I'm sorry, what?"

"On the bottom of Graham's photo, more of that poem or whatever it is. Does this sound familiar? 'One, two, don't be blue, I'll come back to get you?'"

Her mind was now buzzing, an irritating, humming sound.

"You there?"

Adel nodded. "Yes. I…don't recall that poem."

"Well, obviously there's a link between the two men. We need you to come down to the station. Maybe between you and Penny, we can figure out what the connection is."

# # #

The bright and glorious future of Penny Spencer crashed and burned the evening her husband failed to return home.

Usually, Graham went to the restaurant at three in the afternoon to prep for the evening crowd. Usually, he was home by one in the morning. Usually, Penny would be asleep.

Sometimes, if she wanted to talk, she'd tried to stay awake by watching the endless stream of late night talk shows. But regardless of the hour or her state of consciousness, when Graham arrived home, he'd wake her for a murmured hello, or a ten-minute whispered chat as he'd update her on the events at the restaurant or she'd tell him about her day.

On the night he didn't return home, she'd fallen asleep at eleven. Six-year-old Ben had been in an active, obnoxious mood, disrupting her work, keeping her on edge. She had been revising and annotating legal briefs for a friend's new firm. Ben, always underfoot, had been muttering hateful things at her. Exasperated, she'd been forced to set the project aside, give him the attention he demanded. After he had been put to bed, she resumed her seat in front of the computer, working on the files from eight to ten-thirty. Finally, with her eyes dry, heavy and hard to keep open, she had succumbed to exhaustion, climbed into bed, fallen asleep with the TV on.

A little after one a.m., the trebly laughs of a studio audience pulled her from slumber. The TV host was yucking it up with a sitcom star. The clock said 1:07.

"Graham?" Her voice was thick with sleep, sounded like a confused moan.

Penny yawned, felt the tremendous beckoning of dark sleep, like a riptide, circling her, pulling her down. She fumbled for the remote, flicked off the TV, called for her husband again, got the same silence. She turned on the bedside lamp. Glanced around. The bathroom light was off. The open bedroom door showed only darkness. She checked her phone; no texts. She turned the light off, drifted easily back to sleep.

Must be some event at the restaurant keeping him, her mind murmured.

# # #

She awoke with a start at 3:15 a.m., sat up in bed. "Graham?"

She turned on the bedside lamp, shielded her eyes from its glare, looked around. Bathroom and apartment still dark, no texts or calls on her phone. She dialed his number. Voicemail. She texted him, then called the restaurant; it rang and rang until the message kicked in.

Where was he? Her heart was on red alert, her breathing seized up tight. *Am I awake?* she wondered, *or is this a nightmare? Something this bad—a missing husband—doesn't happen in real life.*

"But he's not missing," she chided herself as she pulled on the bathrobe Graham had given her last Christmas. She checked on Ben who was sleeping soundly. His even, undisturbed breathing helped to calm her own erratic heartbeat, but only a little. Once she left his room, the panic rose up again, looming over her.

"Graham," she whispered, pulling the robe tight. "Where are you?" She called, texted again. Waited. No response. Then she did what she had always done when she was in a crisis. She called her older sister, Rebecca, who lived in New Jersey.

On the second ring, Rebecca answered groggily. "Hello? Pen, what's wrong?"

"Graham isn't home from the restaurant yet." Penny clutched the bathrobe, her knuckles sharp, white, no room for blood. Rebecca put the call on speaker so her husband, Michael, could hear.

Immediately, Penny felt as if she was taking an oral exam but without a grade to be given.

Michael's logical questions began, all of which helped to somewhat diminish Penny's mounting fears.

Somewhat. Michael was a pediatrician, so he was used to the unexpected, to late night calls, to hysterical or worried parents. He was an expert at "talking down the adults" as he called it, could quench the fear created over an insect bite, smooth over the uncertainty of a too-high fever, cheerfully explain away a lack of appetite, perk up a listless youngster. He was the doctor, Penny was now the patient.

He told her he was going to call the hospitals, taxi and limousine commission, Uber and other transportation services to see if anyone had picked Graham up from the restaurant. As he rattled off those practical steps to take (renewed anxiety swept over Penny) her eyes burned with tears. This was really happening.

Rebecca said, "Honey, I'm coming over. I'll be there within an hour, okay? We'll find Graham. Okay, Pen?"

Now shaking with fear, her hand sweaty, Penny couldn't speak.

"Pen? Are you there? We'll *find* him."

Penny tried to form words, but all that came out of her mouth was an anguished sob.

"I hear you," Rebecca said. "I'm on my way."

# # #

A lady in waiting.

The phrase flicked on in Penny's mind like a neon light.

Yes, I am a lady in waiting, she agreed.

She was waiting for Rebecca to arrive, waiting for news about Graham, waiting for him to return home or call or provide some evidence that he was alive and well. Her phone sat uselessly on the counter. She gazed at it reproachfully, its silence indifferent to her. It had become a lifeline, a thing that could give or withhold information. She had called Graham several times, shocked at how hysterical she sounded when she left him a message, tried to send calmer texts, but there had been no response.

It was now four in the morning. The stillness in the apartment expanded, a muffled heaviness that rendered her immobilized. What could she do? Or *should* she do, other than stare at the phone, pleading with it to communicate with her. It was her only link to Graham, but it seemed to be broken.

She rocked back and forth on the kitchen stool, whispering his name, a mantra of protection for him, a prayer for his soon and safe return.

At four-fifteen, the doorman called up that Rebecca was there. Penny opened the door, waited for her sister to arrive. Rebecca stepped out of the elevator, the sisters fell into one another's arms. Penny's numb, wide-eyed fright dissolved into hysterical sobs. Her sister took charge, led her into the apartment, closed the door behind them. Although they were close, spoke daily, they hadn't seen one another in a couple of weeks. Rebecca had recently been down in the dumps, a little withdrawn. Penny had inquired the reason, but her sister hadn't been forthcoming. Penny let it go, didn't want to push.

They held hands as if afraid of being separated. They settled on the couch.

"Graham *will* be found," Rebecca insisted, murmured the words into her sister's shoulder as they embraced. "Let's wait to see what Michael finds out."

Ten minutes later, Michael called. No transportation pickups from the restaurant, no one matching Graham's description at any of the local hospitals. "It was a quiet night, so it didn't take long to check," he said. "I think you should call the police."

# # #

After Penny completed the missing persons paperwork for Graham, she spent the next two days in a state of frantic turmoil, unable to sleep or eat much. But when she received the two photographs in the gray envelope in Thursday's mail, the case was immediately prioritized and moved to Willards' group. He contacted Adel, arranged for the two women to meet in his office. Penny arrived first, accompanied by Rebecca. He had asked them to try not to contaminate the photos, hold them and the envelope by the edges, put them in a plastic baggie.

"What's going on?" Penny demanded once they were seated. "You said you have *another* case like this one?"

"Yes, a woman named Adel Daniels. Her husband, Carl, was abducted a couple weeks ago—"

"Two weeks ago?" Penny and Rebecca said as one, alarmed.

"What's his name again?" Rebecca asked. She seemed startled by the information.

"Carl Daniels. Is the name familiar to you?" Willards asked.

Penny looked at her sister. Rebecca said, "No, but…is he all right?"

"As far as we know."

"But if he's been missing two weeks, why isn't this in the news?" Rebecca asked. "Shouldn't you—"

"We've kept it quiet since we think Adel's son, Scotty, may also be in danger," Willards explained. "Unfortunately, since there are now two abductions, it's going to get huge play in the media. I'm sorry for that in advance, but that's why we wanted to get Adel and you together, try and get ahead of the onslaught, see what you may have in common."

"But this guy, Carl, he's all right?" Rebecca asked again, then quickly turned to her sister. "Because if *he's* okay, then whoever did this will take care of Graham too. Right?" She looked back at Willards.

"We hope that's the case," he said. "Let me see the photos you received."

It was Rebecca who handed over the envelope, Willards noticed the sparking wedding band she wore, how it captured the overhead light, almost shooting off sparks. The ring held his attention for several seconds; he didn't often see stones that size up close. It was in a bold, six-prong platinum setting.

He examined the photos through the baggie. Both men were in the same position, hands cupped over their faces, legs secured to chairs, Tuesday's *New York Times* front page positioned on their chests. On the bottom of the front of Carl's photo, in the white margin, nothing was written. Nothing was etched on the black glossy back of the Polaroid either.

On the bottom of Graham's photo was written:
ONE, TWO, DON'T BE BLUE,
I'LL COME BACK TO GET YOU.

His son's name BEN was lightly carved on the black gloss on the reverse side of the picture.

"Do the words at the bottom of the photo mean anything to you?" he asked Penny.

The phrase *Dirty mother, dirty daughter* flashed through her mind but left no impression.

"No, not at all," she answered. "It sounds like a rhyme or something, right? Or a song?"

Willards nodded, shrugged. "We don't know, haven't come up with anything yet."

"What's with the photos?" Rebecca asked, taking

back the baggie, looking at the pictures again with Penny. "Why pose the men that way, with their faces covered by their hands?"

"The photos are actually a way to build trust with you. They're sent so you can see Graham is alive, that he's okay. This person becomes the only contact you have with Graham, or Adel has with Carl. But, no idea why they are posed like that."

"Why is Ben's name on the back of the picture?" Penny asked. "Why does this person know the *name* of my son? Why would he take my husband? What does he *want*?" Her voice was rising with each question, momentum building. Rebecca put her arm around her sister to calm and comfort her.

"We don't know yet, other than whomever is doing this, is keeping both men alive, sending these proof of life photos, yet no ransom demands."

"But is this kidnapper going after the children next?" Penny asked. "Is Ben in danger? Is *that* why his name is on the back of the photo? 'I'll come back to get you' sounds like a threat to me!"

Willards put his hands up. "We're not sure yet, but we have no reason to believe that. There were no attempts at abducting Scotty Daniels in the days before his father was taken, but he and Adel are under police protection now, just to be sure. There have been no attempts on Ben or Graham, nothing at all suspicious, right?"

Rebecca looked at Penny, who shook her head. "No, no nothing at all. Ben's only six, so I'm always close to him. I would know if anyone tried anything."

"They haven't demanded anything to get Carl returned?" Rebecca asked.

"There's been no mention of ransom for Carl. Would there be a financial incentive to abduct your husband,

Penny?"

She shook her head again. "Graham is doing well with the restaurant, but we're working hard just to keep ahead."

Thinking of her ring, Willards looked at Rebecca. "Adel has no other family, and she and her husband are not in the position to pay any significant ransom. Do you think this person or persons would reach out to you on behalf of Graham?"

Rebecca said, "My husband is a pediatrician but with constantly changing insurance plans, we're by no means wealthy."

He nodded. "Okay. It's just that when someone is kidnapped, the abductors don't care *how* the money or ransom is raised, they just want it done quickly. That's why I asked. If Penny didn't have the funds but they knew her sister did…"

An officer tapped at the door. Adel Daniels entered. After introductions were made, Rebecca quickly excused herself to use the ladies' room. "You okay, Pen? Michael's been calling, so I want to talk to him and the girls." She glanced at Willards. "I'll be at the front desk, okay?"

After Penny and Adel were settled in, they sat side by side in front of Willards like nervous school girls called into the principal's office.

Picking up where they had left off, Penny asked, "Why write the names of our children on the back of the photos?"

Willards admitted they didn't know. "But we don't believe child abduction is the ultimate goal because it's too much work for someone seeking to kidnap a child. Traditionally, this type of person would spend weeks or months fantasizing about the target. Then, in a fit of almost uncontrollable rage or desire, they'd snatch a child. And at that point, any child would do."

The two women shifted uncomfortably in their chairs.

"That's because their fantasy is never very specific," Willards continued. "This is true even with family friends or relatives. These monsters don't usually abuse or fondle their niece or grandchild because they want that *specific* child; they do it because it's convenient. The child is available to them, accessible."

Penny asked, "Then why would this person go to all the trouble to kidnap an adult, my husband, if he's really after my son? It's easier to take a child, right? It just doesn't make any sense."

Willards nodded. "I agree, and yet that's what we're dealing with in this case. And remember, we have no reason yet to believe Ben or Scotty are the targets. It's just implied."

After glancing through his notes for a moment, he said, "I thought it might help if the three of us met to talk about what has happened. What we're concentrating on right now is determining if there is any connection between your husbands."

The women glanced at one another again, nervous eyes, a cautious bond forming.

"You haven't met until now, is that correct?"

They both nodded. Another knock at the door startled them. Two members of the task force squeezed into the room. After everyone had settled in, Willards reviewed the two-week-old case, showing Adel the new Polaroids of Carl and Graham. Willards watched Adel's expressions. In the two weeks he'd known her, he'd noticed a profound change in her appearance. There was a hardening, a tightening was taking place, as if she was straining to keep everything perfectly cared for, cleaned, preserved. He had expected her to crumble, break as the weight of each day with no news was stacked on her. Instead, like a tortoise, she had drawn into herself and forged an impenetrable shell. When he spoke, she never broke eye contact with him. The phrase *lights on, nobody home* flashed through his mind, but he shook it away. She was very much aware of what was going on, had simply forced herself to deal with it for the sake of her son.

Willards turned to Penny. Her eyes were tired, had a panicky, wary look to them. Her body was rigid with tension, ready to break, not bend, as the onslaught pushed at her. In just two days, the ordeal was already taking its toll. She seemed desperate for answers, a ship lost in a storm frantically searching for the lighthouse, a safe harbor. He could almost hear her pleading with him, just as Adel had: *Tell me you'll find my husband, that you'll bring him back to me. Alive.*

# # #

Two hours later, when every question had been asked and answered, Willards finished by relating, "We're starting background checks on everyone at Graham's restaurant, staff and customers. And as you've both repeatedly told us, you know of no one who would be after your husbands."

"And there's no connection between them, either," Penny said helplessly, looking at Adel, who nodded. "Graham and Carl don't even know one another as far as we can tell. We have never met…"

Willards said, "There's a connection. Whoever did this knows both of your husband's work patterns and habits, knows your children's names. And there's still something about the 'I'll come back to get you' phrase that is key to all of this. It sounds like a children's song or poem or story. You're sure it means nothing to either of you?"

Neither woman spoke, glanced at one another as if waiting for the other to begin. Bewildered, they looked back at him. He said, "We know that because of where you both live, Scotty and Ben don't attend the same schools or play at the same playgrounds. You've said they don't share babysitters or doctors. Neither of you regularly attend any religious organizations and you've both stated that no one unknown to you has had contact with either of your sons or acted in a threatening way. But I want you to think carefully about this again. You're absolutely certain that no stranger on the street, no store clerk, no random person approached your sons? It may have been casual, an off-hand encounter, someone walking a dog that your child petted or perhaps they complimented you on your child's appearance."

"Well, that happens at times," Adel said. "People may say something *nice*. In the park—"

"Wait a minute!" Penny said excitedly. "Something *did* happen a few weeks ago. But it was a good thing, I think. We didn't feel threatened. This may not be anything but..."

"Go ahead," Willards said, leaning forward. "Go slow, tell us everything you remember." The two members of the task force seemed to wake up. All eyes were on Penny.

"Ben and Graham and I were in Central Park a few weeks ago," she said. "We were watching the model boats in the pond. We each had an ice cream cone. This person came over, asked to take our picture, said it was an assignment to photograph families in natural environments. We thought it was fun, sort of flattering."

"Was this person male or female?"

Penny closed her eyes. Her fists tightened as she

struggled at what she was or was not seeing. She shook her head, opened her eyes. "It's strange. I didn't get a close look or wasn't paying attention. He…or she…had…loose pants on, a cap, sunglasses. Skinny, I think. Hard to tell which gender."

"Age?"

Again, she shrugged. "I'd guess mid-thirties? Only because of the way he acted, you know? Not a kid, not a teenager, seemed older than someone in college, even though they said they were."

"He or she said they were in college? Did they say where?"

"He—maybe it *was* a guy—didn't say, only that he was taking a class in photography."

"Which college?" Willards asked again.

"I don't know, don't remember. Maybe he didn't say college, just a class."

She stopped.

"Penny? Take your time. What's wrong?"

She sniffed, pulled a tissue out of her purse, dried her eyes. "Sorry. I just realized what I was about to say. You see, we thought it was sort of flattering because this guy had selected us out of all the families in the park to photograph." Again, she stopped, cringed, shuddered. "Now I look back and…was that the guy? Was *he* the one that took Graham from me? Was he watching us, stalking us?"

"Keep with what happened," Willards said calmly. "Tell us everything about that day that you remember."

Penny nodded. "Um, he took several photos. He liked that we were eating the ice cream cones by the pond, just took pictures of us enjoying ourselves, all candid shots."

"What kind of camera?"

"Not his cell phone. A real one. It hung around his

neck."

"Remember the brand?"

"No, he was too far away. But it wasn't digital. I remember that. He said he had to shoot a roll of film. I didn't think anyone used film anymore."

"Lot of lenses with him? Or a camera bag?"

"No, just the camera. Not at all fancy, no extra lenses."

"He never said his name?"

"No. When he finished, he thanked us, offered to send us pictures if they turned out. Graham gave him the restaurant business card."

"Smart," Willards said.

"Yeah, Graham said later that with all the kooks in the city, of course he'd never give a stranger our home address or email or anything."

"Did he ever contact your husband?"

"Yes, Graham told me last week that the guy had called, left a message that the pictures had turned out great, he was going to leave prints at the restaurant."

"Did he leave a phone number?"

"I don't know."

"Was your husband planning to meet him?"

"I don't know that either. It really wasn't a big thing. At the time. You know?" She closed her eyes, placed her hands over her face. "God, it was him, wasn't it?"

"We can't know for sure," Willards said, "but we'll check into all of this, whom he spoke to at the restaurant, if he left a number—"

"It was him," Adel said dully. She hadn't spoken the entire time Penny had told of the encounter with the photographer. "There's a connection."

"How do you know?" Willards asked.

"He took pictures of us too," Adel answered.

# # #

"Where were you when you first saw him?" Willards asked. Now everyone in the office was staring at Adel.

"Central Park. Just like Penny. We were sitting on the benches, just as you enter at 72nd Street from Fifth Avenue. He came up to us…"

"Did you get a good look at him? Certain it was a guy?"

Adel glanced at Penny helplessly. "He was dressed like you said, sort of covered up, baggy clothes, with a cap, sunglasses. But I think it was definitely a guy. And like Penny, he never got too close to us. He spoke to Carl, talked to him more than me." She turned to Penny, asked, "Was that what it was like for you?"

Penny nodded quickly. "He wasn't very tall, shorter than Graham, who's five eight. How tall is Carl?"

"Five nine, so maybe he's more our height, five-five or five six?" She looked at Willards. "That helps, doesn't it?"

"Any facial hair?"

Both women shook their heads. Penny added, "But like Adel, I didn't get a close look at him. He seemed intent on only talking closely with Graham, almost like he was trying to hide his face or appearance from me. Kept the camera up in front of him a lot, of course, taking the pictures."

"Yes!" Adel said, grabbing Penny's arm in agreement. "That's it exactly, how it was with me. He spoke to Carl, I was busy keeping an eye on Scotty."

Penny said, "He kept telling us not to look in his direction, don't look at the camera, they were candid shots, just act like he wasn't even there. When he was done, he signaled Graham to come over. I turned away to care for Ben who had grown restless."

Willards asked Adel, "He offered to send the photos to your husband?"

"I…think so. I don't remember what Carl said."

"So, you don't know if Carl gave him his business card or contact information."

Adel shrugged.

Willards and the two other men were jotting notes. "What about his voice? Was there an accent or anything memorable about it? Gruff? High or low pitched?"

Both women pursed their lips, struggling to remember. Penny finally said, "Maybe…he was soft spoken? You know, polite, almost shy?" She glanced at Adel, who nodded.

"How about his mannerisms or distinguishing characteristics? Any tattoos or blemishes or marks on him? Moles, scars? Did he limp, stutter when he spoke, anything at all that would set him apart?"

Adel said, "Nothing at all that I remember. That's why it was so easy to forget it ever happened. And I didn't feel threatened at all. That's why I didn't think to mention it to you earlier."

Willards tried to sum it all up. "If he was in his thirties, then the photo course was probably just a hobby, not anything to work toward for a degree. We'll check into all the photography classes in the area, run a list of students and if there were any assignments like the one you both described. Anything else about him you recall?"

The women shook their heads. Penny asked Willards, "It was him, wasn't it?"

"Maybe," he said, then added, "Probably."

# # #

Rebecca stayed with Penny for two days, doing her

best to comfort her sister, get her to eat something, try to sleep. She FaceTimed with her daughters, spoke to Michael to keep him updated as to what was happening. The police were following up on the Central Park photographer but had quickly learned there had been no photo classes in Manhattan with that type of assignment.

"Tell me more about this Adel woman," Rebecca asked the second night as she and Penny finished a bottle of wine. It was after ten, she was planning to leave early the next morning and neither of them—nor Ben— had slept well the previous evening. It had been Rebecca's idea to put Ben to bed earlier than usual, split the bottle of wine in hopes it would relax them, lull them into a gentle slumber.

Penny shrugged. "I don't really know much about her. The police just keep asking questions, wanted to see if there's a link between us."

"And the photographer was the only connection?"

Penny nodded. "Other than that one event, we seem to live in very different worlds. Graham in the restaurant world, her husband owns a small electronic store."

Rebecca said, "I wonder if his repair shop had done some work for Graham's restaurant, or maybe they had the same customers? Have the police checked that out?"

Penny nodded. "Yes, they are checking into everything we could think of. Repairs, if they shared the same delivery services. All of that."

From the other room, Ben cried out for his mother.

"Coming Ben boy," Penny said. She glanced at Rebecca who suddenly seemed out of gas, slumped over a bit. "Maybe you should get to bed. Looks like the wine has done its duty."

By the time Penny returned, Rebecca was out cold on the sofa, snoring softly. *Too much to drink, too much talking, too much thinking,* Penny mused as she covered her sister with a blanket then crept off to her own bed. Fifteen minutes later, Ben called out for her again.

It was going to be a long night.

#

The next morning, Rebecca returned to New Jersey.

"Hug your kids for me," Penny said after a long embrace with her sister.

Once outside the apartment building, Rebecca hurried to the garage, claimed her car. Twenty minutes later, she was stuck in traffic just outside the Lincoln Tunnel. Her hands squeezed the wheel, tears sprang to her eyes. She had been holding them back ever since she had been in Willard's office two days earlier. Visually, all became a watery mix as she sobbed, an odd mixture of relief and distress. Relief in knowing that she hadn't suddenly been ditched by her lover of six months, distress because that man—Carl Daniels—had been kidnapped two weeks ago.

May 17, 1994

Dear Diary,

She loves secrets, my little angel does! Crawls up on my lap even though I tell her she's too big. Insists that she isn't. Loves to be called my angel.

When I ask her about her life, she quiets down. No word about her father. Not much about her mother or why they spend so little time together. Sometimes she's bruised or her face is streaked with tears. She doesn't like school or her classmates, that she had made clear. But when I ask too many questions, she grows restless, pouts, immediately threatens to leave, never to come back. Of course, I quickly reassure her, tell her it doesn't matter, she doesn't have to answer my questions. She asks me to promise to be there for her every day, and I tell her of course I will, I live here. She still won't tell me her name, I continue to call her my angel.

She asked why I write in here every day. I tease her, I tell her that it's easier to write down secrets and hard things, easier than saying them aloud to another person. "You have secrets?" she asked, wide eyed. "What if someone reads your secrets?" That's when I told her about the special hiding place in the desk. Of course, she immediately had to see for herself, had to feel the latch with her tiny, grubby fingers, watch the way the second drawer popped out. Over and over she tried it until I feared she'd break it. "Our secret?" she begged me to promise her, wanting to establish another bond between us. "Of course!" I assured her, it would be our secret. But it was really *my* secret, one that I shared with her, trusted her to keep to herself. Did she have one to share with me? She scrunched up her face, serious thoughts going on, but then shook her head. No secrets to tell me.

She's a bright, precocious little girl. I still can't fathom why she wants to spend time with me. She should be outside, playing with other children her age, but she insists she doesn't like them, wants to be here with me. How strange and wondrous to be loved by this child who is not mine and yet to be so hated and reviled by one who came from my womb.

The Third Week
Rebecca

Rebecca Roberts and Carl Daniels had met six months earlier. It was March, the chaos of the St. Patrick's Day Parade seemed to be everywhere. Rebecca had brought her children to the city where they met Penny, Graham and Ben for breakfast. As usual, her husband Michael was behind in medical insurance paperwork, so he missed the family outing.

"Too bad, but I'm not surprised," she had said dryly while he dressed in their bedroom. "But I had to ask, for your daughters' sake."

"What's that supposed to mean?"

"It means that when the three of us drive off into the city today without you, they will ask where you are. And I want to be honest with them, tell them the truth."

Irritated, Michael had said, "The truth is—"

"Work comes first," Rebecca had finished. "It's always first, always was, always will be, world without end. Amen. A pediatrician who neglects his own children…"

He sighed, wanted to take a moment, hold back his angry response, but she desired a fight, had already lit the fuse, was eager for the explosion.

Finally, he said, "You always make it sound like I'm *choosing* to be too busy to spend time with them. Or with you. You don't seem to understand how crazy it is right now, how behind we are in so many areas."

"I know *you're* too busy. That's what *I* know."

"Look, Beck, this is just the way it is now, okay? Why do you have to push harder on me when I'm already up against the wall?"

"Nobody's pushing you. I just—"

"Yeah, right."

Six-year-old Melody burst into the bedroom, immediately diffusing the explosion. Michael scooped her up, smooched kisses all over her belly while she squirmed, giggled.

"Stop it! We have to leave for the parade now!" she squealed. "You're coming, right, Daddy?"

"Sorry, monkey, I can't today."

Melody's bright, elated face clouded over. "Work again? You always work!"

He set his now-miserable daughter down. "So I hear. Like mother, like—"

They watched Melody scurry out of the room.

"How long do you expect to keep this up?" Rebecca asked.

"Well, let's figure it out, shall we? How long do we plan to continue paying the mortgage, the private school for Melody, the elite Busy Bees kindergarten for Chasity? *You* decided the public schools in this area were not good enough, remember? And let's see how you feel about the need to update your wardrobe every season!"

Rebecca closed the bedroom door, told her husband to lower his voice. She then glared at him as he continued to gut her with his words.

"That's your answer?" she asked. "Blame me?"

He turned, pulled a shirt out of the closet. "Not blame, just facts," he muttered. He dressed, studied his reflection in the mirror, left the room, called out a goodbye/have fun to his daughters. Rebecca swallowed the bile that had risen in her throat. It settled like a fireball in her stomach. She heard the low clank rumble of the garage door opening, his car roaring to life, leaving them all behind, then the steady sound of the garage door closing.

"Just like that," she said to the empty room. "He leaves you behind just like that. So easy."

# # #

Angry and miserable, Rebecca had driven the girls into the city that March morning. Tears had stung her eyes while the girls sang and played in the backseat. *I can handle this,* she thought grimly, her jaw clenched tight as she drove toward her sister's apartment. *Every marriage has a rough patch. I'll just drive through mine until it smooths out.*

# # #

Penny had made green pancakes in honor of St. Patrick's Day. Once she, Graham, Rebecca and the kids had finished, they all headed to the parade. The weather was spectacular, showcasing a bright blue sky, a dazzling sun, temperatures in the low sixties. The route was packed with an enthusiastic crowd. Rebecca felt her spirits lift. Who could resist the Boom! Boom! Boom! of the marching bands?

She didn't want Michael's hard words—or her own—to spoil the day for the girls. She glanced down to make certain Melody, Chasity, and Ben were still clustered together. They were giggling and talking excitedly about the floats, crowds, and music. She looked at Graham and grinned. He had his arm wrapped comfortably around Penny's shoulders. The sisters smiled at one another. Watching them, Rebecca suddenly became once again infuriated by the earlier encounter with Michael. The realization that he had so casually and with such indifference walked out on her without so much as a backward glance reignited her anger, the flames high, mighty and red-hot again.

"I need some coffee," she shouted into Penny's ear. "You or Graham want anything?"

She made her way slowly though the mass of people to one of the corner coffee stands that was a couple blocks away from the madness. She joined the line of people, feeling agitated and seething as she recalled Michael's behavior. Lately, he so often infuriated her and his behavior and their fights lingered like a bad aftertaste. After she made her purchase, she quickly turned from the cart. A man walked right into her. *Splat!* The cup's lid snapped off, hot coffee splashed all across the front of her sweater.

"Shit! Why the hell don't you look where you're going?" she cried out. The man started to apologize. She looked at him, managed to swallow the flood of choice words that she was preparing to fling at him. He was nice-looking, seemed genuinely horrified by what had occurred.

"God, I'm so sorry. Let me get some damp napkins. Maybe we can get some of the stain out before it sets in." He hurried away, returned in less than a minute, tried to blot the coffee stains. His hands were shaking. He stammered, "I'm so sorry. I'm such a klutz."

Rebecca almost laughed. The guy was sweet, honestly upset at what he had done. Anyone else would probably have shrugged, walked away, blamed the collision on her, called her a stupid bitch. Michael would have made no effort at all.

"Sorry," the man said again, giving up on the sweater. "This isn't helping much. I wasn't watching where I was going. It was my fault. Let me pay for the cleaning of your sweater. It's the least I can do." He fumbled for his wallet, his hands still nervous. He groaned, shook his head. "All I have is a five. Let's find a bank machine."

Rebecca hadn't had someone pay so much attention to her in a long time. It was always about the kids and when it was just she and Michael, it was all about his practice. This was all about *her*. The man gently grasped her arm so they wouldn't be separated as he cut a path through the crowd. She didn't resist, felt herself being slightly lifted, as if a gentle wave had latched onto her, was tugging her up and about. She found she was letting herself go with the flow.

He turned back, shouted, "My name's Carl."

"Rebecca."

Soon they had left the boisterous parade behind, were able to converse without raising their voices.

"Sorry, again. I'm not always such an idiot."

"Well, I could have been more careful myself," Rebecca admitted. "I just turned without looking."

He grinned at her; she liked his smile. When was the last time Michael had smiled at her, or even grinned or looked at her for any length of time? She didn't want to think about Michael.

"You live around here?" he asked.

"No, I'm in Jersey, here with my kids for the parade. How about you?" She was glad Michael wasn't with her, was relishing the time spent with this man, enjoyed the fluttery feeling in her gut. It was fun to be silly, giddy. She hadn't felt like that in a long time.

"Upper East Side, here with my son."

But not your wife? Rebecca wondered, very much aware she had snipped any mention of Michael out of her introduction.

"Here we are," Carl said. He held the door. They were the only two in the ATM booth. It was quiet, calm, another world from the crowded, noisy streets outside. She watched his back as he punched his code into the machine, heard it make grinding noises like it was creating the cash right then. A few pings. He turned, glanced at her, smiled again, she responded. Her weak grin felt tight, fake. *Unused*, she thought. *I really should smile more.* He was a good-looking man. She liked the way he sought her eyes when he smiled. He held her gaze, she knew he enjoyed looking at her.

"How's forty?" he asked, holding two twenties. "Might that cover it?"

Their hands touched. Rebecca felt hot all over her face. Blushing, the tight smile reared up again. She met his eyes. Neither of them looked away. She didn't take the bills, he didn't release them, their fingers continued to touch.

Dazed, Rebecca heard herself speak. "It's not enough."

He blinked. "Oh? Well, then, how much?"

"I think I want…more." Amazed she was being so forward, so silly, so obvious, she also had that sense of buoyancy again, that feeling of being lifted. She knew exactly where this was heading, just as if she was writing down one of the children's events in her daily planner. This was going to happen, she would *make* it happen.

His puzzled expression softened into certain understanding. He closed his hands around hers. *I'm doing this,* she thought, *this is happening.* She never thought about her legs or the effort they went through to keep her upright, but when they started to go soft on her—*weak at the knees,* she realized—she had to take a breath to clear her mind. A warm, sensual tingle nestled over her hand as she remained in contact with his. *How long since I've held another man's hand?* she wondered.

"What about our kids?" Carl asked quietly, never looking away from her.

The world shifted unsteadily for a moment. That's right: Melody and Chasity were waiting for her, along with Penny, Graham, and Ben. She had to get back to them. They'd be wondering where she was. She couldn't do this. What had she been thinking?

Rebecca continued to hold his hand. His grip hadn't changed. She willed him to stay connected to her, to concentrate on one another, to find a solution.

"What *about* the kids?" she managed to ask, wanting him to figure things out.

"What about my wife?" he said, the words soft, sorrowful. "And…your husband?"

The silence in the ATM felt stale, hard, all chrome, grease and machinery, nothing soft or anything close to yielding to what was on their minds. Anticipation, desire, a little magic, it all vanished when there were no answers to the questions. They were simply two people in a gray, metal chamber where people gathered to obtain currency. It was all business. The lift, the rise she had been experiencing was replaced with the solid heaviness of gravity.

She tugged slightly on the cash, he released the bills into her hand, she tucked them into her purse. Now flustered, chagrined that she had actually followed this man down the street to the bank machine…what had she been thinking? What had gotten into her?

"I should get back," she said. "They're going to wonder what happened to me."

Carl smiled again. "Oh, they'll know what happened."

Startled, she said, "What do you mean?"

Carl gestured at the stain on her sweater. She looked down at it. He touched her chin. She felt a powerful thrill surge through her. Again, her legs weakened a bit. He lifted her face to his. He moved nearer to her. He was going to kiss her, but at the same time, he was giving her a brief instant to pull back, step away, put the brakes on, if she wanted to.

Without hesitating, Rebecca stepped closer.

# # #

Soon after they met in March, Rebecca started driving into the city to meet Carl once or twice a week during his lunch break or whenever he could make an excuse to be out of the shop. Melody was in school most of the day and Rebecca arranged for Chasity to have a play date after her shorter day ended, which meant that Rebecca had the morning and afternoon to herself. And she had her car and plenty of prepared excuses to tell any noisy neighbors. Shopping in the city, visiting her sister, waiting in line for half-price Broadway tickets. Any excuse would do if anyone bothered to ask about her comings and goings. Most didn't, just waved if they saw her in the car.

Only two problems were uppermost in her mind when she met Carl, time and location. Since he and his partner were sole owners and employees of the electronics repair shop, they worked hard, so Carl's time was limited, but they made it work.

In early April, over sandwiches at the Farmer's Deli,

they exchanged life stories. He said he loved his wife and son very much but—

"But what?"

"But…there has always been something missing, I guess, between me and Adel. We've never really met in the center, if that makes sense, never crossed over. They always say you become one in a marriage, but we're still very separate. I think of it like a double helix, you know, you twist and turn over the years and eventually…become one united couple. That's just not us. She always…held back a bit."

"Have you talked about it with her?"

He shrugged. "It's hard to put into words without offending her or sounding like an idiot. I've realized over the years that we just don't fit together. And you can't fix that."

"What about counseling? Or leaving?"

Carl shook his head. "No, it's never *that* bad. Besides, it would destroy her."

"Oh, please!" Rebecca said. "No woman is *that* fragile. We all hurt, we all bruise, but men don't destroy women. Eventually we heal."

Carl waited a moment, then said, "She made me promise to never leave her. Never, ever, never."

"So, what are you doing with me?"

"You know what they say: Never say never."

When lunch was over, she left him a block from his store so no one would see them together. As he walked away, Rebecca continued to stare after him, willed him to turn one more time to look at her.

"Look at me, damn it!" she whispered playfully to herself.

He opened the door to the shop. Then, just before he disappeared from view, he turned, looked back at her.

Rebecca beamed. Carl vanished into his store.

# # #

Carl checked for places that rented by the hour, cash only. He settled on the Capri Hotel which was a few blocks from his store. It claimed that "Your Privacy is our Concern." It also promised to be clean, discreet, and very accommodating. The building was old, easy to walk past without noticing. Perfect.

It was May first. Carl told his partner Neal that he was going to scout out some used equipment on the West Side, would be gone for a couple of hours. They were always on the search for used pieces to replace what needed to be repaired or if they were attempting to rebuild and resell an item. Neal nodded as he flipped through a catalogue.

Rebecca met Carl in front of the hotel at 12:15, right on time. He paid cash as requested, and they took the elevator to the fourth floor. Carl opened the door of room four. The double bed sagged, the faded, peeling wallpaper was decades old, the air was stuffy, smelled of stale cigarette smoke. Carl grimaced, struggled to open the tiny window. Rebecca looked around the small, unpleasant room. Out of nowhere, the old song by Ricky Nelson flashed through her mind. *"Going down to lonesome town…"*

Carl turned to her, said apologetically, "Some fresh air should help."

Outside, the bright May sun showed powerfully yet wasn't able to penetrate the dim, dark room. The contrast of light and dark caused Rebecca to think of the bedroom as truly a haunted place, one filled with scents from previous occupants, phantoms somehow not at rest.

Eager to begin, they undressed one another quickly.

They were careful, gentle, not wanting to tear fabric or buttons or pull zippers loose. They knew they had to return to the real world unblemished, unmarked. Carl touched her carefully at first, lightly beneath her breasts, his mouth soft on her, exploring. He stroked her hair, pulled her closer to him, whispered her name, told her how beautiful she was. When she reached down to touch him, he gasped with excitement. As they made love, everything about the room was gradually transformed; now they were haunting it, possessing it, changing it, renewing and restoring it. Their joined presence would drive out all previous specters, it would be their room to claim as their own in the same way they took control of one another's bodies.

When they had finished, when their breathing had calmed down and the sheen of perspiration on their bodies had started to disperse, when they knew it was over, their thoughts settled. The moments had come and gone so swiftly, the ebb and flow of their appetites had finally been appeased. Neither spoke, both knowing lines had been crossed; they would never be able to return from where they had started. They were different now, no longer capable of convincing themselves that they were good, honest people. From the moment they had first had lunch, they had become liars. Now, they were adulterers. Neither felt shame, only altered in some way they were not yet able to discern.

Sleepy, half-awake, Rebecca felt she had lost sight of herself. Now out of focus, who was she? A mother? Yes, that was the same. A wife? Yes, but...not so much anymore. She had driven off the road she had been on for so many years, taken a detour, had no idea where she was now. Nothing was familiar. Not now that this man had touched her or kissed her, not how he had tasted or his scent. All new territory to explore, the curves and depths and wide expanses of skin. All wondrous to her. She had changed, been transformed. The peculiar nature of her surroundings baffled her. The Capri Hotel. Cheap and seedy. Convenient. Served its purpose, like a plastic cup or paper napkin.

Why am I here? she wondered. *Because of Michael? Has he driven me to this, pushed so hard against me that I ended up here? Or was it Carl, a chance meeting that had immediately gone so out of control that I am now lying next to him, his steady heart beating so close to mine? Or am I here simply because of me, because of what I want?*

Carl turned to her, touched her breasts, feathered his hand down her stomach, between her legs where she was already ready for him. Again.

He wants me, she marveled as he murmured his pleasure, kissing her deeply, stroking her.

She glanced out the tiny window in wonder as the sensations of pleasures rippled over and within her body. Rebecca saw a square of bright, blue sky. She saw a bird fly by, followed by another.

Flight.

That was the sensation she found with Carl.

Rebecca closed her eyes.

She soared, cried out.

# # #

Thinking back on her first time with Carl as she drove home from Penny's brought tears to Rebecca's eyes. She couldn't see through the watery onslaught, thought she'd have to pull the car over, exit the New Jersey Turnpike, just sit there, have a crying jag.

She hadn't expected to fall in love with him, but she had. It was as simple and as complex as that. They were never able to figure out how or why it happened, although they talked about it every time they were together.

"I don't even *like* parades," Carl had said, "or crowds."

"Me neither," Rebecca would agree. "We went for the kids."

"Exactly! Scotty loves the marching bands for some reason."

"Melody and Chasity do too, as does Ben. What is it about marching bands?"

Carl turned over in the lumpy bed, embraced her from behind. "I don't know, but if it wasn't for their love of all that noise, I never would have met you."

"Actually, it was my love of coffee," Rebecca had reminded him. "If I hadn't gone for a cup—"

"—and I hadn't splashed it on you—"

"—we might not be here now," Rebecca had finished.

But where are you now, Carl? she wondered anxiously as the traffic in front of her came to a standstill again. She took the opportunity to fish a cigarette out of her purse. She had started smoking again as soon as she had found out Carl had been kidnapped. It was an old, old vice that Michael hated, had insisted she quit before he would even consider marrying her.

"After all, I'm going to be a doctor," he had kidded. "Can't have my wife smoking."

And she had stopped, happily—if not easily—with great discipline and enthusiasm. Anything for Michael. But that a long time ago.

Once she learned of Carl's abduction, the craving abruptly returned like a friend request on Facebook, one that she immediately accepted. *Yes, I remember you*, she had thought after she had reacquainted herself with the coolness that swept through her body as she inhaled, the gentle buzz that soon followed, the sense of calm. It was as if she was watching her life, not living it, so she had perspective as the nicotine did its work; the stress left her. It was like closing a window on parts of her life she didn't want to deal with; for a few minutes, it was like a blissful isolation tank.

When she returned home, she hid the cigarettes in a make-up bag in the bathroom. Michael would never find them there. Like so many things in her life, she was a pro at keeping secrets, revealing only what she wanted Michael to know on a need-to-know basis.

Why did I ever quit this, why would I ever want to? she mused. She knew Michael could probably smell the scent on her—if he got that close to her, which was rare—but she didn't really care. Besides, he wasn't around much anymore; when he was, it was all business, all about his practice, the bills, the kids. Not really her, or them. Hadn't been *them*—or her—for years.

She inhaled deeply, felt it tighten around her chest, a fierce embrace. She tapped the steering wheel impatiently, waiting for the sludge of traffic to move. She lowered the window, exhaled slowly. It sounded like a weary sigh. She could feel the weight of her life experiences bearing down on her. Bearing down hard.

# # #

When Carl abruptly stopped texting and calling Rebecca at the end of September, her stomach burned nervous acid for days. Had his wife learned what had happened? They had both been careful to delete their phone calls and steamy text messages as soon as they had finished. Just in case. Was he ill? Had there been an accident, second thoughts brought on by regret, guilt?

She realized there was so much she didn't know about him, so much he didn't know about her. After that first lunch in early April, they hadn't shared much about their spouses, just vague sketches, outlines of what life was like. She knew his wife's first name, he knew Michael's, who their children were. The rest remained untold. Ignorance and denial would serve as a form of bliss; what they didn't know couldn't hurt them.

Carl's sudden silence drove Rebecca swiftly into a black hole of anxiety and depression.

Over the phone, her sister Penny would ask her what was wrong, what had happened. Was it Michael? The girls? Her health, was she ill? What? What? *What?*

"Just a rough patch," Rebecca would say, "a bad funk, a lousy time. You've had those, right?"

Finally, in desperation, Rebecca had called Carl's repair shop, hoping he would answer. When Neal picked up, she had calmly asked for Carl Daniels.

"He's…not here," Neal had said, his voice tight, sounding surprised. "Who's calling?"

She ended the call, deleted the digits from her phone, her fingers sliding off the slick phone screen. Her eyes filled with tears. *Where was Carl?* The thought was like a prayer that was not acknowledged, never answered. He couldn't have just disappeared or suddenly dumped her. Their last time together had been fine, no signs of him pulling away, no vague response about when they'd get together again, no sense he was about to ghost her, not after so many months together.

It was hell without him, the upset, nervous stomach, the dull, ever-present headache, the restless nights, the physical yearning for him, for his touch. For the children's sake, she had to act as if nothing was wrong. Michael didn't really notice or if he did, didn't really care. Only Penny was concerned, maybe a bit suspicious.

Then, Penny called early in the morning. Hysterical. Sobbing. Rebecca had actually managed to fall into a deep sleep, was dreaming about Carl who was in a phone booth, trying to find loose change to connect with her again. The image slipped away as she listened to Penny say that Graham hadn't made it home, he was missing. Rebecca forced herself to switch lanes mentally, to get on a new track, to focus on her sister's ordeal, setting aside her own heartache and unbearable despair. Yet even in the midst of sharing her sister's agony, she never stopped worrying or wondering about Carl.

And then, in the most extraordinary and unimaginable way possible, information about Carl was revealed. A few days later at the police station, she had been told that Graham and Carl had been kidnapped by the same person. Terrified yet relieved that Carl was still alive, Rebecca had to be careful how she responded to the news, needed to confirm Carl was okay yet keep the focus and concern on her brother-in-law.

But all she was thinking was *Thank God Carl is okay!*

# # #

Rebecca needed something to occupy her days and focus on anything other than the raging anxiety over Carl and his abduction. She felt helpless, immobilized, and that wasn't her way. She was a doer, a fixer, and she needed to get in gear because the cigarettes were now being greedily consumed at an alarming rate. She no longer cared if Michael or anyone knew about her returned addiction. Her husband had tried to reach out, comfort her over Graham, her-brother-in-law. She pretended to show weary appreciation, embraced him, but longed to be held by Carl. Although she had compassion for all her sister was going through, her thoughts were only about Carl. She slept poorly, which left her cranky, short-tempered with the girls. She called and texted Penny too much, feeling she was missing out on any breaks in the investigation.

"Thank you, Beck, but you don't need to call so much. I know you've got your own family. You know I'll call you as soon as there's any news about Graham. All we can do now is hope and pray."

"I just want to know what's going on," Rebecca said. "I love you, I just want to know as soon as you do if anything happens. Just call, okay?"

She could tell no one that she knew Carl, had to keep everyone in the dark. Ironically, the only one she could share her grief, pain and uncertainty with—the only person on earth whom she could commiserate with—would be Carl's wife, Adel.

Then, swiftly unfolding like a paper map that she had just discovered, a plan came to Rebecca. It provided a path to follow, simple directions that would allow her to get as close as possible to Carl. What the police wouldn't tell Penny about Carl, they would reveal to Adel. And Rebecca was desperate to get in touch with Adel.

Since the story had made all the papers—the media had dubbed the abductor the Comeback Kidnapper due to the odd poem written on the Polaroids—many details had been made public and Rebecca read that Adel worked at Second Hand Rose in Brooklyn. She lit a cigarette, took a few puffs, allowed the mellow rush to sweep over her. Without knowing exactly what she was going to say, she punched in the digits.

"Hello, is Ms. Daniels there?"

"Yes, speaking. Who's this?"

"My name is Rebecca Roberts. My sister is Penny Spencer. I saw you at the police station the other day."

"You did?"

"Yes, you arrived just as I was leaving Detective Willard's office. Remember?"

"Oh, yes. Of course, Ms. Roberts. I do remember. Is there any word about your brother-in-law?"

"No… nothing yet. Anything about…your husband?"

"No…"

Rebecca cleared her throat. "This is such a terrible thing. Penny is having an awful time about it, as am I. When the detective was speaking with us, he mentioned you had no family and…I was wondering if I could possibly come to see you some time. To talk about all of this."

Silence. Disappointment surrounded Rebecca. *This was a bad idea,* she realized. *I said it wrong, she'll never want to see me.*

"Ms. Roberts?"

"Yes?"

"I'm so sorry. I'm just…scattered. Your call—and your suggestion—caught me off guard, I guess …"

"I apologize. This is so abrupt. We all feel so helpless. I'm sorry to have intruded."

"No, it's fine, actually. Really, very kind of you, in fact. And you're right, I have no family. Our friends have been supportive, but no one really understands what this is like unless you're living through it. As you and Penny are. Thank you for reaching out to me. It's so kind. I *would* like to talk with you. When would you like to get together?"

"Actually, I could be there today, if you're available. I was planning to be in the city, but I could meet you in Brooklyn where you work." Another silence. Rebecca waited.

Adel said, "Just a moment, Rebecca." The phone was muted.

She called me by my first name, Rebecca thought as she inhaled deeply. *That's a good sign.*

After several seconds, Adel said, "I'm planning to leave early today, why don't we meet at my apartment?"

Adel provided the address, told Rebecca the best time to meet, ended the call. Rebecca took a breath, exhaled, relieved yet keyed up, excited yet uncertain about what she had put into motion. What she was about to do wasn't something she planned on telling Penny or the police if they asked. Really, she wasn't going to tell anyone. And she'd ask Adel not to mention it either. Was it really a big deal that she was making contact with Adel Daniels?

"No, it's *not,*" Rebecca said firmly.

It was just another secret in her life.

# # #

Michael's receptionist put a call through to him at 2:30 p.m. "It's Chasity's school."

"Dr. Roberts? This is Macy Abbott from Busy Bees? Your wife hasn't arrived yet to pick up Chasity. We were wondering if other arrangements had been made?"

"No, she didn't say anything to me. When was she supposed to have been there?"

"School is dismissed at 2:00, but parents are asked to be here early, no later than 1:45."

"Have you tried my wife's cell?"

"Yes, but it only goes to voice mail and she hasn't responded to any texts we've sent. Chasity is here in the office so she's fine, we just need to know what your arrangements are to have her picked up."

Michael said he'd call back, texted Rebecca, tried her cell, but like the school, no response. He thought back to anything she had said that morning. Was she going to be away in the afternoon? If so, surely she would have made arrangements for the girls knowing he couldn't leave the office. Nothing came to mind, but he hadn't really been listening too closely to her the past few months. She had pushed him further away for some reason, and now things had become even worse when her brother-in-law had gone missing.

A second call was pushed to him, this time from Melody's school where she was in first grade. Was someone other than his wife picking up Melody?

Michael called a neighbor, asked if she could pick up the girls, keep them until he got home.

"Of course," the woman said. "Is everything okay? Has something happened?" Stories of the kidnappings of Carl Daniels and Graham Spencer were all over the news, and the neighbors had been protective of Michael and Rebecca's privacy.

"Everything's fine," he lied, "she just got stuck in the city longer than expected with her sister."

"I saw her leave earlier this morning," the woman volunteered. "She drove past, I waved at her. I'll pick the girls up now, feed them, keep them as long as needed."

Michael called the schools with the updates, then phoned Penny, hoping his lie might have been the truth.

"No, she isn't here." Penny said. "She called this morning like she always does but that was it. Is everything okay?"

"She left this morning but I have no idea where she went. The schools just called, she hasn't picked up the girls. A neighbor's taking care of it."

"Michael, that doesn't sound like Rebecca. If she

wasn't going to be there…she's always early. To *everything.* She didn't answer her phone or texts?"

"No, she didn't. Look, let me finish up here at the office and I'll call you when I get the girls."

# # #

It took two hours until he was able to gather his family together. He called Penny back. "I didn't want to alarm the girls. I told them Rebecca was spending the night with you. I'm calling the hospitals in the area in case something happened, but I don't understand why no one called me if she was injured."

"Oh, Michael, why is this happening to us?"

Taken aback by her fatal tone, he asked, "What do you mean?"

"First Graham is taken, now Rebecca…"

"She's just missing, Penny. We don't know what's going on. I've got to make these calls, find out what I can."

There were no women matching Rebecca's description admitted to any of the hospitals, no arrests made, her white BMW didn't match any automobiles involved in accidents. When he had checked every phone number off the list, Michael poured himself a Scotch, checked on the girls. They were sleeping. He and Rebecca loved their children; there was no way either of them would ever put them at risk or not be certain they were picked up after school. It would never happen. He and Rebecca may have been separating from one another for months, wildly adrift, but they both remained tightly tethered to their children.

He finished his drink, dialed the police.

# # #

Ten residents at the Manhattan apartment building used the same housekeeper, Sylvia Camel.

Monday through Friday, for almost five years, she would arrive around six in the morning, greet the doorman on duty, then start her tasks. She worked long, hard hours, scrubbing, scouring, vacuuming, polishing, sweeping, wiping and anything else that was required to leave the apartments she cleaned looking sparkling and well-cared for.

On this particular morning, she started on Mr. Johnson's residence. He was young, worked eighty-hour weeks on Wall Street, was up and gone before dawn most days so she never had to worry about him being under foot when she arrived. He had left the stuffed bag of dirty clothes by the front door. She fetched the detergent, the laundry card, the paperback mystery she had brought with her, headed for the basement. She liked doing laundry, sitting there alone, reading, which was her favorite pastime.

The odor—more of a stench actually—greeted her as soon as she opened the door to the pitch-black room that housed a dozen washers and driers. She flicked on the light. There was a hesitation, then *ping, ping, ping* as the old, overhead fluorescent lights flicked on. She dumped the bag of dirty clothes into one of the carts. She looked around, wondered if there was a dead or dying animal hidden away somewhere. She took another whiff, almost gagged. It was a foul, sour smell, like food that had gone bad or had been left outside in the hot sun. It was intense. *What is that?* she wondered, taking a step deeper into the basement.

Smells like something died, and then died again, she thought. She didn't venture any further into the room, only looked from where she stood. All the washing machines had their lids open, invitations to be used, like baby birds with their mouths wide, ready to be fed. The dryers were all closed. In the back, two huge industrial dryers were available for oversized loads; she never had to use them. The one on the left was closed, the one on the right was opened just a bit.

That was odd since she knew the building cleaned up the room each night when it closed at ten, everything was in its place, washers open, all dryers closed. Even the big ones. Sylvia swallowed. The smell was so bad she squeezed her nose closed, forced herself to breathe through her mouth. Still felt like gagging. She cautiously took a step, then another. Curious now as to the source of the odor.

She continued forward, soon was halfway down the aisle of washers on the left, driers on the right. The smell was increasing in its ferociousness, like a beast that was rearing up, ready to attack. Sylvia suddenly pictured some unbathed homeless man who had come here for shelter. Would *that* be the origin of the odor? If so, she'd turn around quick, get the doorman or one of the staff.

"Calm down, don't embarrass yourself," she murmured, trying to quicken her pace, get a look see, then get out of the room. "Don't start making any crazy claims or no one will want to have you clean their apartment. Homeless men living in the basement, beasts ready to attack…"

Finally, she stood a few feet from the two industrial driers. She wrinkled her nose. The scent was brutal now. It was coming from the machines, probably the one on the right whose door was opened a few inches. Trembling now, she grabbed her hands to settle herself. She took two steps. She was in front of the dryer on the right. Sylvia leaned closer, peered into the darkness of the barely opened machine. It took a few seconds to adjust to the dim interior, then a few seconds for it to register what she was seeing inside the large drum. It was a nightmare. She was staring at a nightmare.

"Ah," she gasped, backing away, trying to scream. "Ah!" The volume wouldn't come, only panicky pants, grunts of terror. Crying and whimpering, Sylvia ran from the basement, didn't bother waiting for the service elevator, clamored up the steps, noises coming from her that she knew made no sense. She had to get away from that thing in the dryer, had to get the stench of it out of her. She had breathed it in, hadn't she? It was inside of her now, wasn't it?

She burst into the lobby from the side door. Joe, the doorman, turned to her.

"What? What is it, Sylvia?"

"The dryer! In the dryer. And the smell. Oh God, the smell!" She finally managed to scream. It was like a broken lock, the sounds she was finally able to make, a dam freed as she trembled, wept in the doorman's arms as he tried to calm her.

At that early hour—it was now just 6:30—they were alone at the front desk. He supported her as he walked her over to the couch. Her legs were wobbling, she leaned heavily against him, murmuring, muttering crazy things.

He thought he heard her say, "It was dead! Roasted! Red! There was hair! And an eye! I think a face! And that smell!"

#

The police arrived within five minutes. Joe escorted them to the laundry room while Hank, one of the maintenance men, took over the front desk, tried to hurry along the departing residents who found their lobby and the front of the building filled with New York's finest.

"What's going on?" "What happened" "Why are the police here?" Everyone asked over and over and over again as they stepped off the elevator.

"Everything is fine, just a problem in the basement," Hank had been told to say. "Everything is fine." Two police officers glared at the tenants, their stoic expressions pushing the crowd out the door. Only a few turned toward the service door, sniffing out the bad odor that had just started to rise from beneath them.

When Joe and the officers returned to the lobby, their expressions were grim, faces pale white at what they had seen. Joe joined Sylvia on the couch, put his arm around her, whispered in her ear.

"Joe?" Hank said, stepping away from the desk, letting the police handle the exodus of residents. "What was it? What's going on down there?"

The call went out for homicide assistance and an ambulance, no siren needed. At the nearby precinct, a steady buzz rose up once word got out that a female body was discovered in the dryer of a building. Willards picked up on the excited activity, asked what was going on.

"Toasted woman in a dryer over at—" and then glanced at the police sheet report, told the address. It was familiar. It took Willards only a few seconds to place it as Adel Daniel's building.

#

The laundry room was sealed off, yellow and black police tape bandaged across the enclosure. Five officers were in the basement, taking photos, measurements, brushing black, lift-powder all over the large dryers, talking in low voices. The stench had only grown worse in the past hour. One of younger officers had hurried away to vomit in the maintenance bathroom.

The dryer door was now wide open. Willards and the other officer looked closer. The heat had inflamed the body a bright red. *Broiled lobster,* Willards thought, *only without the protective shell.* The corpse was badly bruised, bones were broken, deep red marks covered every exposed portion of skin. However long the body had been turning and bouncing in the stifling hot enclosure, it had managed to bang loose skeleton from skin. *Bag of bones,* Willards thought.

The face had been sheered to a white-pink from the constant blast of heat. The body had ended up on its back, the face turned toward the opened dryer. The eyes and tongue had swollen.

Dried blood and excrement lay splattered throughout the metal cage. Various parts of clothing had been shredded or torn loose.

When Willards stepped back from the gruesome scene, he noticed the ring. "Harry, can you bring the left hand out?" he asked one of the gloved attendants.

"We're ready to bring the whole thing out if you're ready," Harry replied. With a nod from the homicide detective, they all stepped back. It was a woman's body. They carefully extracted her from the dryer. Within seconds, the corpse was atop the gurney.

Willards moved closer. "Can you clean off her left hand, let me see the ring finger?"

The unnaturally bright, red-orange hand was lifted, the gore wiped away. Willards peered closely at the diamond wedding band. It was in a bold, six-prong platinum setting. He held his breath, looked closer. He had seen it before, recognized the expensive wedding band.

#

"Somebody stabbed Rebecca Roberts more than a dozen times then put her body in the dryer last night after ten, set it on high for a couple hours," Willards told Tony over the phone. "She bounced around for a while. It was horrible."

"What was she doing in Adel's building? Did they know one another?"

"I think the only time they met was in my office very briefly when we spoke to her and Penny. Where's Adel been lately? Have they been seen together?"

Tony said, "Nothing in the reports. She keeps to her usual pattern. Walks her son to school in the morning with the police escort, drives to her job, leaves there around two-thirty, gets home in time to pick up her son with the officer. No change."

Willards checked his watch, asked the doorman not to call up to Adel; he wanted to tell her about Rebecca without her having any prior knowledge of the incident. When he arrived on her floor, he took a moment to compose himself. He really wanted to be on point with her, able to quickly key in on any strange behaviors or odd reactions. He knocked at her door. After a moment, her muffled voice, uncertain, called out, "Who is it?"

He identified himself, she opened the door. "Detective! I didn't know you were here. The doorman didn't—"

"May I come in?"

She moved aside, appeared flustered but no more than anyone would be with the unexpected arrival of a police officer. In the background, he heard cartoons were on.

"Scotty's not at school yet?"

"Just getting ready, actually," she said. "Scotty, are your teeth brushed? We leave in five minutes!" She turned to Willards. "You have news? What's happened?" She turned off the TV.

Scotty appeared. "Hey, I was watching—"

"You remember Detective Willards, don't you, Scotty?" she asked smoothly.

The boy nodded, his eyes wide. "Have you found my daddy yet?"

"Not yet, Scotty, but we're looking really hard."

"Do you think he's okay?" the boy asked, his voice flat. Willards wondered how much Adel had told her son about the investigation.

After a moment—Willards expected Adel to chime in, distract the troubling question, but she only watched him—he said, "I don't know, son. We're doing everything we can. Did you brush your teeth like you mother asked?"

Scotty shook his head, tromped off to the bathroom.

Adel asked, "What's happened?"

"There's been a homicide in this building, in the basement."

She didn't respond.

"Rebecca Roberts was found there, dead. Penny's sister? You saw her briefly when we met in my office."

"She…lived here?" Adel asked. "I don't understand."

"No, she didn't. She lived in New Jersey."

"Then what was she doing here?"

"We're figuring that out now, taking to the doormen, seeing when she arrived, whom she came to see."

"What has it got to do with Carl?"

"Did she come to see you?" Willards ask, ignoring her question.

"Me? Why would she want to see me?"

"That's what I want to find out. Did either of you speak to one another after you met in my office?"

"Why are you asking me these questions? Shouldn't you be out searching for my husband?"

"We're investigating every aspect of the case, Adel. And you haven't answered my question."

"Yes, I have. Or I thought I did. Roberta hasn't been here to see me. She—"

"Rebecca."

"What?"

"Her name. Her name is Rebecca Roberts, not Roberta."

"Okay. Whatever her name is, does it matter? She hasn't been here."

Surprised at her dismissive response, Willards grew angry. "Of course it matters! She had a name, she was married, she had two daughters, and a sister, Penny, whose husband was taken by the same person who took Carl. It *all* matters, Adel. *All of it.*"

"Why do I feel like you're accusing *me* of something?" Adel asked, standing up straighter, now defiant.

"Have I given you a reason to feel that way?"

"Well...I know you're following me."

"You are under surveillance," Willards admitted, "for your own protection."

"There's a difference, though, isn't there? Between police protection and police surveillance. Am I under suspicion?"

"Of what?" Exasperated, she squeezed her fists. "Am I a suspect in this case, in the death of this woman? Do I need a lawyer?"

"No, you're not a suspect," Willards said, knowing he was probably lying now but couldn't figure out what had suddenly changed between them. He watched her hands wrestling with one another, trying to settle down. Hands could convey so much, too much, if they weren't under control, still and calm. "However, if it's determined you have lied to us or withheld information, you will be looked at differently. Do you understand?"

Adel's forearms quivered, her fingers intertwined, struggled with one another. "Yes, I understand. Do you have any more questions? I really should get Scotty to school and I should get to work."

"No, that's all for now," he said.

At the door, she pleaded with him. "Find my husband, detective. I don't care what you think of me, but I want my husband back, Scotty wants his daddy home. I'm…sorry about this other woman. Rebecca. But I don't have anything else to *give* right now. Do you understand? It's not that I don't care, it's that I have nothing left inside of me."

#

After Michael Roberts had been informed of his wife's death, he gathered up his daughters, drove to Penny's apartment in the city. He needed her as much as she needed him. The girls didn't really understand what was going on, but wept in response to their father's unsettled, tear-stained faced. Scared by what was not known, they all huddled together in grief once they reached Penny's home.

"Oh, Michael," was all Penny could say when she opened the door, fell into his arms, the girls grabbing the adult's legs. The two broken families finally settled in the living room, Penny and her son Ben with no husband or father, Michael and his daughters with no wife or mother. His parents lived in Westchester, would be arriving at any moment. They would stay with the children while Penny and Michael went first to the police station, then to the morgue. Michael still had to identify the body. Penny and Rebecca's mother and step-father lived in Florida and would fly up later that day.

An hour later, after Michael's parents arrived, he and Penny left for the police station.

"I don't know how I'm still holding it together," Penny said as they closed the apartment door behind them. They started down the hallway to the bank of elevators. "I went numb after Graham was taken, just shut down, and when I heard about Rebecca, I felt turned inside out. I...I can't believe all of this is happening to me, to us."

He put his arm around her, didn't know how to respond, felt hallowed out, in shock.

"I can't sleep anymore," Penny continued. "I take a sleeping pill, lay down, stare at the dark ceiling, watching it until dawn arrives. I've had a...*sense* that something horrible was going to happen, equally bad to what has gone on with Graham, but I never suspected it would be Rebecca. I was leaning on her, she was my rock, but now she's gone...I just feel like I'm falling but can't hit ground. And still nothing from the kidnapper. Not a word. Three weeks, Michael! Graham has been gone *three weeks*, and the other man, Carl, has been gone almost a month. The police have no idea what to do, no idea who's done this or why. None! The papers and TV keep reporting about this Comeback Kidnapper but there's nothing new, but it's all they talk about! And now Rebecca. My sister..."

Once they were outside, they became part of the rapid street flow of people, jostled along like pebbles in a fast-moving stream. No one acknowledged their strained, distraught faces, their slow, awkward movements as they tried to find their footing in this new world of violent loss. Michael was grief-stricken over the death of his wife, but the emotion was nudged aside by the guilt of their failed relationship, the indifference they had shown one another in the past few months. *Or year,* he thought bleakly, *or years.* While Penny continued to voice her sorrow, he admitted to himself that the overwhelming concern he had was over his daughters, growing up without a mother. Not the loss of his wife, the loss of his children's mother. *It's still grief,* he defended himself as Penny grasped his hand. *It's still pain, but it's just not* my *pain.*

Penny had come to hate the police station with the warped, chipped linoleum floor, the overflowing baskets of paper, dirty computer terminals, harsh overhead lights. She had come to think of it as a broken machine, useless, inflectional, yet still in service. Each week that passed with no word about Graham caused her to step deeper into despair, succumbing to a bog of quicksand that slowly, patiently pulled her under. All the police did was ask her questions, ask her friends questions, file statements and then, when the net of suspicion had been cast far and wide, it was pulled in tight but no one was brought into view, everything of promise just slipped away. Even the person who had taken photos of her and Adel's families, he was never identified. The added attention of the media once the story broke open seemed to taunt her, constantly reminding her of what she couldn't forget.

She hesitated for a moment, staring at the front doors to the police station, thinking, *It is all useless, pointless, this building of inept fools and idiots, and yet here I am, about to be asked questions all over again, but not about Graham this time, only about Rebecca.*

Once she and Michael were seated and two other

detectives had joined them, Willards expressed his remorse over their loss. He was struck again by the toll the ordeal had taken on her. Her hair was pulled back, exposing the pressure and distress that was now deeply etched on her face. She had lost more weight, her eyes had a hollow, glassy sheen to them; unfocused, dull, as if she had gone partially blind. Her movements were slow, listless. She exhibited a nervous habit, constantly tapping her fingers against her legs, a silent, frantic beat.

He asked if either of them knew anyone in the building where Rebecca's body was found. They looked at one another, then shook their heads.

Michael said, "When Rebecca goes to the city, it's just to see Penny or do errands. We live in Jersey, so all of our friends are there."

"Did you know she was going into the city the day she didn't pick your children up?" Willards asked.

"No, I didn't."

"Have you and your wife fought recently?"

"What? No. Why? Things are fine."

"Did she often drive to the city during the day, not telling you, forgetting to pick up your daughters?"

"Stop it!" Penny said. "Rebecca was a wonderful, caring mother! She loved her daughters. Someone…probably forced her to leave home, drive to the city."

Willards shook his head. "We have an eyewitness, a neighbor, who waved at Rebecca as she drove away, alone, that day. We just want to put together a timeline, learn where she was and when. And then we can determine the why. I'm still not clear on your wife's patterns during the day. Was going to the city something she would mention to you?"

"Yes. She would have told me if she was going in to see Penny, or had plans in the city."

Penny added, "Or she'd phone me if she was coming in. We'd meet for lunch or at a store or something. She would have called ahead of time. Especially with everything going on now."

One of the detectives asked Michael, "As you know, since Graham's disappearance, we've interviewed Penny's family and friends, and yours, your neighbors, trying to see if there are any crossover relationships. Two of your neighbors said in the past few months—specifically since the end of March or early April—your wife has left her home for several hours at a time, two or three times a week."

"I don't understand," Michael said, glancing at Penny. "Why does that matter? She had things to do during the day, didn't need to stay home all the time."

"A few times, your neighbors chatted with her," the detective said. "Sometimes she said she was going to the city to see Penny, other times, it was shopping, to get tickets to a Broadway show. Lots of different reasons, but she always would return home later that afternoon with your daughters after picking them up from school."

Michael mumbled something.

"What?" Willards asked.

"Broadway. She said that? She'd never get a ticket for a show. I hate that stuff. We never go. She's never even seen a show as far as I know."

"And if she told them she was coming into the city two or three times a week…it wasn't to see me," Penny said, her voice trailing off.

Everyone in the office was looking at Michael. Penny felt a thin rush of doubt flash across her heart. What *was* the relationship really like between her late sister and Michael? Rebecca had told her things were cooling off between them, that sex and affection had departed months earlier, that he was always busy at the office, worried about changes in healthcare, profits, billing issues, had to cut some of the staff a year earlier. The girls missed their daddy, that came up a lot, putting Rebecca in the role of having to defend Michael's schedule while at the same time, resenting him for the time he spent away from the family. But none of that explained why Rebecca was coming into the city so often without telling her.

Michael sighed, brushed back his thick brown hair, adjusted his glasses, shifted in his seat, and finally said, "I…don't know what to say. If she was going into the city so often, she would have told me. At least, I think she would have. But if she wasn't telling Penny any of this…"

Willards asked, "What about a doctor? Maybe she was seeing someone for treatment, didn't want you to know?"

"She'd tell me," he insisted.

"Or me," Penny added. "We really didn't keep things from one another."

"Besides, if it was a doctor or psychiatrist or whatever, she'd go to one in Jersey, near where we live," Michael said. "There's no shame in getting help, detective. But my wife wasn't seeing a shrink or any doctor."

"Are you sure the neighbors said she was going to the city?" Penny asked. The detective nodded. "I mean, it's an hour drive and having to be back to pick up the girls from school, it's a big chunk of her day to get there and home. She kept the house herself, you know, and that was a lot of work, and I knew she saw friends in Jersey, too. It doesn't make any sense she'd make so many trips in…"

Penny felt like too many questions were being asked, none were being answered. If Rebecca was coming into the city, why hadn't she told her? A contemplative stillness settled over the room; she could almost hear the gears clicking in everyone's mind as they sorted through the information they had heard.

Willards said, "There's something else you need to know. The apartment address where Rebecca was found, it's not familiar to either of you, correct?" He read it to them again. Michael and Penny shook their heads. The detective waited a moment, then said, "There is one person who lives there that Rebecca met once, someone Penny knows too. Adel Daniels."

Penny straightened up. "Carl's wife?"

Willards didn't respond, only watched her.

"How did Rebecca know this woman?" Michael asked.

"They met here, briefly, when Adel and I first spoke to the detective," Penny answered.

"Barely met," Willard said. "I remember now. It seemed as if Rebecca couldn't wait to get out of the room once she realized who Adel was."

"Did you speak to Adel?" Penny asked. "What did she say about Rebecca?"

"I spoke to her this morning, found out later that she lied to me, told me she hadn't spoken to or seen your sister since that day here in my office."

"How'd you know she was lying?" Michael asked.

"Simple. We've located the doorman who was on duty during the time your wife would have entered the building. That's why I wanted you to email me some recent photos of Rebecca to show him. He did say that a woman asked to see Adel during his shift; it was easy to recall since during the day there are not a lot of visitors. Plus, with the kidnappings, Adel's name is now well known to everyone. We sent the photo to the doorman, he confirmed Rebecca was the woman."

Shocked, Penny asked, "Did she kill Rebecca? But why?"

"All I know is what the doorman told us. He called Adel's apartment, said she had a visitor, Adel said to send the woman up. And that was it. Rebecca took the elevator, was never seen again until her body was discovered."

Michael asked, "But why would Adel want to hurt Rebecca? You said they barely knew one another."

"That's what I'm going to find out," Willards said. "Adel's under surveillance, we're keeping tabs on her, but I didn't want to go back to her immediately before telling you all of this. Since you have no idea what the connection is between Adel and Rebecca, we're going to bring her in for questioning. And this time, we'll get the truth."

May 23, 1994

Dear Diary,

Took the train into the city to see Deena yesterday. Came home to find a nasty, filthy note from my "angel" slipped into the secret drawer. Won't write down in here what she said, want to forget it if at all possible. Suffice to say that she's a jealous, demanding little girl if she doesn't get her way. She expected me to be here. When I wasn't, it seemed she had a tantrum.

Didn't know at first how she got into the house. Billy said he hadn't seen her. Then I found some very small, white pieces of cedar on the floor near the window. She had climbed up the garden lattice work and slipped into my room! It made for an unsettling day. Not sure what to say to her when she returns, but I won't tolerate that behavior or her breaking into my home.

Billy just called out that she's here. I better put this away. Don't want her to know I've been writing unpleasant things about her.

Wish I hadn't shown her the secret place I keep this. Oh, well.

The Fourth Week
Adel

After Willards walked Michael and Penny out of the police station, he lingered outside on 67th Street, enjoying the fresh air, the rapidly setting sun. After four weeks on the case, he was thinking there was finally a break, a bit of daylight. They had now positively identified that it was Adel who admitted Rebecca into her apartment. Soon, he'd find out why the two women had met, what their relationship was, and why Adel had killed Rebecca, then dumped her body in the basement dryer. If it wasn't Adel, he had no idea what to do next.

The use of a knife was curious. He knew that anytime someone committed a murder by stabbing somebody to death, it always spoke to a high level of intense rage and perhaps an emotional connection to the victim. The experience was visceral, graphic, and usually aligned with someone who was experiencing a fit of paranoia. Stabbing was close up, personal, something that shooting someone with a gun doesn't allow.

But why such rage at Rebecca? he wondered, gripping the iron guardrail in front of the station.

When Willards returned to his desk, he found a gray

envelope addressed to him with no return address on it, no postage. It was the same type of packaging Adel and Penny had received. A knot formed in his stomach. His name had been in the paper enough so if the abductor wanted to reach him, it was easy, but he was still apprehensive seeing an envelope addressed to him.

He asked at the always chaotic front desk where it had come from. The frazzled officers on duty—surrounded by more than a dozen citizens filing papers, asking questions, arguing amongst themselves, elbowing one another for assistance—said they had just found it under a stack of paperwork and left it on his desk, no idea where it had come from or when.

"Really? No idea? So, it could have been here all *day*?"

A woman yelled, "Hey! I was here first!"

Frustrated, Willards returned to his office, turned the envelope over a few times, feeling its weight, looking for anything of interest. It was probably pointless to dust for fingerprints since it had already been handled by so many people and previous examinations had been fruitless. Whoever this Comeback Kidnapper was, he seemed to wear gloves when preparing these packages, maybe even wrapped himself in plastic. The envelopes were always clean. *Everybody watches too many cop shows, knows too much.*

Willards snapped on some gloves anyway, opened the envelope.

A Polaroid fell face down on his desk. He turned it over. Stared at it, not comprehending what he was seeing. He held it closer, breathing heavily. It was Adel Daniels, hands covering her face, legs secured to a chair. Her newspaper had fallen over onto her lap so he couldn't confirm the issue date. Same deep, black environment as the other photos.

When had this happened? When had she been abducted? She was under surveillance. Every morning she and a police escort walked Scotty to school, then she took her car, drove to Brooklyn, worked her job, drove home in time to pick-up Scotty from school, along with the cop assigned. Other than her time at work, she was watched over all day.

Under her photo in thick block letters was written:

THREE, FOUR,
WATCH THE DOOR,
I'LL COME BACK,
WITH ONE MORE.

Willards couldn't help but hear the nursery rhyme or whatever it was dancing through his mind. With every photo delivered, he felt he was able to make more sense of the meaning of the words. *"One, two, don't be blue"*—that was Carl and Graham, the first two to be kidnapped— *"three, four, watch the door, I'll come back, with one more"*—if Adel was number three, would Penny Spencer be number four? Logically, it made sense. This person was after the husbands, and now the wives.

He flipped the Polaroid over. Lightly etched into the glossy black panel on the back he saw the name SCOTTY.

What role did the children play in all of this? Why were their names written on the back of each picture? Their abduction had always been implied since the case had been opened more than a month ago, but no attempt had ever been made to abduct Scotty or Ben. Was it just misdirection? Were they *ever* the targets?

Tony appeared in the doorway.

"I was just going to call you," Willards said as he slid the Polaroid across his desk to Tony. The detective exhaled when he saw Adel's image.

"How'd this happen?" he demanded. "We've been watching her!"

"That's what I want to find out. And *when* did it happen? Her newspaper isn't showing the headline, so it's masking when she was abducted."

Willards made some calls, immediately confirmed that Penny and her son, Ben, were all right, then he spoke with the police escort who said Scotty was delivered safely home after school hours ago."

"What about Adel? Didn't she meet Scotty?"

"No, his baby sitter, Sally, showed up."

"Where was Adel?" Willards almost shouted into the phone.

"Sally told me Adel had left work early, felt sick, gone home, asked if Sally would pick up Scotty, keep her with him and she'd pick up later this evening, said she needed to rest. Is everything okay?"

Willards tried Adel's work number, but the store had closed. He dialed the cell phone of Second Hand Rose owner Nedra Whyler.

"Ms. Whyler, I just want to confirm that Adel showed up for work this morning?"

"Yes, she was here this morning, but left just before lunch, said she didn't feel well, thought she was coming down with something. Is everything all right?"

Willards thanked her, ended the call.

"So, it sounds like she was abducted this morning between the time she left work and arrived home," Tony said.

"Maybe," Willards said. "I just find it so convenient that now that we need to talk to her about Rebecca's death, she's kidnapped. And this picture doesn't show the headline like the others did."

Tony nodded. "It might not be a proof of life photo."

"It might be staged by Adel. Let's see if her

neighbor, Sally Erickson, knows anything."

\# \# \#

Willards and Tony arrived at Adel's building ten minutes later, checked with the doorman if Adel had arrived home earlier that day. He hadn't seen her, checked with the relief doorman; he hadn't either. They were escorted up to her floor by the building superintendent. They knocked on her door, rang the bell, no response. The super let them in. All seemed in order, but there was no evidence that she had been home that day or had been resting to overcome her sudden illness.

They knocked on Sally's door.

"Is everything okay?" she asked, her eyes wide. She was small, no taller than five-three with thick, unruly red hair, dramatically painted on, high-arched eyebrows. Freckles everywhere, deep green eyes. She had been questioned several times over the weeks, was used to it by now.

"Scotty's here, right?" Willards asked.

She nodded. "He's watching TV. Adel's going to come over and—"

"When's the last time you saw Adel?"

"Saw her? Last night, when she stopped by to pick up Scotty after she got home from work."

"Did she call you today, ask you to pick him up after school?"

"Yeah. This morning. Said she was leaving work early, wasn't feeling well. She was going home to sleep it off and asked if I could pick him up, keep him here."

They explained to her about receiving the photo of Adel, apparently abducted, but said they weren't yet convinced it was authentic.

"Obviously, don't mention it to Scotty," Willards

said, "but we wanted you to know since we have to make arrangements for his care." He made some calls, placed Scotty in protective custody at a foster home since he had no living relatives. He told Sally she could apply for the program and he had already granted her access visits with Scotty for as often as she desired.

Tony added, "He doesn't have any other family, so it would help him a great deal at this time if you could visit him." He emailed her the information on whom she could contact.

Sally's eyes welled up. "I...can't believe this is happening. I've know the Daniels' for years. They are such nice people. Why is this happening to them?"

"We don't know," Willards admitted, told her social services would be by shortly

He and Tony returned to Adel's apartment.

"What are we missing here?" he asked, looking around.

Tony said, "Either Rebecca knew something about Adel, or Adel knew something about Rebecca and killed her because of it."

"It's like all these people are connected by this 'I'll come back to get you' phrase yet we can't make the pieces fit," Willards said. "And now we have a six-year-old with no parents."

# # #

It was after nine when Willards and Tony arrived at Penny's apartment.

"Would you like a drink?" The men declined, watched as the vodka bottle clinked against a glass. "What did Adel have to say about my sister?"

"There's been a development," Willards said, then told her about the photograph of Adel he had received.

"*She's* been kidnapped?" Penny said, stunned, the glass halfway to her mouth.

"Maybe," Willards said. "We're not yet—"

"—but she was the last person to see my sister alive and she lied about that! She probably killed Rebecca, right? Isn't that where all this was leading? And now—" She finished her drink in one gulp instead of her sentence. She set the empty glass on the coffee table, tapped her fingers on her legs.

"And you think *I* might be the next target?" She took a breath. "He took Adel? But how could he do it? I thought we were all under police protection?"

"We don't know yet, but we want you to think carefully about everything you've told us. Is there *anything* new you've remembered the past few days?" Willards asked, pleading with her.

Penny stared at the floor, exhaled deeply. "No. I...don't have anything else to say. Believe me. I try, but it's hard to think, to focus, on *anything*. Ben is falling apart; I'd do anything to pull him back together. He's so different now. His behavior. You always hear children are resilient, but it's not true. Neither are adults. I know I'm not. With Graham gone, Rebecca...dead, I feel like...I feel like...I'm *dissolving*."

Her hands twitched as she played out her nervous beats, tears rolled down her face. She didn't bother to wipe them away. She looked at the officers, held her trembling hands up. "Look at me. You *must* find my husband. I'm barely here anymore..."

# # #

Outside Penny's building, Tony and Willards took in the moonlit October evening. The overly hot, brutal Indian Summer had finally surrendered to the seasonal change. Around them, people chatted, laughed as they strolled the streets, the after-dinner crowd on the move.

"Now what?"

Willard scratched his chin. "Adel lied to us about Rebecca, and then, perfect timing, she's abducted, removed from us so we can't question her. My gut says there's got to be more to Adel Daniels then we've found. She part of this, maybe not the victim she said she was or we thought she was."

"Same with Rebecca Roberts," Tony reminded him. "Those frequent trips into the city, not telling her husband or sister? Think she was seeing someone?"

Willards nodded. "Had to have been, right? No matter how 'nice' all these people are, there are some not so nice connections between them. We're missing something, so let's do a deep dive into Adel Daniel's past. She's involved in this more than we ever suspected. Let's start from scratch, double check everything she's ever told us because I think most of it has been a lie."

# # #

Early the next morning, Willards looked over the report he had on Adel Daniels, turned the pages to her parent's profile. "Fresh eyes," he murmured to himself. "Like I've never seen this information before."

Her father was marked as unknown, deceased, mother was Olivia Nelson, deceased.

Wait, that's not right, he thought. He found the notes he had taken when he had first interviewed Adel. She had said she still spoke to her mother occasionally, "on her good days." Her mother had dementia, was cared for at the Ferncliff Memory Care Facility in Hartsdale, New York. But the case file stated Olivia Nelson had died

June 16, 1994 while riding the Metro-North train into the city. She had had a heart attack. Sam Burton, the medical examiner at the time, had scrawled his name on the death certificate.

Willards tracked down the phone number for Sam Burton. Turned out he was widowed, had moved upstate to be closer to his sister and her family. Now in his early eighties, he had retained a robust, raspy voice. A woman answered, he identified himself. A moment later, a voice exploded on the phone.

"Willards? Who the hell is Detective Willards? Do I know you?"

After identifying himself again and briefly providing a background on the case which Burton was familiar with due to the media coverage, Burton said, "But how can I assist you, detective. The Comeback Kidnapper. God *damn* but this case is a puzzler."

"That's why I'm calling, maybe you *can* help. There was a woman by the name of Oliva

Nelson who died of a heart attack on a Metro-North train, back in 1994. She's the mother of Adel Daniels."

"No, she wasn't," Burton said at once.

Willards frowned. "What do you mean?"

"Olivia Nelson was a big time Westchester socialite, very much New England lockjaw, plenty of money. But no kids."

"But the information I have—"

"Olivia helped out with a lot of neglected, abused kids back then," Burton continued. "Orphans and such. Had a real heart for abandoned kids. But she was a widow and after she passed, all of her money—and there was *plenty*, believe me—went to whatever children's charity she was involved with or had established."

Willards shifted in his chair. "But Adel told me her mother *was* Olivia Nelson."

"Maybe there's two of them. Did you check Adel's birth records?"

"No," Willards admitted. "Didn't really think it mattered, but I know better now, and clearly, it matters."

After he ended the call, Willards Googled the Ferncliff Memory Care Facility in Hartsdale, New York. All he was able to locate in Hartsdale was the Ferncliff Cemetery. He went to the Find Family and Friends section, typed in Olivia Nelson, confirmed she had been entombed there in 1994.

# # #

An hour later, Tony rapped on Willards' door, sat down with a sigh. He held a rolled-up set of papers in his hands, tapped them against his leg.

"What took you so long?" Willards asked, grinning. "I found out in ten minutes that Olivia Nelson wasn't Adel's mother and that she's been dead since 1994." He explained all that Sam had told him.

"You had Google and a phone. I had to check old files, birth certificates, then photocopy them, then double check a few things since it wasn't adding up."

Tony unfurled the pages. "Okay, listen to this. Says here that Adel Daniels' maiden name—her *real* maiden name—was Burk, not Nelson, which confirms what Sam told you. Olivia Nelson was not her birth mother. Adel was born in 1987, no brothers or sisters, and her mother's name was Merrill Burk, born in 1965."

Willards leaned forward. "Who the hell was that? And why would Adel lie to us about her mother?"

"Maybe she was ashamed or embarrassed. Or both. I used Adel's social security number and it lists Burk as her mother, father as unknown, likely deceased."

"At least *that's* consistent with what she told us, a

dead father."

Tony said, "Turns out Adel's mother had a long police rap sheet for petty larceny, habitual drunkenness, prostitution. Surprised she had the time or inclination to even have Adel. She started young, in the late 70s, barely a teen, and just continued on."

Willard glanced through the pages of offense: Engaging in sexual conduct with another for a fee, sidewalk solicitation, loitering for the purpose of engaging in a prostitution offense, lewd and indecent acts.

"Just a common White Plains hooker, trouble maker," Tony said. "She was arrested a few times each year, her life was going nowhere, and then it just ends. Seems that she and a fellow by the name of Nick Engersteen—probably her pimp—were murdered in Merrill's home on July 7, 1994."

"Same year as Olivia Nelson," Willards said. "Where was Adel when this happened?"

"Couldn't find that out, police report didn't say, simply states that her mother and this guy Nick were found stabbed to death. A neighbor reported a bad odor coming from the apartment. They had been dead a couple days when they were discovered. The investigation had been closed two weeks later due to the nature of the people killed."

Willards nodded, thinking, *Who would bother to foot the bill or put the time in to find out why they had died? Who'd care about a pimp and the woman he was sending out?* The detective started to fold and unfold the printout of the Merrill Burk's arrest record, finally said, "Why'd Adel latch on to Olivia Nelson, tell us she was her mother? Any ideas? Did she ever meet the woman?"

"Maybe she was looking for the ideal mother figure, and compared to Merrill Burk, Olivia Nelson would be perfect. She was pretty, well known in the area at the time, so maybe Adel saw her on TV or something, wished she was her mother."

"Yeah, but I don't like that both women died in 1994, her real mother and her pretend mother. That can't just be coincidence, can it? Adel was what, only seven at the time? We have to find out where she was at the time her mother was killed and when Olivia Nelson died, and who raised her after her mother was gone."

"We're looking into that," Tony said, standing up. "It's strange about her, isn't it?"

"What do you mean?"

"Pretty much everything we know about Adel Daniels is a lie."

Willards added, "Including the latest development that she's been kidnapped."

"You don't believe the picture?"

Willards shook his head. "I'm at the point where I don't believe anything about Adel Daniels anymore."

# # #

After Tony left, Willards pulled out the photo of Adel that supposedly the kidnapper had taken.

He studied it closely, whispered to the image, "Who are you, *really*? Why have you lied so much about so many things? Have you really been abducted or is it all a game you're playing?"

He read the last sentence under the image:

**I'LL COME BACK
WITH ONE MORE.**

What did that mean? He leaned back, rubbed his eyes, stretched. He tapped his pencil against the computer screen, willing an answer to jump out at him. And it did.

When in doubt, write it out.

It was an old police maxim he leaned on, much like missing the forest because of the trees. Sometimes, too much information, too many facts, names, could cloud and confuse a case, bring it to a standstill in the same way too little could bring it to a halt.

He opened a Word document, a clean slate, then started working the keyboards:

Olivia Nelson
Wealthy widow [who was her husband?], worked with abandoned/orphaned children, left estate to children's charities

Adel Burk Daniels
Born 1987, orphaned at age 7 [where was she from 7 to 18?]

Merrill Burk
Adel's mother, prostitute, petty crime, murdered July 7, 1994 [by whom?]

Nick Engersteen
Check on him; probably just handled Merrill

Adel marries Carl Daniels -- > son, Scotty
Carl kidnapped; implied threat about abducting Scotty?
Adel kidnapped? Staged? Threat of "one more"

Penny and Graham Spencer -- > son, Ben
Graham kidnapped; implied threat against abducting Ben and maybe Penny now that Adel was kidnapped?

Rebecca Roberts, Penny's sister

Murdered in Adel's building

Why so many trips to the city? Seeing someone????

Connection to Adel?

What did she know or what did Adel know about her to be murdered so savagely?

"And what will happen next?" Willards muttered. "'I'll come back, with one more.' Does that mean he'll try to take Penny, or one of the kids?"

He took up his pencil, tapped it against the screen, waited for the answer. He had been in doubt, he had written it out. Now, the solution should appear.

He waiting. Tapped. Sighed.

No answers came.

# # #

Penny Spencer was surrounded, and she knew it.

She knew one police officer was posted in the lobby, another was at the school with Ben. She knew the FBI task force were doing all they could to get Graham back to her, protect her and Ben from abduction. She still shivered whenever she thought of Adel Daniels, taken by the kidnapper even with the police around her. But why didn't the police believe she'd been kidnapped?

Surrounded, watched, protected. Penny knew she should feel safe, but she took no comfort from the attention, derived no sense of security. A steadily increasing counterbalance of doubt and fear kept tipping the scale against her. This Comeback Kidnapper was getting away with it. First Carl, then Graham, then Adel. There was no stopping him and he was getting closer.

I'll come back to get you.

The words made her shudder. They sounded like a children's rhyme yet there was also an implied threat that terrified her. The phrase had a whiff of revenge about it, the promise of fulfillment. Person by person, she was losing everyone she loved. Graham, her sister…

I'll come back to get you.

# # #

Growing up in a broken home, she and Rebecca had managed to survive the difficult situation by playing a game they had made up. They called it *In the Future I See* and it compelled them to look ahead, to gaze past their current pain and misery toward a more pleasant tomorrow or day after tomorrow. Rebecca saw a house with palm trees in the front, a kidney-shaped pool in the back. Penny envisioned a farm with horses to ride, fresh eggs to collect, a barn to play in. They each imagined grand bedrooms with huge picture windows, closets full of the latest toys and clothes, and a maid to make their bed every morning and keep their rooms clean.

Penny had promised herself that when she grew up and married, it would be for life, forever, no separation. And yet that was exactly what had happened to her: She and Graham were now separated, taken apart, not by choice but by an outside force. Torn apart, actually, against their will. Even Rebecca, her rock, sister, best friend, was gone. *Dead,* she thought. *Be honest. She's dead.* The absence, the black void left by the two people she loved most in all the world remained, a growing, living sorrow. How was it possible that everyone she loved in her life had been swept away like crumbs off a table? Why had she lost two people, why her? Why was this happening? She was a good person…

She thought about what the detective had asked her, almost accused her of: Was there anything she wasn't telling him? Anything at all? Of course she had said there wasn't, she had told the police—over and over as if she were speaking a language they were too dumb to decipher—everything she knew, or at least what she could remember. But there just wasn't much to tell.

It was close to three, soon Ben would be home, walked from school with the policeman, Officer Jennings, whom Ben had come to adore. She had wanted to accompany her son to and from school, but after Adel had been taken, the detective had wanted to limit her movements. Ben felt the same way, much preferred to have the policeman walk with him alone because it impressed his friends so much. Penny had let everyone have their way. Ben was safe, that was all that mattered. Her son was safe.

"There's really nothing for me to do," Penny said idly as she had said so many, many times as she stared out the window. The vodka had managed to dull all motivation and slow down her thoughts; she appreciated its company, knew they had grown too close, too comfortable, but really, why not? That's what old friends were for. She was surrounded by police protection but they couldn't help the frantic thoughts in her mind. A few drinks quieted down the chatterbox in her head.

"Graham would *not* have approved," she said to the empty apartment as she finished the drink, her heart now tight at the mention of his name. He was the one and only in her life, her prince, the man who had rescued her, taken her away from her gray, painful existence just as it was crumbling beneath her. *Just like in a disaster movie*, she had marveled at the time. When all was collapsing, when there was no hope, he arrived, carried her swiftly to safety.

# # #

Penny had been 23, still living at home with her mother. Then, at the very last minute, the final second before the bomb would have exploded, Graham had cut the right wires, snatched her from her dreary life.

Rebecca had been saved two years earlier when Michael had asked her to marry him.

"Go!" Penny had encouraged her sister. "Flee this place." They had laughed excitedly, yet Rebecca had expressed concern, even then, over her sister's drinking and limited prospects for the future.

"I'll be fine," Penny had assured her sister, holding the glass up. "*This* is just to help me through the rough patches. And most of the time it's not *too* rough, is it?"

Rebecca had given her sister a fierce hug. "Well, if it ever gets to be too much, just call me and I'll come back to get you."

Penny shook off the memory and the now-familiar phrase. When Rebecca had said it, it had been wonderfully freeing, a safety net that was promised if life got too hard. It was a place to fall into, to be held, to be safe. When said in the right circumstances, *I'll come back to get you* could be a lover's whisper or an older sister's pledge to care for you if you needed her to help you with your gloriously planned future.

Not the menacing statement from a crazed kidnapper...

She flopped down on the couch, fought back the tears as she thought of Graham. She was so terrified for him. One day, he *would* return to her, she had to believe that. She kept clinging to that hope. Absently, she found herself muttering, "One, two, don't be blue, I'll come back to get you. Three, four, watch the door, I'll come back, with one more." Her voice took on the sing-song meter, a tone and cadence she hadn't used since she first sang the song as a child playing the game. But what was the game?

Dirty mother, dirty daughter. The phrase crept across her mind, was quickly extinguished before she was able to fully acknowledge it.

Her mind began to track backward, carefully avoiding the dark closets, trapdoors, and miserable places marked Parents Fighting, Dinner Table Silence, Household Tension, Bill Collectors on Phone, Drinking, Yelling, Things Being Thrown. She hurried past all of that; she ignored The Separation, The Uncertainty, The Bad Moods, all the things that loitered in the house she and Rebecca grew up in, awful events that lingered like monsters ready to jump out from closets or grab you from under the bed. Of course, there were some good times, pleasant memories, but they occurred when away from home, or at school or with Rebecca, the Big Sister, always to the rescue.

And the game, what was it, how was it played? She strained to remember. It was a combination of several: a little Hide and Seek; some Musical Chairs; tag; Duck, Duck, Goose; maybe Red Rover too. Penny closed her eyes, struggled to recall. She forced herself to relax, to let it come to her, knowing if she stalked it, she'd never capture it.

She waited. Then, in her mind's eye, she saw several young children in a circle facing outward, shoulder to shoulder, hands over their faces, hiding their eyes. Giggling. Excited. Nervous energy. A game in progress. One person, eyes not covered, walked around the inside, tapping the backs of those gathered.

"One, two," Penny said aloud, eyes still closed, seeing one child, then another, being touched on the back, "don't be blue, I'll come back to get you." She continued with the numbered counting. When the final word *more* was shouted—"I'll come back, with one more!"—whatever child that had last been tapped was It. All the other children would scatter. The child who was It had to chase them all down, calling out, "I'll come back to get you!" as he or she raced after the others in the game, tagging them and sending them back to the circle where they all remained until the chosen player returned with the final child. The first child who had been tagged and returned to the circle became It and would tap the backs of the other children.

As she reclined on the sofa, it all came back to Penny. She could see the playground, could hear how it would be awash with the breathless cries of, "I'll come back to get you! I'll come back to get you! I'll come back to get you!" Where had the game come from, who had taught it to her and the others at school?

Penny opened her eyes, wondered why the chant from some long-forgotten children's game would end up on the proof-of-life photographs of three kidnapped adults. Images of Graham and Carl's hands placed over their eyes rose up. Penny whispered, "Exactly like in the game." Someone knew the game, knew how it was played. It had stuck with them all those years. *But why this game?* she wondered. *Why would this one be used in such a threatening manner?*

"I'll come back to get you," she said quietly, trying to think back to how she felt when she played the game. It was exciting but sort of scary to be chased by the kid who was It. Hearing him or her screaming after you, shouting, *I'll come back to get you!* Something about it was a little creepy she admitted, especially when...

A flicker of a memory, quickly extinguished.

Dirty mother, dirty daughter.

An unpleasant feeling was quenched. What had happened? What didn't she want to remember? What had they done sometimes? What had *she* suggested they do some times? Penny closed her eyes again, tried to settle in on what she was avoiding. Her thoughts marched on, boot marks in memories that hadn't been disturbed in decades.

Sometimes…

She cleared her throat, thought it would be easier to form words, to say it instead of think it through. "Sometimes, I'll come back to get you…could become a nasty game for one girl. Sometimes, when she was It and thought she had tagged all the kids and they'd be waiting for her at the circle…sometimes, they weren't. We all hid from her. She'd run back, there would be no one there. That was when we'd all jump out from where we had hidden, jeering at her, calling out, 'No one came back for you!' Over and over…"

Penny forced herself to stay with the memories, the raw feelings. *Sometimes, we'd leave you all alone, never even return to mock you, just spy on you as you wandered around, looking for us. We'd all watch you crying and sobbing...* A tear eased out, slid down her face. "Sometimes, it was a mean game. You were abandoned by us. And sometimes—this might have been even worse than hiding from you—sometimes nobody chased you, no one wanted to tag you," she said, realizing she had to call Willards immediately.

She sat up. Ben would be home any second; she wanted to fix her hair, brush her teeth, be alert for him. Unsteadily, she made her way to the bathroom, the childhood images of the game clear, stark, haunting in their cruelty. One child wandering the fields or playground, weeping hysterically, left behind, calling out for the others to come back, come back, begging them to come back to get her.

# # #

"A game?" Willards said after Penny had repeated to him the children's rhyme and the rules. She sat across from him in his office, her eyes wide with the excitement of discovery. "We've Googled the words, looked into the phrasing and nothing came up that related to a game."

Penny shrugged. "All I know is what I recalled, and how we treated this one playmate."

"Who was it?"

"I can't remember. I think it was a girl, back in first grade maybe, but it was so long ago."

Her mother was a witch. That's what you and Rebecca told everyone.

"You know how cruel kids can be. I must have blocked out what we did, leaving her all alone, running away from her, hiding, watching as she broke down. I have these really stark images. These kidnappings must have something to do with that game, don't you think?"

"Kids can be cruel bastards," Willards agreed, an idea forming. "Many adult criminals start out as bad kids reacting to abusive or violent childhoods, but I want to find out more about this child you said was tormented by the other kids. What do you remember about her?"

"Not much. It's all vague; I remember more about how bad it felt to treat someone like this, yet we did it anyway."

Not we. It was you, she corrected herself. *Admit it. It was your idea to torment the girl.*

Dirty mother, dirty daughter.

"Kids usually gang up against others if they are different from them," Willards said. "Just like adults, we put them down if they are a perceived threat or aren't like us. There are many reasons. We need to—"

Tony knocked, entered the room. Willards told him all that Penny had remembered about the game, focusing on how cruel the kids had been to one girl. Tony said he could get the records from her school. "Maybe looking at the pictures of your classmates will jog your memory," he said, "help us ID the girl you're thinking of."

Willards could see the gears in Tony's mind turning. "What?" he asked. "Before you get the school records, what do you know?"

"I've got some information about Adel Daniels—rather, Adel *Burk*—that's going to surprise you both, and may tie-in to what Penny just said."

"What was her name again?" Penny asked.

"Adel's real last name was Burk," Tony said.

Penny stared into the middle distance for several seconds while the two men watched her.

"What is it?" Willards finally asked.

"That name. Burk. Adel Burk. There *was* a girl I went to school with for a short time and her last name was Burk. But the first name isn't right." She looked at both men. "I didn't know anyone named Adel until you introduced me to Adel Daniels."

Tony said, "Let me get those school records now," and he hurried out of the room.

# # #

"Adel Burk was enrolled in the White Plains Elementary School in the fall of 1993," Tony told them fifteen minutes later. "Just for a year, when she was seven years old, in the first grade. She was registered as Adel Burk but the records showed that a few of the teacher's comments on her report cards and documents referred to her as Addy. Here's her picture."

"That's her!" Penny said, her eyes widen as she looked at the old photo of an unsmiling girl with a thin, narrow face. "*Addy* Burk, not Adel! That's the name! She was the girl we played the game with as a child."

Her mother is a witch, Rebecca had warned Penny. *Stay away from her! Dirty mother, dirty daughter. Her mother has a garden of herbs that she uses to cast spells.*

"What do you remember about her?" Willards asked eagerly.

Penny griped her hands tightly, tried to control her breathing and keep her thoughts to herself until she was able to sort through them. "We only knew one another in first grade. She showed up to school, a new kid. I *do* remember she was different from the rest of us, stood out on her own…"

She closed her eyes for a moment as vague recollections began surfacing.

"Something about her face…or her eyes… What was it? A scar or some deformity."

Was she fat, an obese piggy girl? They were fun to tease, make cry. Or maybe it was an ugly girl, Horse Face you called her, the one with the big teeth? Or maybe the kid with the thick glasses, the terrible scar on his mouth?

Willards said, "Just try to remember."

She was a dirty girl. She smelled. Her clothes were dirty, torn, not clean. Her mother was a witch. Rebecca was older, knew these things about people in the neighborhood. Penny just passed the information on to her friends. It made her more popular. Didn't want the kids to find out about her own home, her own mother, the drinking…

After several seconds, Penny said, "*Poor.* I think Addy was poor, came from a poor family. She was sick a lot. Breathing problems. But not much money, so we noticed that. White Plains was a pleasant, middle-class area back then, everyone more or less looked alike, made the same money, all the husbands rode Metro-North to commute into the city for work, most all the mothers stayed at home during the day…"

"What about Addy's mother? Do you remember anything about her?" Tony prompted

She was a witch. She'd put a spell on you. She had a garden of herbs she grew to create her dark magic potions. She did something with men all the time. Wasn't married, did sex stuff with men.

"I remember Addy always boasted to us how much her Mama loved her."

I started it, she admitted to herself. *Everything Rebecca told me about Addy and her mother, I repeated it as if it was fact. I had no idea how far it would go, neither did Rebecca. I told everyone what Rebecca was saying. Better we all made fun of Addy and her home life and her mother before any of them ever found out about mine…*

Penny paused, straining to recall events from decades earlier. "She said her mother loved her so much, more than our mothers loved us, even had a nickname for her."

That made me jealous, she remembered. *That started it. Even though we found out it was a lie. To have a mother love you so much, more than any other mother. I asked Rebecca about that, how much did our mother love us. She just rolled her eyes, said it didn't matter. But it mattered to Addy, and to me. I wanted that kind of love…*

"What was the nickname?" Tony asked.

"Something to do with her face. When she'd be out of breath, her face would turn red and she'd point to it, say, 'See! See!' I remember that. Her red face, pointing at..."

The room was silent.

"A bell?" she finally murmured. "Something about...a tiny shape would appear on her face when she was upset or had difficulty catching her breath. Her face would turn red from the effort to breathe. On her cheek. Her *left* cheek! I can see it now, stark white against her blushing skin. It *was* in the shape of a bell. Now I remember. When she'd get upset with us for ditching her or hiding from her, she'd scream that it didn't matter what we did to her, her Mama loved her, she was her bell."

From far away, she heard Willards asked, "Her bell?"

Behind closed eyes, Penny was able to see it all much more clearly. The bell worked as a shovel, allowed her to dig up more odds and ends from the murky depths. Penny saw herself telling the children Addy's mother was a witch, Addy probably was too, said that Addy's mother used her body for men, worked hard—"on her back and on her knees!"—all the time, not even knowing what that meant. A fit of nasty giggles would follow the statement. Penny hadn't really understood at the time, yet she remembered she had joined the other first graders in taunting Addy with it. All her classmates said it. And Addy didn't have a father, just a man who lived with her.

Why was I so cruel? she wondered, feeling sick to her stomach, disgusted at all that was surfacing, all the garbage and filth.

Penny said, "Sometimes we invited her to play with us. Maybe the teachers forced us. They had to know how we were treating her. I'm sure she had no idea what to expect from us. Sometimes we'd play the game by the rules, all return to the circle after she tagged us. But...

other times, I know we often would all abandon her."

Yes, use the we *word, don't let them know* you *were the one who started it all, kept it going.*

"No wonder that game—those words—were so hurtful to her, saying I'll come back to get you, but we usually didn't…"

"Do you remember whatever happened to her?" Willards asked.

Penny shook her head. "I don't think any of us saw her over the summer, not that we'd seek her out. Then second grade started and she just didn't show up for school. I don't even think we cared what happened to her or where she had gone. We all just forgot about her." She looked at Tony. "Do you know from the school records?"

"There's a lot I couldn't find out, thanks to the sealed court records. But we do know that in July 1994, her mother and Nick Engersteen—the guy that lived with them—were murdered."

"My God, how horrible!" Penny said as the words *ice cream and berries* drifted to the surface. She pushed away the thought, asked, "Where was Addy when it happened?"

"Not at home, thank God," Tony said. "She was seven at the time, was sent off to the White Stone Juvenile Detention Center."

"Detention center? That's harsh for a kid," Penny said. "Why not foster care—"

"Don't know, we're checking. But what I do know is that Adel was at White Stone until 2005 when she turned eighteen. Then, as an adult, she legally changed her name from Adel Burk to Adel Nelson, to solidify her false connection to Olivia Nelson, I guess." He explained to Penny who Olivia Nelson was. "The name familiar to you?"

Penny shook her head, thinking, *I told everyone your mother was a witch, a whore. After she died, no wonder you wanted to find a new mother. How you must have hated us. Hated me...*

"I guess she thought a new name would give her a fresh start," Penny said.

Tony nodded. "She married Carl Daniels a couple years later, in 2007. He had moved here from Michigan. They had their son, Scotty, in 2010."

Willards said, "And I'm certain Adel never told Carl anything about her past or name change. She probably told him the same story she told us, that her only living relative was her mother, Olivia Nelson, but she was housed in a memory care facility in Westchester, only spoke to her occasionally by phone."

Tony nodded. "Probably right. I've got a judge looking at the sealed record now. It's been so long and since Adel is a suspect in the murder of Rebecca Roberts, we hope he won't see a need for its contents to be kept from us."

Penny asked, "Whoever took her, must have been part of my first-grade class, right? To know the game? You said you hadn't found any source for it online or anywhere. What if it was just some local game we played?"

"Do you remember how you started playing it?" Willards asked.

"I think Addy taught it to us," she said. "I think when she first showed up, she wanted to be part of the gang, said she had this special game that no one else knew."

And we played it with you just long enough to learn the rules, then we twisted it around so we could torment and abuse you with it.

"What if this is all about people in my class or those we're married to, and our children?" Penny asked. "Are you going to track them all down, ask them? Wouldn't that explain why we're targeted?"

Tony nodded, gestured at the school records. "After all you've told us and with this information, we'll immediately start making the calls to your classmates and teachers."

"Maybe he's trying to create families?" Penny said suddenly.

"What do you mean?" Willards asked.

"The kidnapper. He's getting the parents first. He has Carl and Adel and Graham and…perhaps he's after me now. And then the children. Scotty and Ben's names are on the back of the Polaroids. And he's never asked for a ransom, so he's…just *taking*, asking nothing in return."

Willards and Tony watched her, gave her room to speak.

She sat up straighter. "I just remembered something else. The guy who took our photos in the park, he mentioned something about the importance of family. He said…he said that it was what he liked so much about the assignment, that it focused on something really important, family. How nothing was more important than family. It was such a cliché to say that I didn't really think about it until just now."

"If he's trying to create families, he'll be delivering on the promise of the game," Tony said, "'I'll come back to get you.'"

"I think you're on to something, Penny," Willards said. "Tony, we better focus on speaking to everyone in Penny and Addy's first grade class. Maybe that's where this all began."

# # #

Penny left the police station, thirsty for a drink,

wanted the blanketing warmth that would cover and comfort her, weigh down all that seemed to be attempting to surface. Ben was being cared for by a neighbor in her building; she needed to look after herself. She sneaked into her apartment, poured a lot of vodka and a little cranberry juice into a glass, stirred it with her finger, sucked her finger, and downed the drink. She closed her eyes and felt the alcohol buzzing about, looking for a foothold, a place to embrace her and take her under.

She mixed a second drink, lighter on the juice. *Who am I fooling?* she thought as she took the glass to the living room, sat on the sofa, stared out the window, sipping, sipping, sipping. *Drinking won't bring Graham back safely or Rebecca; she was forever lost.*

"Why is this happening to me? I'm a good person, a good wife and mother, a good daughter and sister. Rebecca always said I was..." Speaking aloud only made it worse.

You're a terrible person and deserve all that is happening to you, her mind whispered furiously. *The way you destroyed Addy Burk's life, the lies you told about her and her mother.*

Penny shook her head, silencing the poisonous accusations.

Ice cream and berries.

She imagined herself with Rebecca, huddled together at night in their shared bed while their then-single mother would drink herself asleep night after night in front of the television. Sometimes she'd be alone, sometimes she'd have a sleepover guest, but for some reason, the TV was always on. That was a hard and fast memory, falling asleep to whatever was on the television.

Maybe your mother was a witch too, the voice in her

mind suggested. *Maybe she also worked on her back and knees all the time. You weren't as bad as Addy, you were worse. Think about what you led everyone else to do to her...*

Penny stood up unsteadily, weaved a bit on the way to the kitchen, a stumble here, a stumble there, the old soft shoe. "One more for the road," she said, then changed it to, "One more for Ben." *Three drinks in under five minutes had to be a new record*, she thought, trying to ignore the depression that was subtly beginning to settle around her like black snow. It piled up quickly; if she wasn't careful, she'd soon be buried beneath it. But anything was better than the old memories that were resurfacing.

"Be careful," she whispered. "Don't want to be like mother." She started to pour the vodka, stopped. The cranberry remained on the counter. She thought of Graham. Of Rebecca. Of Ben. "I'm all that's left," she realized. "And it's come to this. Again." She stared at the half-empty glass. Her mouth was dry, a brackish taste, her eyes were heavy with exhaustion, alcohol, anxiety and bad memories all remembered. She should go get Ben; he needed her, not a babysitter. Why was she sneaking drinks? Why was all of this happening?

You're no different from Addy Burk. You both had witches for mothers, have both been abandoned by your husbands, soon your children will be taken.

She poured what was left of the bottle down the drain, took a deep swig of the juice, filled the glass with water, drank that. She grabbed her phone, scrolled through the contacts, finally found the name, dialed the number.

It had been years since she had seen or spoken to her AA sponsor.

# # #

Penny attended her first AA meeting the following afternoon while Ben was in school. It had been more than five years. Her sponsor, Flora Applegate, took the train in from Westchester to meet her at the Madison Avenue Presbyterian Church at 12:30.

They hugged quickly, then Flora held Penny away from her. "I'm sorry I haven't kept up with you, your life, especially after reading about Graham in the paper. I guess when I moved out of the city years ago and we didn't communicate much…"

"No, it was my fault. You *did* reach out to me. Several times. I couldn't expect you to keep knocking on a door that never opened. And I really *was* doing well. Until all this…"

"And Rebecca," Flora said, tears in her eyes. "Oh, honey." They embraced again, tighter, longer. Finally, Flora said, "Come on. Let's go." She took Penny by the arm, led her around the side of the church. She opened the heavy, ornate wooden door leading to the basement. Penny hesitated at the first whiff of the familiar scents: disinfectant, stale cigarette smoke, floor polish, dust, the woodsy smell of stacks of construction paper from the nursey school, and, strongest of all, burnt coffee from the centuries-old post church-service coffee hour of fellowship and all those decades of AA meetings. Not everyone smoked at the meetings but most everyone drank coffee; had to drink something.

Penny and Flora settled in the back, nodded at familiar faces they hadn't seen in years. *Didn't anyone ever get better or get out of these meetings*, Penny wondered, alarmed that she was back now too. *Have they all continued to return, day after day, week after week, year after year, decade after decade, world without end?*

Tense, she stiffly sat in the metal folding chair while Flora held her hand like they were seated in a roller coaster, the ride about to start. Two terrified, apprehensive women. Penny glanced at Flora; she actually was calm, relaxed, her eyes clear, her expression alert. *Okay, only one terrified, apprehensive woman,* Penny thought as she modified her observation. *But you did fail me,* she mused cruelly, *didn't keep up with me, and look what happened? Here we are, back in the basement. I blame you. I didn't do anything wrong.*

The slang returned abruptly: *Back in the basement.* You were never on the wagon or off the wagon, or in or out of your cups. There was no wagon, no cups. You were either out and about, living your life above ground with the rest of the population, exposed to the trees, seasons and sunlight, or you were buried here, below ground, in the darkness, hidden away in the basement. Here, you were of no use, or you were broken beyond repair, needed to be fixed or stored away until you could get worked on. In the basement, you were at the bottom. *The losers are here,* Penny acknowledged as she glanced around. *We're all here.* Whatever broken or twisted gene or addiction or screwed up childhood had been experienced, whatever the reason or cause, the truth was, the losers ended up here, at the bottom of the stairs. *Can't win at life or love, can't even control the greedy love for the buzz,* she recalled. Was that a song?

Love for the buzz.

Another expression. How many years had it been since she even thought of the terms, much less said them? Five or more years since a meeting, but had she really blocked it all out so completely in the same way she had her horrid, cruel behavior in first grade?

"Good afternoon," a man said. "I'll be chairing this

meeting." *I remember you,* Penny thought, looking at the short, rotund man with the black, bushy goatee. Max. That was his name.

"My name is Max."

He had been there years ago when Penny used to come two or three times a week. She settled into the chair. *I got out, Max,* she thought. *For a while, but now I'm back where I started from.*

# # #

Outside, an hour later, she and Flora were on Lexington Avenue looking for a place to get a sandwich.

Once they were seated in a diner, Flora asked, "So, how did you feel?"

"Awful. Nervous. Sweaty. Like a failure, I guess. Which I am."

"Which you are *not*. God, but this brings back memories, Penny. Your greatest hits, trashing yourself, belittling yourself—"

"And you rescuing me, fighting me."

"With you. Fighting *with* you, every step of the way. Remember? Shoulder to shoulder?

Penny nodded. Another cliché: Every day, every step of the way. But it had worked, as cynical as she was, it *had* worked. *Did* work. Millions of people, one day at the time, kept coming back. It works if you work it, work it 'cause you're worth it. And so on. With Flora's help, she'd start all over again, back in the basement. She *would* quit drinking. Again.

They ordered. Chatted about nothing much. Penny knew Flora was honest enough to admit that Graham and Rebecca were two very good reasons to resume drinking.

"Tell me about Ben," Flora finally asked. "How's he

handling all of this?"

"He's…the only reason I've gone back to the basement."

"No, you do it for *you*," Flora said firmly. "Remember?"

They worked their way through lunch like this, fits and starts, detours mixed with familiar routes of conversation. When they were standing outside again, Flora asked, "I'll meet you tomorrow. Same time?"

"You don't have to come back in, Flora. It was important for my first time, but I can't ask you to make the trip in for each meeting. I should a get a sponsor here in the city."

"Thirty days, thirty meetings. With your sponsor. That's me, it's *still* me. You know that."

Penny agreed quickly, wanted this to be done. Suddenly tired, she wanted to be finished with all the AA discourse. She was wrung out from it all, from seeing Flora again, the basement, the smells, the memories, the people, the stories. She hugged Flora, said thank you, waited until a cab arrived and whisked her friend back to Grand Central.

She turned, felt lighter, as if the weights had been left outside the doors of the diner. She *had* been to the basement, that was true, but now she was above ground, again. Functioning, still breathing. *One meeting down*, she thought, heading toward Third Avenue, passing a liquor store with bright cardboard displays in the window, oversized bottles, so many of them, so many different shapes and sizes. Penny stopped, stared, felt her willpower and clarity dissolve like a tablet in water, sensed it crumble, fizzle, almost disappear.

She turned, walked the opposite direction, took a different, longer way home.

# # #

Penny pulled her phone out of her bag once she was home to check messages since she had turned it off during the AA meeting. She had two voicemails from an unknown number.

"Penny? Penny Hawthorn?" a female voice asked. Nervous, breathless, then shouting, "IT'S ADDY! WHERE ARE YOU? WHY'D YOU LEAVE ME HERE ALL ALONE? WHY'D YOU TREAT ME THIS WAY?"

The message ended. Shaking, Penny replayed it. The hysterical screaming behind each word was unsettling to hear. When it stopped, she poured herself a Diet Coke, her hand trembling so badly the can tapped the glass several times. Had Addy escaped or had she faked the photo like Willards suspected? Was Graham free too? Was it all over?

The second voicemail was from Willards, asking her to call him.

# # #

"We're already working with yours and Adel's phone services and are receiving a live feed of your phone records," Willards told Penny. "The voicemail message was made from a payphone in Brooklyn."

"I didn't know there were any payphones left," she said.

"The city collects revenue from calls placed from pay phones, and the city *always* needs money. I think there are only a couple thousand pay phones in Brooklyn, if that. But we located it, have a team over there now, checking for prints," Willards said.

Anxiously, Penny asked, "Do you think that her

ability to make the call from the payphone means she's free or escaped? Is there any news about Graham?"

"We haven't had any more contact from anyone. She might have been forced to the make the call under duress, and then was taken back to wherever she, Graham and Carl are being kept," Willards said. "But we suspect she faked the photo, to misdirect us."

"So, she wasn't kidnapped. Then, where is she? Where is Graham?"

Willards said, "We don't know."

"How'd she get my number?"

Willards said, "Probably from Rebecca's phone?"

Fighting to hold back tears and a hysterical edge to her voice, Penny said, "And she used the name Addy, not Adel. She called me by my maiden name. Why would she do that?"

"I think she's just confirming what we suspected, that whatever had triggered these events all goes back many years, to when she was seven and in first grade. Any idea why'd she single you out, Penny?"

"What do you mean?"

"She called you. Asked specially where you where, why you left her there all alone, why'd you treat her that way?"

Your past is coming back to get you, her mind warned her. *No more secrets.*

"I have no idea," Penny said. "I haven't even thought of Addy Burk until Tony mentioned her name."

Willards sighed. "Yeah, that's what we've discovered to. We've reached out to teachers and your classmates, and very few have any recollections. The teachers acknowledge they didn't do a very good job protecting her from bullying and the few of your classmates who even remember her don't recalled playing the game much."

"I'm sure they don't want to admit the terrible way we treated her, either," Penny said.

"You're probably right."

The way you *treated her. It was all you, Penny Hawthorn.*

# # #

The next afternoon at 12:45, Flora called Penny.

"Where are you?"

"Home."

"Then you're not coming." A statement of disappointment, not a question.

"I should have called. I'm sorry…"

A weary sigh. "Forget it. Look, I know this is an awful time for you, but slipping back will only make things worse. You know that, right?"

"She called me, Flora. Yesterday, while we were in the basement, Adel Daniels called me! If I hadn't had my phone turned off at that meeting, I would have been able to talk to her!"

Penny was miserable, angry. Flora heard it, said, "No, Penny. If you hadn't been *drinking* in the first place, you wouldn't have been at the meeting. Own it, okay? Don't blame me or the basement. It always goes back to what's in your glass, remember? It always does. Don't act up by being angry at me or deciding to skip meetings, deciding not to get healthy. If you're not ready to do this for you, then you're not ready. And I get that. You have too much on your plate." Flora hesitated, went softer. "Focus on one thing at a time, all right? Let's get things settled with you, Penny, okay? Meet me at two, Trinity Baptist on sixty-first street, okay? We'll go to their meeting."

Penny declined the offer, regretted shutting Flora out

of her life, but it was too much to deal with at the moment. "When Graham is home safe, when this is over, I'll reach out to her again," she said minutes later as she fluffed the pillows in the apartment. She looked out the window; it was a sparking bright, beautiful fall day. She thought of going outside, yet wasn't able to hear her phone very well on the streets. What if Addy called again? What if—

Her phone jingled. She snatched it up, didn't recognize the number, pressed the green *accept* button, waited.

"Penny?"

"Addy—"

"WHY'D YOU LEAVE ME HERE ALL ALONE? WHERE IS EVERYONE? WHERE HAVE THEY ALL GONE?"

The call disconnected. Penny stared at the phone, couldn't look away. It rang, it was Willards. "The call was made from Brooklyn again, a different area, different pay phone. Dozens of prints on the first booth that we're pulling, but it'll take time."

"Why is she calling me, screaming at me, then hanging up?"

"We don't know—"

"And when she asked 'Where is everyone? Where have they all gone?' I know that was about the game..."

Willards said, "I agree. She's obviously regressing back to that time when she was in first grade, reliving the time she played the game, felt abandoned by all the kids. But there have been some developments I want to tell you about. First, I need you to stay in your apartment and wait until a police officer arrives. It'll be Officer Denton.

"Why? What's happened?"

"I just sent you his picture to confirm his identity,

and I also notified your front desk. Did you get the photo?"

She checked, looked at the photo, confirmed with Willards she had received it. "But we already have an officer with Ben. Why do I—"

"Because we received another gray envelope."

She almost dropped the phone, her hand was shaking do hard. "Is Graham okay?! Was there a picture—?"

"There were no photos of Graham or Carl or Adel," Willards said. "It was a Polaroid of an empty chair. For some reason, the photograph was cut off at the right edge. On the chair was a hand-lettered sign. The words were written in big, bold letters and read 'Reserved for Penny'."

"Me?"

"Don't worry, Denton will be there at any moment. We just got this photo and I wanted to let you know. It seems to support the theory that Adel—if she really is behind all of this and we are beginning to think she is— wants to create families, bring in the adults first. But I wanted to make sure you're all right. Penny?"

It took her a moment to respond. "Yes. I'm here. Were any of the words from the game included?'

"No, not this time. And I meant to ask, did those words and numbers mean anything when you played the game? 'Don't be blue, watch the door'?"

"None of it really meant anything, other than counting out the numbers as we tapped the kids on their backs. Just a rhyme."

Willards nodded, made some notes, said, "Okay, good to know, one less piece of the puzzle to go after."

She had to ask. "Was Ben's name written on the back of the photo of the chair?"

"Yes, it was," Willards admitted.

Penny didn't respond.

"Penny?"

After a moment, wearily, she said, "Yes, I'm here."

"Remember that court order, the one that was sealed from when Addy was a child? It was opened. A lot of surprises."

Penny sat down on the couch, put the phone on speaker so she wouldn't have to hold it in her trembling hand. She set it on the coffee table.

Willards said, "According to the police records, it was the court's finding that Addy Burk killed her mother and that man, Nick, who was acting as her pimp."

"Killed them? But she was just a child…"

"Did it with a butcher knife," Willards continued, "which I found hard to believe but her mother and the other guy had been drinking, so if they were drunk or passed out, it wouldn't have been too difficult to overpower them."

"But she was only seven…"

"And due to the nature of the crime and her age, that's why she was committed to the White Plains institution—not an orphanage—until she was eighteen. She was obviously mentally unstable."

"And after she turned eighteen?" Penny asked, trying to picture a seven-year-old doing these crimes.

"Like Tony told us, they released her. She'd been locked away about ten years, hadn't caused any problems, had been raised in a horrible home with child endangerment written all over it. I think she was probably discharged after years of psychiatric evaluations and treatment, they concurred that she was not any threat to society, was only required to check in with some social service organization."

"What happened to her after she got out?"

"She filed with the state to change her name, which

was approved, and like we figured, at some point she met her husband, Carl, told him—and later, us—that her mother was Olivia Nelson, who of course was dead by then, as was her still unknown father. There was no reason for Carl to doubt anything she told him. At that point in her life, Addy Burk no longer existed. She was now Adel Daniels."

# # #

After Officer Denton arrived at Penny's apartment and checked in with Willards by phone, the detective ended the call, laid his head in his folded arms, rested on his desk. It was just as exhausting working a case when it was breaking wide open as it was when it was log jammed at a standstill, as this one was. So much information was coming at him but it also seemed to be rushing past, a blur of images and words that made no sense to him.

Was it possible Adel had kidnapped her own husband and Graham, then faked her own abduction, but for what reason? All of the first-grade classmates had alibis for the times of the kidnapping. Most barely remembered Addy Burk or playing the game. If Adel did it, why was she so focused on Penny? What had gone on between them that was still bothering her decades later? And were Carl and Graham still alive?

He stretched, glanced down at the court records he had just read to Penny over the phone. He couldn't help thinking about Adel. Her terrible childhood, the murders, the time in the mental institution, growing up in such a place, changing her name to start over new, adopting a fake mother to replace the one she had killed. Still, from a thirty-thousand-foot view, she seemed to have done all right. She married a nice guy, started a family, just living her life, her debt to society—if it was even a debt—paid in full, all was going fine for her, the past long gone, buried, left behind, until the day her husband was kidnapped.

If only changing a name could change a past, he thought. He couldn't blame her for trying to forget or block out her early years. Her childhood must have been hell; who knew if she had been sexually or physically abused? Did her mother even protect or love her? Sounds like the kids at school were unbelievably cruel to her, taunting her, mocking her and her mother, hiding from her when they played the game. No wonder the poor kid went crazy. Just seven when she went after her mother and Nick; such rage for a little kid. He hadn't shared the gruesome details with Penny but Addy Burk had gone after the two adults with a vengeance, just like Adel had repeatedly stabbed Rebecca. He read again from the report:

"Almost beyond comprehension that a seven-year-old could inflict such wounds on two adults. The mother was stabbed a total of 27 times, several in the face, resulting in both eyes being gouged out, and then her head was almost severed due to the number of times her neck was attacked. The man suffered the majority of injuries to his chest and stomach, a total of 17."

"Jesus," Willards said, closing the report, wanting the images out of his head. But a lingering thought held his attention: Seven. "Seven," he said. Addy was seven when she did this. Just a seven-year-old kid. The thoughts were barely registered when all the lightbulbs in his mind lit up. "Seven," he repeated. "Could that be a trigger? Seven years old…the same age as her son, Scotty, is about to be…"

He jabbed some numbers into his phone, left a voicemail for Gail Skillman, the Virginia-based FBI profiler assigned to the case. Two minutes later, Skillman called. She had been a consultant for the task force from the beginning so Willards didn't have to give her any background. They had spoken on the phone many times, exchanged emails and texts, but never met, just two voices on the phone, trading information.

"Hi, Gail. I had an idea I wanted to run by you. As you know, we think the abduction photo of Adel is a fake, used to misdirect us."

"Especially now that she's made the phone calls."

"Exactly," he agreed. "It makes no sense for her to imply she's been abducted, then call Penny—"

"Unless she's so confused, she can't think logically. She's behaving like a child, impulsively, so she probably wasn't aware that once she made the first call, it destroys the illusion that she was kidnapped."

"That was the question I had for you, about her regression and child-like behavior. Addy Burk was seven years old when she killed her mother and Nick Eagersteen. When she called Penny, she now refers to herself as Addy, her voice almost sounded like a child; she was enraged on the phone, screaming at Penny, accusing her. You've heard the recordings."

"Yes, it's as if she's throwing a tantrum. She's no longer thinking like an adult, so she's going to be much more reactive, spontaneous in her behavior. One thing I am curious about is why she is directing her rage at Penny. Any ideas?"

Willards said, "Not yet, but I was wondering, do you think Adel devised this kidnapping of Carl and Graham because it coincided with her son Scotty turning seven? Did one event trigger the other? I checked, his birthday is next week. Could there be something in her subconscious that would be…reawakened by the fact that her son is turning the same age she was when she killed her mother and Nick?"

"Hmm. Yes, Scotty turning seven could be a trigger that could send her spiraling backwards in time. In many cases, psychotic mayhem can be set off by the anniversary of an event. Those involved in the original situation may repress all memory of it, live normal lives, but something will activate what was suppressed, bring it to life again and the only way to tamp it down is to act out the episode again, get control over it."

"Not sure I follow."

"Most of us are able to put an unpleasant experience out of our conscious memory, file it away somewhere so we don't have to be exposed to it all the time," she explained. "Above all else, we want to avoid painful memories. Penny is the perfect example. She found it unbearable to admit how terribly she and her friends treated Addy in first grade, right? She locked away those experiences, the words to that game, for decades, right? It was only the constant stress she's under with Graham's abduction and seeing the phrase 'I'll come back to get you' that finally broke open that locked memory. To help her husband, she had to relive what she and her classmates had done, had to allow the pain to reawaken so she could uncover what she had buried."

"Yeah, that all makes sense. But what about Adel? Where do you think she is at now, mentally, since she's in this regressive stage?"

Skillman said, "I can't say with certainty because we have no recent psych evaluation of Adel. I don't know her recent or current mental state, only the reports we have when she was first admitted at age seven and a few follow-up reports. But here's one way to look at it, to guess at what may be happening. I use this in class, so bear with me. I take a common life experience and use it to see how the majority of the population, the mentally healthy, deal with it, and how a psychotic individual handles it. I ask my class, by a show of hands, the question, have you ever had your heart broken?"

A perfect image of Willards' ex-wife, Sara, rose up, fully formed to the last detail. Thick blonde hair, bright blue eyes, a happy, healthy smile almost all the time, a great, athletic figure that she worked hard to keep in shape. She was beautiful, kind, loving…until the day she betrayed him, shattering his spirit. He never saw it coming, never suspected. His heart never really fit back together again after that.

"My hand is up," he said into the phone, eyes squeezed tight against the reawakened pain.

"And no matter how bad it was at the moment, as the years passed, it became a little more tolerable, right?"

"But only a little. *Maybe…*"

There was a pause, then Skillman said, "But the point is, you allowed yourself to heal and deal with it. Like a bad scrape or wound, pain needs time to heal. There will often be a scar but it does take care of itself, eventually. That's how a healthy body takes care of itself and how a mentally well person deals with emotional injury.

"However, with a psychotic individual, their effort goes into eliminating whatever is discomforting to them; that's where their energy goes, suppression. But they can only do that for so long, the stress only increases over time, eventually becomes overwhelming.

"I say it's like blowing up a balloon that's filled with confetti. As long as the balloon fills with air, all is well. But soon it's going to have too much air, it'll pop, and everything inside—all the pain which is represented by the confetti—explodes, goes everywhere. Or, like a leaky boat in a lake. Sooner or later the water will get in. It always does. The hidden things begin to surface until they can't be ignored anymore. For many psychotics, the only way to once again suppress their misery and rage is to reenact the event, recapture all the pain, try to create a different or better outcome."

Willards said, "They try to fix what went wrong or change what happened?"

"Exactly. Once the trigger is activated, they know what's about to happen, they want to change it through a force of their own will."

"So, right now, Adel may be preparing to recreate the events she went through when she was seven years old?"

"Possibly," Skillman cautioned. "Remember, this is only theory based on what we know about her, and we only know what happened when she was in first grade."

"And while we keep focusing on her, I'm still confounded over how and *why* she abducted Carl and Graham in the first place."

"The *why* is crucial," she agreed with him. "I think once we can determine the why, the reason that all these events have occurred with these specific people will be clear. There's one other idea I have that could be a severe trigger for Adel."

"What's that?"

"Betrayal. It's what drove her to such rage playing the game as a child. When the other kids hid from her or wouldn't return to the circle after she tagged them, it was a form of betrayal. They didn't play by the rules. Someone like Adel could go into a rage if the rules as she sees them are broken."

"So, if she felt betrayed by someone close to her—"

"—it could take her all the way back to the state of psychotic violence she expressed when she was seven. Only now with the experience and cunning of an adult."

# # #

Once Willards was home, he poured himself a tonic water, stared out the window as the city darkened around him. He missed his children terribly; it was always worse at night. When they were younger, it was his great joy to tuck them in to their beds, to hold them, touch them, confirm they were real, that he and Sara had created them out of nothing other than love and passion. They were innocent, unblemished by the filth and crime of the city, the underside of Manhattan that he dealt with every day.

He had always been out of the apartment by 7 a.m., always with the hope that the extra time in the morning might work in his favor so he could get out of the station by seven, home by eight. Rarely worked out that way, but still, he felt better that he was trying. Bedtime was eight-thirty, had to be home for that. Didn't always make it, but it was the effort, the desire, that counted. The kids knew it, Sara knew it, he knew it. He tried. Every single day he tried to get just an hour ahead of a job that was like quicksand, always sticking to him, pulling him away from where he really wanted to be.

Sara was drifting from him. He knew that, knew she resented the life she had signed up for. Didn't like the road she was traveling. She resented Steve that he pretty much always failed in his attempts to get home in time for dinner or bedtime. He left her alone all day, called or texted if/when he could, then called later in the day to say he wouldn't make dinner, or bedtime, or the worst, don't wait up for me…

Willards finished his drink, shut his mind from those dark, dark nights. He had always had a thirst for alcohol, it brought quick comfort, especially after Sara left with the kids. But he knew too many cops who drank their way through the evenings, didn't want to be a member of that club, began to swig tonic water instead. After witnessing Penny Spencer up close and personal, saw how she handled stress, he was more grateful than ever for the choice he made.

The sunlight was gone, his apartment was now dark, no lights turned on. He preferred it that way, found any illumination to be a bit of a distraction. The dark helped clarify his thoughts, brought them into focus. He worked out the toughest puzzles and mind twisters in the blackness behind his eyes; in shadows, he could drift, float above the circumstances, the clues, the bewilderments that made so many cases so fuzzy. Darkness usually brought him a better perspective since there was nothing there to begin with.

Sara's departure and the kids' absence increased the size of the apartment. It was as if he had discovered a whole other wing of rooms. Everything echoed now when he walked or moved about, there was no one there to absorb sound other than him. No one spoke to him; he hated the silence, would have preferred the hushed, frantic arguments that they had, whispered rage so as not to wake the children.

Ironically, for the first weeks after she had left, he was able to get home to the empty apartment pretty much every night by seven-thirty. It was as if now that it didn't matter anymore, everything worked in his favor. It was bad karma or a bad joke, but it was what it was. More time at home in his huge, alarmingly vacant home. Sara and the kids were now in New Jersey at her parent's house. Phone calls were made, arrangements were made, plans were made. It was all about scheduling time. He saw their children on the weekend, tried a dinner, alone, with Sara, but he couldn't restart what had already run out of gas.

"Nothing will change, with you, with the job, we

both know it," she had said. "I'm a single mother, a wife with no husband. That's not what I wanted, or what we wanted. I'm angry all the time because I am alone all the time."

He didn't respond, knew he had to keep his mouth shut, just listen. What she was saying was true but he wanted to put his foot in the door before it was permanently closed. He still loved her, wasn't angry with her, knew she was right, but wasn't sure how to respond when she told him she was seeing someone.

"Been seeing someone," she corrected herself, reached for her wine, gulped it. A good Catholic confession. No tears. Between the salad and the pasta, at Bella's, their favorite place over on Amsterdam Avenue. He thought the familiar surroundings might soften things a bit, break up the bitter, jagged concrete that they were both stuck in.

Hurt, surprised, speechless at her admission, his appetite gone like a train off the tracks, he could only watch her. He wanted tears, regret. Instead: "We love each other. He likes the kids…"

"He's met them?"

She gave him a look of such dismay, such rage, such pain, that it knocked the breath out of him. "Of course. You were never home much, so we all went bowling after school one day. It was fun. When was the last time we had fun? Or you had fun with the kids?" She could see she was hurting him; she stopped, pulled back. That wasn't like her, to be cruel, to twist the knife. "You weren't home, remember? It was phone calls all the time, you'd be late, put the kids to bed, you'd be home by ten or don't wait up. Did you even want to come home?"

"Of course," he said immediately, on cue, but wondered. Had it really been that bad? Had he really stepped so far away from his wife and family that they were no longer in view, decided to move along without him?

It appeared so.

Quietly, Sara said, "We all got tired of waiting for you to come home."

In the darkness of the apartment, Willards wandered around in boxer shorts and a t-shirt. Opened the refrigerator. It was so bright with the light on in the pitch-black kitchen. He pulled out another tonic, twisted the cap. It hissed a bit, sprayed, bubbled up, furious, angry like he was angry. He collapsed into his easy chair, gazed into the darkness, drifted.

What else could he have done or should have? Or would do if he had another chance? Past, present and future were locked together, nothing was ready to give an inch, only to take from him, his wife, his kids.

"Have you ever had your heart broken?" Skillman had asked.

Oh, yeah, big time.

# # #

Finally, to bed, to listen to the cable news arguments with their panel of talking heads, then flipped to one of the late-night hosts, then dark silence. He drifted, bobbed towards sleep, his thoughts careless as they meandered about, no filters or concerns. He wondered about Adel's mother, Merrill Burk. What kind of woman would raise a child in that horrible environment? Did she make any effort to clean up her act or did she simply not care?

Sad.

Was she so desperate for cash that it didn't matter to her what her daughter was exposed to? Indifferent to those around her. Same with Nick; was he to blame too, did he drive Merrill forward, force her to generate income for him? Probably. Of course, why not? That was how it worked. *He made me do it…*

Willards turned over and flipped the pillow. The cool side felt good. He felt himself easing toward slumber. What really happened that night? Adel—Addy—just seven years old. Had there been an argument, had she begged her mother to stop whatever she was doing? Was Nick abusing Addy? Had Merrill seen it, fought with Nick? But the report said Addy killed them both. Why the rage at her mother? Was there no love between them at all?

Again, Willards turned the pillow. His usual portion of the mattress had worn itself into a familiar hollow, form fitted to him. He wasn't comfortable on Sara's side, reminded him of how big the bed was, how huge the apartment was. Her side didn't feel slept in; it was still firm, hard, unyielding. He sighed, started into the blackness, didn't want to look at the clock on the night table next to him, wanted to be pulled under by sleep. Couldn't help circling back to Addy, age seven, one more time.

What had compelled Addy Burk to kill her mother? Matricide. He had looked up the stats. The incidence made up less than 2% of US homicides. It was most always committed by sons, only a very small number of girls aged eighteen or younger did it. For daughters over 18, mental illness was most often to blame, but girls under that age, mental illness was the least likely root of the crime. It was usually traced back to severe abuse by the mother in more than half of the cases. The next most likely cause were girls who were ostracized from their peers or classified as dangerously antisocial.

That's you, Addy, he thought as sleep finally pulled

him under. *At home or at school, nobody liked Addy Burk.*

#

The next morning, Willards awoke feeling melancholy. Something about the previous night's musings had made him blue. Too many unanswered questions in the case, in his own life. He was lonely. There, he admitted it. It made no difference. The few years before he married, he had fought it with eighteen-hour days, but that still left six hours alone. Sleep helped nip some of that off, but it wasn't until he met Sara, had the kids, that the loneliness withdrew so significantly that he wasn't even aware of it. But then the ten-hour days turned to twelve, the distance between himself and Sara and the kids increased and...

Coffee helped. Strong and black. The taste of something hot and harsh helped aid in chasing away emotional distress. Planning the day also pushed the blues aside since he needed to be engaged, focused. Skillman had been right: We don't like to experience pain, think about it or examine it. We'd prefer to bury it six feet under and never visit the grave.

Today, his plan was to call Sam Burton, the old medical examiner, the one with the long, long memory, one Willards hoped was still intact.

#

"Knew you'd be contacting me again," Burton said heartily over the phone. "Or I'd call you if you didn't."

"Why's that?" Willards asked, bemused, smiling at the sound of the cagey old timer.

"Loose ends. You got plenty of them. And I got a

theory I want to run by you. But those loose ends. All your fancy computers can't close them up, can they?"

"You're right. They can't figure out what's going on if they don't have the information to begin with. They can't think, or solve crime, that's for sure. The world still needs us for that." He quickly updated Burton on all they had learned since they had spoken. After Burton asked some follow up questions, Willards said, "My reason for calling is to see what else you may know about Olivia Nelson and this fellow named Nick Eagersteen."

"What about 'em?"

"You have any insights into them, anything you remember that we don't have in our files? We don't have much…"

"Sure do. In fact, after we last spoke, I went back over my journals."

Willards sat up straighter. "You kept case journals?"

"Well, more like a diary I guess. Been writin' in them for more than fifty years, my day to day comings and goings, as well as cases, local and national events." He chuckled. "My life, as you can imagine, was much like anyone's so it's a bore to read, but I went back into them to check a few things after we last spoke."

"And?"

"This Olivia Nelson woman. From what I jotted down, her maiden name was Lowrey. Nothing special about her, came from a middle-class family in Ossining, but then she married the transportation millionaire Reggie Nelson and everything changed. His name ring a bell?"

"No, why? Should it?"

"Before your time, I guess," Burton said. "Funny how it's the important things people *don't* know that always matter, isn't it? Reggie and his family's old, old,

old money was heavily invested and they owned a significant amount of the New York, New Haven, and Hartford Railroad, the largest passenger and commuter carrier in New England. Eventually, they were bought out by J.P. Morgan and then the whole thing came under the authority of New York State and is now known as the Metro-North Commuter Railroad.

"What's fascinating is that Olivia almost didn't marry Reggie Nelson. I heard all this from Dexter Ponds, the reporter for the *Ossining Gazette*. He's dead now, so's the paper, and what I'm about to tell you wasn't even printed so don't bother looking for it. The paper spiked it. This was back in the sixties, when things like this were routinely kept quiet, especially if great money and influence were involved."

"Things like what?" Willards wished Burton wasn't so long-winded, yet knew it was the only way to hear the old man out.

"In the sixties, there was a bunch of escapes from Ossining State Prison. It was called Sing Sing back then, named after some Indian tribe. Anyway, blocks B and D of the prison housed the mentally ill, with B-block known to be where the most violent offenders were kept. This reporter, Dexter Ponds, he told me that back in 1966, one of these fellows got loose, managed to rape a couple of the women in town before he was recaptured. None of the women came forward, of course. Too ashamed and back then, people didn't talk much about such things in public or the papers. One of the women became pregnant and since this was before legal abortions, she found it difficult to find someone to help her end the pregnancy."

"Even under those circumstances?" Willards asked.

"Yep. Didn't matter. It was a different time and place back then, so it was all very hush hush. Still, she was pregnant, unmarried, had nowhere to go in her life, would never say who the father was. Can't blame her, can you? What would people say if she told them the father was some escaped lunatic!"

Trying to move things along, Willards asked, "I'm thinking one of the pregnant women ties into this case, right?"

"Yep, Olivia Lowrey, of course. That's the woman. She hightailed it up to Boston until the baby was born."

"Her family or friends took her in?"

"From what Ponds told me, I believe she had a sister who helped her, but once the baby—a boy—was born, the sister wanted her gone. Olivia returned to Ossining, the only place she knew, with the infant. Her first stop was Stony Lodge hospital where she left the baby in a cardboard box in the waiting room. Pond found out about all this from a nurse he was dating at the facility. As soon as the baby was discovered, they tried to track down the mother, couldn't find her because of course, she didn't *want* to be found. But Ossining was a very small town and everyone knew—or assumed—it was Olivia Lowrey's baby. After all, the very day she returns to town—"

"A baby is abandoned at the hospital," Willards finished the sentence even as he was typing the story into his computer. "I follow. Who was the father? The convict, right?"

"Yep. Fellow by the name of Clay Thomas. Crazy as they come, violent streak a mile long, just as wide. Homicidal, bottom of the barrel. Cunning, smart son of a bitch, in his own, twisted way. Escaped twice more, finally died in Sing Sing in the early eighties."

"And his son? What happened to Olivia's abandoned baby?"

Willards could hear Sam Burton lick his lips, heard

the smile in his voice.

"Well, the son was adopted by Mr. and Mrs. Floyd Eagersteen of Yorktown, New York."

Willards leaned back in his chair. "Shit! You're telling me Nick Eagersteen was Olivia's son!?"

Burton let out a short laugh. "Yep! Told you there were some mighty loose ends! But remember, none of this was publically acknowledged. After Oliva gave up her son, she never, ever looked back, never admitted to ever having a child. She wanted to be thought of as pure as the driven snow and once she met Reggie Nelson, there was no way in hell she was going to admit having an illegitimate son, let along that she had been raped by a convict."

"He'd never have married her," Willards said.

"Hell no! And the only reason my newspaper buddy knew any of this was that when the engagement was announced, everyone wanted to know the background of Olivia. That small town—like any little village—started to whisper up the old story, and Pond's nursing lady friend filled in all the gaps."

"And Reggie Nelson never heard about this?" Willards asked. "Wouldn't his family have—"

"Guess not. He was head over heels crazy for Olivia Nelson and she for him. Any nasty rumors were ignored since the family genuinely liked Olivia, and Reggie was his own man, even at a young age. What he wanted, he got. His family didn't listen to the lowlifes who were whispering this story. Olivia denied it, of course. Plus, there really was no actual proof. The names of the women who had been raped were never made public. Reggie was in love with Olivia, she was in love with him, so they were married."

"And you think this story is all true?" Willards asked.

"Oh, yeah. And it also probably explains why Olivia

never had any children."

"Why was that?"

"There's always some truth in local gossip," Burton explained. "She wasn't able to conceive; some thought she was frigid, which would make sense after the rape. In any case, she and Reggie never had kids, so when he died, all the money went to her, and perhaps, to ease her conscience about abandoning her own son, she spent most of her time and money on orphans and abused or abandoned kids."

Guilt money, Willards thought. "Whatever happened to her son, Nick? Did he ever—"

"I know what you're going to ask, and yes, I'm pretty certain Nick found out Olivia was his mother. The family who adopted him wasn't very wealthy, had a dodgy relationship with the law. As the years went by, Nick—like his blood father—was in and out of jail, a dangerous sociopath from what I learned. He probably leaned hard on all sorts of people until he heard the story about Olivia abandoning a baby in the hospital, an infant that matched his age, and I expect his parents finally told him all they knew about his adoption. Knowing she was loaded, Nick contacted her, proved who he was, blackmailed her, told her he'd go public, tell the world that he's her bastard son. How do you think she'd respond?"

"With cash to keep him silent?"

"Exactly," Burton said.

Willards was taking notes as quickly as he could. "This is incredible information, Sam. Do you know if Nick ever found out his real father was Clay Thomas?"

"Probably not," Burton said, "but there's really no way to be certain about that. But it does lead me to one thing I have learned that shook me up a bit. It's this theory I have. It'll sound kind of crazy but hear me out."

Burton cleared his throat. "It's a bit unsettling, but here goes. I saw a news show last week that had this theory that genes carry a lot of the personality and disease traits of people, both good and bad. Alcoholism, breast cancer, autism, and so on. I didn't understand a lot of it, but I began to wonder why the people in this case are all so god damn violent. I got to thinkin' if there was any sort of gene that Clay Thomas might have passed on to Nick that would give him an inclination for violent behavior. You think that's possible?"

"That sounds like the nurture versus nature idea," Willards said. "You know, the question of is our behavior based on the environment we're raised in or the gene pool we come from."

"Right."

"Actually, the consult on this case is an FBI profiler and she spoke to us about this recently. Adel Daniels seems to be regressing back to who she was when she was in first grade, taking on the traits of Addy Burk. She's called Penny twice, hysterical, screaming at her, saying she's Addy Burk, wanting to know why Penny left her all alone—"

"Adel escaped?"

Willards sighed, explained that they now suspected the entire kidnapping of Carl and Graham had somehow been conceived and carried out by Adel. "That's a whole other can of worms. Our main concern—in addition to Adel's whereabouts—is that we haven't had any proof of life photos of Graham or Carl in weeks, just the *Reserved for Penny* photo. But Adel is involved in all of this in some way that we never suspected before."

"Wouldn't be surprised, after all we know," Burton said dryly.

"Anyway, we didn't know anything you've just told me, but the profiler brought up the nurture and nature information for us to consider. Let me find my notes on it." He checked the file folders until he came across what Gail Skillman had written.

"Okay, here it is. She said that more and more research is suggesting that some people are just biologically primed to be more aggressive, and specific kinds of stress or pressure can encourage them to act on that tendency.

"She said that some research indicates it may be one gene, known as the warrior gene, or it may be two that have been identified. If these genes are present, they can make the person up to thirteen times more likely to have a history of violent or aggressive behavior. But the presence of the genes can't be used as an absolute to screen criminals because many more genes may be involved in violent behavior. And of course, environmental factors may also play a role."

Burton asked, "So, she was saying that even if someone has a high-risk combination of these genes, the majority will never commit a crime, so the theory might not be true?"

"Correct."

"Well, I think that's bullshit in this instance. From what I know, it seems pretty likely that Nick inherited something awful bad from his father since he became just like him! Got into a lot of violent crime, drugs, ran a prostitution ring that included running Adel's mother, Merrill Burk. Unless you call all of that just the way he was nurtured."

"That would really be up to Skillman to determine. I'm just sharing what she told us."

"I gotta another question for you, and maybe an answer."

"Go ahead."

Burton said, "Last time we spoke, you said Adel had

claimed Olivia Nelson was her mother. Any idea why she latched on to that particular woman?"

Willards said, "No, we never made that connection. But if what you said is true about Nick being her son, him blackmailing her, he was probably talking about Olivia a lot around Merrill and Addy, right? Making a lot of threatening calls to her, or mentioning her when he talked about money. Now it makes sense why Addy would seek her out. She had probably become this mythical mother figure who had money, could solve life problems, meet needs."

"Yeah, that's what I was thinking too."

Willards agreed. "It makes sense. I also think—"

Burton cut him off. "I have another idea to run by you. A suspicion I suppose. It's been gnawing at my gut for a while, and I have no solid proof, but it confirms what I saw on that TV special, that these bad genes get passed along."

"Okay, what's your suspicion."

"I think Nick may have been Adel's father."

"What? Where'd you get that idea?"

"From her behavior," Burton said. "The rage she exhibited at age seven, the way she tore apart her mother and Nick with that butcher knife. Where do you think that came from? Think about it. She had the bad genes of Clay Thomas, her grandfather, mixed in with the evil stuff Nick passed on to her. She had a horrible childhood from all we know, an abusive home life, and was also tormented and ridiculed at school. It's like she was in a pressure cooker every single day of her childhood. Put all those ingredients together, wouldn't you have one fucked up kid?"

Willards thought about it for a moment. "I guess it's possible—"

"—and you don't know who Adel's father is,

correct?" Burton reminded him.

"No, we don't," Willards admitted. "But since Merrill worked for Nick, if he got her pregnant, why'd he allow her to keep the baby since she couldn't be earning for him as often if she was pregnant?"

"I thought about that too. I think Nick had Merrill keep the baby to use as additional leverage against Olivia," Burton said. "If she ever wanted to end whatever payments she was making to Nick, he could tell her she now had a granddaughter. He'd threaten to screw her over by announcing she not only had bastard son but now a granddaughter too."

Willards nodded. "Yeah, that could be, I guess. We can't prove it without DNA, but it makes sense. If all we've talked about is true, can you imagine the tension, the hate and the rage in that household? Makes you feel sorry for Addy."

Burton said, "She was a smart kid. Damaged and broken beyond repair, but intelligent in a cunning, nasty way. You told me how cruel the kids at school were to her, playing that game and often hiding from her, abandoning her. She got that at home too, I'd guess..." Still mulling over the past, he added, "Who knew what Nick was doing to Addy in that house? Was Merrill aware, looked the other way, abandoned her daughter to the abuse? Poor kid. Addy Burk was *born* with the motivation to kill Nick and her mother."

"And Addy could also hold a grudge for a long, long time," Willards said.

#

"Skillman here."

Willards had dialed her immediately after finishing up the call with Burton. He scrolled to the top of the notes he had taken.

"Hello?" she said. "Steve?"

"Hi. I need some help with some new info that just came in about Adel Daniels."

"Okay. Hold a sec, I have another call I need to finish."

He looked over what he had written. Much of what Burton had said was intriguing and explained a lot, but it was really more hearsay and speculation. He needed someone like Skillman to sift through it with him to see if it was something to add to the foundation of the case, more building material, or just more odds and ends. But it all made sense. It all fit together, which was the first time he had been able to even think such a thing in weeks. He updated his notes, uploaded them into the system and also sent them to her email so she'd have immediate access to them.

"Hi. Sorry about that," she said. "It was my travel agent, had to finish the call."

"Vacation?"

"I wish. Speaking at Columbia University tomorrow."

"Here?"

"Yes, a friend from college teaches there, I'm speaking to her poly-sci class."

"What's your connection with political science?"

"FBI. Law enforcement, hacking, identity theft. The science of it all. It all bounces off each other a bit, and I have some Washington stories she wants me to tell."

"Good gossip?"

"Some of it is. Politics is so hot right now. I can bring a bit of a spin to the usual stories, drop some names."

"I hate that word 'spin'."

She laughed, her voice light, gentle. "Actually, I do, too. It's shorthand for misdirection."

"When do you arrive tomorrow?"

"Tonight, actually."

Without thinking—that train had already left the station—he asked, "Are you free for dinner." He had spoken to her for weeks but all at once, he wondered what she looked like, then wondered where that thought had come from? Was she married? Divorced? Single and dating or just single? Thin? Blonde? The questions flickered along. He had no idea, but he realized at that moment that he had always been attracted to the sound of her voice. "Tonight?"

"Yes. Or are you seeing your friend?"

"No, we're getting together for breakfast to catch up." She went silent just long enough to either check her schedule or think of an excuse. "But yes, to dinner tonight. I land at seven-thirty. Probably won't be ready until around nine. Would that be too late?"

"Is French food okay?"

# # #

Willards arrived at Le Compteur at 8:45. Reservations were hard to come by, he hadn't been there in two years, not on his salary and he had no reason to book a table since he hadn't had a date in that long. Hadn't had sex, either—now that he was making a tally—in more than three years, but who was keeping track of such things?

The restaurant was attractively laid out. The front tables faced the windows so you could watch the fashionable people of Madison Avenue strolling past. He ordered tonic water at the small, cramped bar. He drank it too fast, was nervous, was excited, was anxious. But he felt good, glanced at himself in the mirror, thought he looked presentable. Plain, but acceptable.

Although he didn't stand out in the fashion-conscious, buzzy crowd that swirled about him, he actually thought that he at least fitted in. Sort of.

Blue blazer, white, medium starch shirt, designer maroon tie that he had paid too much for years ago. He didn't know if it was too wide or too narrow, didn't really care. Gray slacks, brown shoes that he had actually shined. He stood at the bar, sucking on the ice from his empty drink. She had said she was blonde, his weakness. She had said she was five seven. Perfect height to his six feet. She had blue eyes. Trim. Single. Never married. Perfect. Perfect. Perfect.

He had started to describe himself over the phone, Gail had stopped him. "Doesn't matter, Steve."

"Why? Are you blind? Or not as shallow as me?"

"Not as shallow, but it was nice you didn't just Google me."

Playful sense of humor. He glanced around, jittery. He was surrounded by attractive women in little black dresses. He had never noticed just how many styles of little black dresses were being manufactured. Most of the men were in suits but he spotted some blazers. A few women glanced at him, a few of them lingered, a shy smile or two. *I should come here more often…*

His phone pinged. A text. *I'm here.*

Willards looked at the entrance, found her. She was perfect. Just as she had described herself.

Once they were seated, they ordered a bottle of wine, then their dinner, then there was a slight break in the conversation while they looked one another over. She was attractive, no doubt about it. Heads had turned when they were being ushered across the crowded, chaotic restaurant to their table. She too was wearing a little black dress, filled it out perfectly. They looked good together; they were both aware of it, they had an eager glow about them.

Giddy, Willards thought, couldn't help smiling. *We're giddy together, and we just met.*

"Why are you smiling?" Gail asked, smiling.

"Same reason you are," he teased.

They talked backgrounds, cases, colleagues, pros and cons of New York and Virginia, goals for the future, managed to share off one another's plates as they finished off their bottle of wine. Half-way through the main course, conversation lagged, but it was more of an easing off the gas, not at all running out of fuel. Nothing to panic over. The comfort that existed between them was relaxing, calming. Willards couldn't help grinning to himself. Again.

"Let me in on your thoughts," she asked.

"Just realizing that I don't usually invite women out for dinner sight unseen. I'm glad I did in this case," he added hastily.

"In this case, meaning me, or this case meaning the actually case we're working on?"

"Both."

"Good answer. Now, as for the latter, tell me more about this theory the medical examiner said that so intrigued you?"

Willards thought for moment, wanted to be coherent in what he was going to say. "I guess this idea of moral behavior is what keeps coming to mind. How it might or might not be passed down through our genes."

She grimaced. "Sounds like a thesis I had to write in college."

"I was hoping it was." She had read his notes, so they discussed the family lineage that Addy Burk had come from: Clay Thomas her grandfather and Olivia Nelson the unwilling mother of Nick, who may have been her father. Gail leaned forward to make a point. Willards stole a glance at the top of her little black dress, started down, stopped, dragged his eyes back to her face. She knew what he was doing but didn't seem to mind.

After several minutes, she summarized where they were. "There *is* a theory that all human behavior—the good and the bad—is a product of our genes. You have to add in home environment, geographical location, and conditions of course, but the majority of behavior can be laid at the feet of our gene pool. It's a hypothesis that is gaining ground in evolutionary psychology." His blank look prompted her to say, "Evolutionary psychology is focused on how evolution has shaped the mind and behavior. It's close to the hearts of FBI profilers like me."

Willards nodded. "Got it."

"Science is intent now on discovering the genetic seeds of destruction all of us may carry, both physical— like muscular dystrophy, autism or breast cancer—and mental or emotional, which could include homicidal tendencies. It's a big, huge leap, however, to say that these proclivities can be passed down, whole, to the next generation."

"So, you don't agree that the violent, psychotic bent of someone like Clay Thomas could be passed along to his and Olivia's son, Nick, and then to his daughter, Addy?"

She shrugged, sipped her wine. "I think it's *possible*. I think that all science, all proven fact, provides the truest and most complete account of life. Of *a* life."

He watched her.

"What? You're staring."

"No, I was waiting for you to finish."

"Well, it's complicated. There really aren't any definitive yes or no answers yet in this field. And I feel like that's what you're asking of me, or what Burton was suggesting to you."

"No, I don't mean it to sound like that. I don't think he did, either. It's just an idea he had that I wanted to hear your thoughts on." The waiter arrived, reached over, topped their glasses off, and offered another bottle. Gail shook her head. When they were alone, Willards said, "Okay, you said it's complicated. Try me."

"You've heard of the Human Genome Project?"

"*Heard of* completes my knowledge base."

"The project was an international effort to discover the exact makeup of the genetic material that controls the way we develop and grow. Scientists from around the world worked together, sequencing thousands of human genomes."

He put his hand up to stop her. "What's a genome?"

She smiled. "A genome is the genetic material that makes up a living organism. It's contained in chromosomes, which are made from DNA. They finished the Human Genome Project in 2001 and the results, and ongoing genomic studies, will hopefully lead to the diagnosis and treatment of diseases as well as provide new insights into many fields of biology, including human evolution."

"Does any of that help with this theory about Adel?"

"It can. It may," she said. "You see, DNA combines to form genes, which contain the instructions that are passed on from one generation of an organism to the next, through reproduction. So, in a roundabout way, what I'm talking about *can* support your theory."

The waiter returned, cleared their plates, left dessert menus.

Gail said, "One thing we do know, specific to this case, is that genetic factors play a major role in the etiology and development of schizophrenia and other mental illnesses. Some genetic linkage studies have estimated the heritability of schizophrenia to be up to 90%."

"Wow. What about violent or psychotic behavior?" Willards asked.

"There are some likely pathophysiological mechanisms that, when added to existing DNA with a curve toward aggressive behavior, could be passed along from generation to generation."

Willards nodded quickly.

This time, Gail put her hand up. "Wait. I said *could be*. But you're talking what, three generations?"

Willards counted on his fingers. "Clay to Olivia, Olivia to Nick, Nick to Addy. Yes, three."

"*If* Nick is Addy's father," Gail reminded him. "Remember, it's not proven. You have a *lot* of connections between these people that haven't been established yet. And remember, for this potent transference to occur, microscopic pieces of information need to occur in exactly the right order, the right amount."

"Like a recipe?"

"That's one way to look at it."

They ordered dessert. When it arrived, they sipped their decafs, mulled over the conversation. Willards asked, "Now that they have this project done, are they working on eliminating the negative conditions?"

"The work is in the early stages. No one knows how successful it will or won't be."

"But like you said, this violent, homicidal behavior could be—*could be*—passed along from generation to generation. It is possible, right?"

"Possible, yes. Likely or provable?" She left the statement hanging. "Why are you so stuck on this theory that Addy's behavior was inherited? Couldn't she—"

"Because it makes sense," he said. "There is so little

that makes sense in this case, but this…this works for me. It explains so much. I want this piece of the case to be true."

\# \# \#

Outside the restaurant, the evening air was fresh, cool, the street relatively quiet after the restaurant. Willards inhaled, deeply satisfied. He glanced at his watch. Just after eleven. "How you holding up?" He had a plan.

"Fine. Wonderful dinner. Thank you, again. You didn't have to—"

"Wanted to," he said. "Besides, you helped me with the case. All that science talk, put some legs and padding on my theory. If we could deduct dinners, if I had an expense account…"

She continued to look at him, her smile dazzling, her eyes shiny with anticipation. She was so attractive.

"Up for an after-dinner drink?"

She slipped her hand into his. He turned away, didn't want her to see the grin that threatened to tear his face in half. *She likes me,* he shouted inside, recalling Sally Fields' Oscar speech, added, *she really, really likes me!* They started down Madison, on their way to 57th Street and the Four Seasons hotel. A nice, quiet, in-the-round square bar that was pleasant, low key at that hour.

They didn't speak, didn't need to. Holding hands, keeping pace with one another as they strolled, everything was communicated without words. Willards thought, *Don't lose her. Don't chase her off, embarrass yourself, corner her or pressure her. Just invite her along for an after-dinner drink—check!—and then, maybe, sometime in the near future, invite her to become part of your life.*

But not too fast, he cautioned himself, thrilled to be holding her hand. *Not too fast.*

# # #

Too soon, they finished their Himbeergeists. They were facing one another, each perched on a plush, comfortable bar stool. By now, they were reluctant to let go of one another. They had already kissed quickly, somewhat discreetly after toasting one another. He had placed his hand on top of hers, they played with one another's fingers. He was so attracted to her, so aroused, so mildly drunk that he kept reigning himself in. *Not too fast, not too fast, not too fast.*

She stifled a yawn. "Excuse me. Long day..."

"And I've kept you out way past your bedtime."

"True, but it's been worth it." She patted his hands, leaned in for another kiss.

He didn't want the night to end. She yawned again, then he did. They chuckled.

"Enough!" he said, tossing the bills on the bar to cover the drinks, helped her off the stool. "We've both had enough."

Once outside, they paused on the street.

"I don't know where you're staying," he said.

"Westin," she said. "Let's walk. Do you mind?"

Hands joined, they strolled to 42nd Street, easy silence between them. Willards couldn't think of anything to say. Not a word.

It was well after midnight when they arrived in the lobby. Their eyes tired, their smiles lazy, they held hands facing one another.

"Thank you," she said. He led her away from the harsh lights that glared above the front desk to a more private area surrounded by a clump of large potted plants.

He whispered, "You're welcome," and pulled her into his arms for the long, deep kiss he had desired all night, hoping she felt the same way.

She did.

#

Willards took a taxi home, his heart pounding with excitement. He felt like dancing even though he had never mastered the skill very well. He would have taken Gail Skillman out for an all-night night on the town, but she was tired, he was tired, and she had an early breakfast with her friend before her lecture. Besides, he hadn't tried to dance in years, didn't even know of a place to dance, didn't know if he still could.

But at least he felt like it. That was something he hadn't felt in years.

He paid the cab fare, gave such a generous tip—why not?—that the driver actually turned around to thank him. Willards unlocked the door to his empty apartment. Immediately, he felt lonely, depressed, as if the night had only been a dream. How had he managed to live alone for so *long*? It was awful to come home to a silent, dark apartment. He tugged off his tie, shed his blazer, undressed for bed.

What a night, what a woman, he thought. *I gotta believe there will be a second date.* He had turned his phone off for dinner, didn't think a few hours would matter. Tony knew where he was if anything occurred. He checked for messages. Maybe Gail had had sent him a goodnight text? Maybe she had—

A voice message. Was it from Gail? He didn't recognize the number. Put it on speaker, pushed playback, heard a young woman's voice, maybe even a child. It started as a whisper, then quickly accelerated into a scream.

"Hello? Detective Willards? It's me, Addy. I'm all alone now. Where is everyone? Help me! FOR GOD'S SAKE, HELP ME!"

He played the message back twice.

You should have left your phone on, he chastised himself. *You could have engaged her, found out something, anything to help locate her. But you were too focused on Gail…*

"Why Adel…or Addy?" he murmured to the ceiling. "Why are you regressing now? Even the voice had a little girl quality to it, you sound like a child." He closed his eyes, saw himself wandering down a long, long corridor with doors on either side. Each one was locked, but he knew he had to try them all. If even one opened, then he'd learn something, discover some information, something he may have missed.

It wasn't until after 2 a.m. that he finally fell asleep, dozens of doors still to check and those behind him, all sealed tight. He hadn't learned a thing.

June 3, 1994

Dear Diary,

Need to see the eye doctor. For the past week or so, my vision is either blurry at times or I find the sunlight too harsh when I'm outside. It's the strangest thing. Sunglasses help, but the bright light hurts my eyes. Billy said he'll schedule something for me.

I hope it's nothing serious. I simply must feel well enough for Deena's party on the 16th. I'm lucky to have a friend like her. She has been so dear since Reggie died. Billy too.

What would I do without Billy? I'm so glad he stayed on after Reggie passed. He's a part of the past that helps to keep memories of my husband alive. Billy could never understand why a man with such wealth insisted on taking the train from Westchester to the city instead of calling on Billy, his driver, to take him in, or drive himself. He knows where Reggie's money came from, of course, which was why he still supported the transportation lines he helped build. I'm the same way; I like the trains, the passing views, the announcement of the stations. Riding the MTA makes me feel closer to Reggie. Billy drives me to the station and picks me up when I return. When the train is delayed and I arrive home late, he has a smug look on his face. "Not a word," I say as he helps me into the back of the car.

Ever since my angel left the nasty note about me not being here for her visit, our relationship has changed. She seems intent on watching me as if I'll slip away from her if I have the chance. It breaks my heart to see how insecure she is. If I'm not going to be here, I tell her a day before. Those are the rules we've agreed to. I do want to know her name, who her mother is, where she lives, but she refuses. I've had Billy attempt to follow her home after our visits, but she seems wise to him. Twice he's come back bewildered as to where she went once she entered the fields behind our property.

I think she may regret the awful note she left me but doesn't want to apologize or discuss it. Instead, she started to bring me a peace offering each time she visits. She comes almost every day after school. She brings the crushed ingredients in a baggie, I supply the boiling water, she makes me her special tea. She learned to make the tea from her mother, telling me, "You know all tea is made from the *Camellia* plant? My mother grows it in her garden."

I never liked tea that much, maybe a few times a year, but now it's each time she visits. She prides herself in bringing it to me. It's really not a big deal and I admit I don't want to deny her this pleasure, this ability to give something to me. She seems so miserable; something is wrong at school too. The other children don't like to play with her or are mean to her, one girl in particular. Her home life seems very unhappy too. I only get snatches of information from her. If I ask one question too many, she shuts down.

I still don't even know her name.

The Fifth Week
Penny

Late the next morning, Willards was at his office looking at his desk calendar when his phone rang. It was now the fifth week of the investigation. He had written the number five on his calendar, underlined it, wondered if he'd be writing six the following week, and then seven.

It was Gail. "I wanted to thank you again for dinner. I had a wonderful time."

"Me, too. Sorry I kept you out so late. How was breakfast with your friend?"

"Fine. I speak to her class at one, so I still have a couple of hours to figure out what I'm going to say."

Willards asked, "When can I see you again?"

"When will you be in Virginia next? I fly out this evening, leaving when the lecture is done."

"Actually, I *am* planning to come to Virginia."

He could almost hear the smile in her voice, which was exactly what he wanted.

"Really? That's great. When are you coming?"

"As soon as possible."

He told her about the call from Addy in case she hadn't had time to check the updated file."

"That's the third call from her referring to herself as Addy. It's classic regression. It's so complicated, but with her background, she sounds like a fuse that has been lit, is ready to go off." Gail sighed. "I wish there was more I could do to help."

"What you said last night helped a lot."

"What did I say?"

"The parts about the possibility that Clay Thomas' homicidal tendencies were passed along to his son, Nick, and then to his granddaughter, Addy."

"Key word possibility. Like I said, there's a big difference between that and what's provable. Besides, just because Adel may have had homicidal tendencies, how would that affect this case now?"

Willards said, "I'm a firm believer in career criminals. You know the stats: Within three years of release, almost 70% of prisoners are rearrested. You might say it's in their blood."

"Or their genes," Gail said, teasing. "Wait, forget I said that."

"When Adel—or Addy—was seven, she killed her mother and Nick, the guy who may have been her father. With her regressing, I think she still has it in her to do something terrible, and probably sooner rather than later."

# # #

Penny made an effort, a real effort. She managed to attend two meetings in four days. She was proud of herself. Flora wasn't.

"You can't do this half way," she scolded Penny over coffee at a diner. "I know how much stress you're under, but you must do everything you can to pull yourself together."

"It's easier to do that with a drink in my hand," Penny said, trying to keep the conversation light. She really was proud of herself.

"Spoken like a true alcoholic," Flora said. "That's not funny, Penny."

The silence between them was sharp, like a slap in the face that had just landed, the sting still felt.

Changing the subject, Flora asked, "How is Michael doing?"

"He seems more upset for the girls losing their mother than he is for losing his wife. You know, it's really not until someone dies that you realize the many different roles they play in your life. I know at Rebecca's funeral, there were so many of her friends that I didn't know, as well as neighbors. We all touch so many people…" She stopped speaking. Thinking about Rebecca was such a raw, unsavory wound, one that wasn't healing. She still felt lost, despondent without her sister.

"Michael is probably setting aside his own grief to focus on the children," Flora said.

"I don't know, it just seems…off. I expected him to be devastated, but he seems to be functioning all right. He did ask me if Beck and I told one another everything."

"What did you say?"

"Said I thought so, but then he told me that their marriage hadn't been very good for a while, did I know that."

"Did you?"

Penny shrugged. "No, other than they were both busy. They hadn't been connecting much, but that happens. I didn't get the sense that things were *that* bad…"

"Did Michael have any idea why Rebecca was found

in Adel's apartment building?"

"No, neither do the police. No one does. I keep calling Detective Willards because I feel if I don't stir things up, nothing will happen."

Flora said, "It all seems to confusing. I read the papers, watch TV, but it just doesn't make any sense, why this is happening to you and your family."

Penny nodded, then leaned closer. "Some things have happened that they haven't made public. Adel has been calling me—"

"What?"

Penny shushed her. "Listen, no one knows. But they now suspect that Adel somehow arranged for Carl and Graham to be kidnapped, but they don't know how or where they are." She took a breath. "Or even if they are still alive. There have been no pictures of them in weeks…"

Flora started to ask a question. Penny put her hand up, had her wait.

"There's more. They received a Polaroid of an empty chair with a sign on it that read *Reserved for Penny*."

Shocked, Flora's coffee cup clattered on its saucer. "Oh, my God. Penny, why didn't you tell me sooner?"

"Because no one is supposed to know. About *any* of this. But don't worry, I'm being protected."

Puzzled, Flora started to ask what she meant.

"See the guy a couple booths behind me? Red hair? He's a cop. Follows me all the time."

Flora nodded. "You know, I've seen him around when we've been together, but it didn't really register."

"That's their skill, to be there, but not there, as they say. Anyway, not that it matters, but don't mention what I told you to anyone. It's just to let you know how horrible this all is, how confusing, how much worse it seems to get every few days." Her eyes filled with tears.

Penny dried them with a napkin. "Anyway, that's why making *any* meetings feels like a victory for me. I know two meetings in four days is not working the program, is not thirty meetings in thirty days—"

"Oh, honey, forget working the program," Flora said, grabbing Penny's hand, squeezing it. "Forget thirty days. I didn't know about the photo threatening you, or Adel possibly being the one behind all this madness. Let's just get *you* through one day at a time."

# # #

For several days after Rebecca's funeral, Michael had sequestered himself with the girls. The three of them talked and then wept. Since the girls were having nightmares, they all slept together. He did the best he could to answer their questions, comfort them, just be there for them, even though he knew he himself was dangerously close to falling apart.

He desperately needed time to sort out his own grief while also remaining strong for Melody, Chasity, and for Penny. Privately, he doubted that Graham would ever be returned to her alive. If Adel was the one behind all the kidnappings as the police had told him in confidence, and she was now threatening Penny, Adel didn't seem to have an endgame: no ransom, no contact with the police, no threats, nothing. It left Carl and Graham at the mercy of a madwoman.

The events surrounding Rebecca's death had sent him into a dizzying, downward spiral. He felt like he was in one of those cartoons where he had been pushed off a cliff, was grabbing branches all the way down. He'd survive the fall, but little was left of him. He could no longer be strong for everyone. Finally, admitting to physical and emotional exhaustion, he called his parents to see if they would take the girls for a few days.

Grief and guilt urged him to blame himself for Rebecca's death, a simple matter of cause and effect. For whatever reasons—and there were many—he and Rebecca had grown distant, lost touch and affection for one another, lost respect. Passion had cooled, then chilled. It was easier to stay at the office and work late than come home and try to converse with Rebecca while pretending everything was all right. It was easier to withdraw and simply convince himself that she was the one to blame for the state of their marriage. It had lost its shine, was lackluster, not engaging anymore. Like so many things in his life—skiing, the monthly book club, exercise equipment, the wine tasting group they had joined—he had simply given up on it, allowed it to collect dust due to not being used.

So, she had found someone else, snuck off to the city to meet her lover. But who was he? How and where had they met? The police had asked about it, but Michael had no idea who it could have been, neither had Penny. It was a question or allegation that was hanging out in the breeze, flapping about, only now just getting his full attention.

With the girls at his parents' house, he paced the house, thinking, obsessing. Had Rebecca met someone online with Match or with one of the swipe left or right dating apps? Was it just sex she wanted, or a relationship, affection? Did she perch on a barstool in the early afternoon to find some boring business man, stuck there between meetings? Was she planning to leave him and take the girls if she found the right man?

He and Penny had had lunch the day after the funeral. He'd carefully deduced that Rebecca hadn't told her sister the rock bottom truth about their marriage, had never mentioned the lack of physical affection or the terrible silence that had invaded their relationship. It wasn't until he had found out Rebecca had made so many trips into the city without Penny's knowledge that the alarm went off and he suspected another man.

Now alone in a house that seemed to expand the more he paced around it, he decided to search through his wife's personal belongings to see if he could find a number, an address, a name, something, anything.

The police had never recovered her phone, hadn't bothered to search her belongings in the home, only questioned her family and friends. Michael started with her closet, went through every dress, every skirt, every pair of pants, every blouse. He checked the pockets for slips of paper, ticket stubs, any scrap of paper. Then he went through her dresser drawers, bras, panties, scarves, summer shorts, t-shirts. Everything. Anything. He pulled out her purses, dumped the contents atop the bed: make up, coins, gum, mints, little treats for the girls, coupons, a tattered daily diary.

The pages were filled with her shorthand jottings that he knew so well. Parties, playdates, hair appointments, school events, two or three things a week. He flipped back to September, the previous month. Then further back to August. July. June.

May. April.

Beginning last April, the initials CD appeared once or twice a week each month.

CD? Michael thought about it for several seconds. C.D. Nothing came to mind.

He flipped to the back of the planner where addresses were. Most of the names he recognized. Rebecca was somewhat friendly with the neighborhood women since they carpooled the kids around for playdates, school, movie and shopping events. But under D in the address book, he found no one with a first name that began with a C. He turned to the inside back cover where there was a pocket to store loose pages, business cards or coupons. Tucked in the flap were some certificates for free ice cream at McDonald's, a dry cleaner receipt, and a card for First Avenue Electronics Repair. *"Come to us First!"* read the tagline.

Michael stared at the card, wondered why she'd have a business card for a Manhattan electronic repair shop. If they needed anything to be serviced, they'd do it in their own town, not cart it to the city. He looked at the names of the store owners, Neal Jacobson and Carl Daniels.

Carl Daniels. CD.

"No." He shook his head, pulled the card closer as if the name would change.

Carl Daniels. If it was the same man who had been kidnapped, then he wouldn't be available to answer the call, but Neal Jacobson would still be around. Michael punched the number into his phone.

# # #

Ninety minutes later, Michael walked into the shop. The door activated a chime. Behind the cluttered counter, a voice called out, "Be right there."

Michael looked around. The small space was cluttered with electrical equipment of all shapes, sizes and brands. Boxes of wires, speakers, guts of DVD players, TVs and computers were stashed everywhere, along with cartons of parts.

"Hi, can I help you?"

"Neal Jacobson? I'm Michael Roberts, we spoke on the phone."

Neal stiffened for a moment. "Is…anyone with you?"

"No, why?"

"I've just been through hell with the police with all of

this. I really have nothing else to say other than what I told you on the phone. I'm so sorry about what happened to you wife and brother-in-law, but I really don't know anything."

"Actually, I'm not here about them. It's about Carl." Michael wanted to talk to Neal face to face, read what he could into any body language, so he hadn't shared anything on the phone. Neal pulled a chair out from behind the counter, gestured at Michael to sit. When they were settled, Michael said, "I'm just going to have to ask you this straight out, and please, please be honest with me. Was Carl having an affair with my wife?"

Neal didn't blink, didn't turn away, and stared straight at Michael as if he hadn't asked the question. Michael pulled out a photo of Rebecca, put it on the counter between them.

"Did you ever see my wife here? Or with Carl?"

Neal looked down at the photo, didn't touch it. He closed his eyes. His hands flickered on the counter as if he was about to play the piano. He nodded and spoke so softly Michael had to lean in. "Carl never told me. I just…sensed something had changed, something was going on. She came by, a couple times. It was awkward, like they were acting in a bad play. You could tell there was something going on. I wouldn't ask. I've known Carl for years, he was my best friend from college. And I knew Adel, of course. Something was happening, I just couldn't bring myself to ask what exactly was going on. It wasn't really my business, you know?"

Michael swallowed, waited.

"Carl would go on these long lunches, said he was following up on notices about used equipment. We always needed parts. He'd concoct some story. I'd watch him leave, then look out the window, see him meet up with her at the corner. Once, I know Adel saw them, too."

"She *saw* them?"

Neal nodded. "She works during the day in Brooklyn, at a thrift shop, so I don't know what she was doing around here. But one afternoon, just after Carl had left and I was looking through the window, I saw Adel was across the street, in front of the Dunkin Donuts."

"You're sure it was her?"

"Positive. It was odd. I watched her and it was like she was arguing with someone, her head jerked back and forth a bit, her hands were squeezing into fists, her arms were gesturing about. But there was no one there, just her."

"And she saw Carl and Rebecca?"

"Yes, she was looking directly at the corner where they were."

"Where'd they go?"

Neal sighed. "There is a little hourly hotel tucked in the street a couple blocks away. It's old, you'd barely notice it. Look, I'm so sorry—"

"What's the name of the place?"

"The Capri Hotel. I wasn't snooping, either. Like I said, I didn't ask, didn't want to know. But one day, Carl came back after lunch. He was going through his pockets, looking for something. He pulled out a receipt for the hotel, added it to the pile of junk on the counter, found what he was looking for, stuffed everything back in his pocket except for that. He smiled to himself, crumpled it up, threw it out. I saw the name of the place."

"Do you know how long they were seeing each other?"

"A few months, maybe? Since last April I'd guess. After he...was taken, I'm pretty sure Rebecca called once. I remember because it's rare if anyone ever calls asking specially for either of us. But this woman wanted to speak to Carl. She was anxious, so upset. I could tell that in just the few words she spoke. I don't know why, but thinking about it later, I thought that she probably felt he had dumped her, ended everything. She didn't know at that time that Carl had been taken. It wasn't in the papers or anything."

After several seconds of silence, Michael asked, "Did Adel ever stop or come by to ask you directly about Carl and Rebecca? You said she saw them together."

"No, she never did. Even after Carl was kidnapped, she'd call a few times but it was never anything about your wife, nothing was never even hinted out. That's why I didn't say anything to the police; I didn't want to hurt Adel, could see no connection with the case."

"But there *is* a connection. You're *certain* she knew? *Positive* that she had seen them together?"

Neal nodded.

Michael said, "Adel might not have asked you about Carl and Rebecca, but I think she *did* contact my wife, wanted to meet with her, to confront her about the affair. That's why Rebecca went to Adel's apartment."

It took Neal a few seconds to catch up. "Wait, Adel…you think…no, she couldn't do that. You think *she's* the one who—"

Michael said, "I don't know for certain, but—"

"No, not Adel," Neal said, shaking his head. "She was a gentle, kind woman. She couldn't have done what you're saying."

# # #

Outside the shop, the fall sunlight was blinding after the dim, crowded interior. Had it been as harsh before he'd entered the store? Michael fished in his breast pocket for his sunglasses. His eyes were watering, from the glare or all that he had just learned, he didn't know. He started up First Avenue, no destination in mind. He needed to walk, to move, to put distance between all he had just been told even though it all travelled with him.

Rebecca and Carl. She really had been seeing someone and that relationship had led to her death. He felt sick inside. Was it his fault for pushing her away, not even trying to keep their marriage together? Was Carl the only one? Was he her first?

He stopped walking, wanted the questions to cease, needed to talk it all through with someone. He called Penny, asked her to meet him for lunch, had to talk to her, get the information out of his gut and mind, pass it along. Maybe then it would dissipate a bit. Then, with clarity, he would tell the police.

Penny told him to meet her at Baker Street Pub in fifteen minutes

# # #

He had already been seated when Penny hurried in. She sat across from him in the booth. They each ordered a Bloody Mary. When the drinks arrived, they took sips. Then, from nowhere and unexpectedly, the tears appeared. They inched their way down his cheeks behind his glasses.

"Michael? What is it? What's happened?"

He bent his head down as the first sobs shook themselves free. Penny scooted around the booth, sat next to him, rubbed his back, patted his shoulder. Later—minutes or seconds, he didn't know—he was able to lift his head. Penny pulled him closer.

"What is it?" she whispered.

He closed his eyes again, took a breath. "Carl," he

managed to say. "Adel's husband. He and Rebecca…" Then he told her everything he knew. When he was finished, he said, "I have to tell Willards about this, but I wanted you to know first."

She nodded, stunned. "I'm…so sorry. She never said anything to me. I had no idea. I'll go with you to the police." She glanced around, caught sight of the red-haired cop. "Sid?" She gestured him over, introduced him to Michael, explained that they were going to the police station. "Can you call Willards, tell him we're on our way?"

# # #

Michael told Willards all that Neal had said but it was as if someone else was speaking, telling the awful truths. Penny sat next to him, occasionally interjected some information, but the majority of it fell on his shoulders. It was as if he was betraying the memory of Rebecca, exposing her for her infidelity. If the girls ever found out… *But of course they will*, he thought miserably. *One day, of course they will find out.*

When Michael was finished, Willards said, "Okay, we'll follow up with Neal. I want to find out why he didn't tell us any of this in the first place."

"Why would he?" Michael asked. "When you interviewed him, only Carl had been taken. Graham and Penny—and Rebecca—weren't even involved yet."

"But Neal told you he saw Adel watching Carl and Rebecca one day, so Adel knew back then they were seeing one another. He should have told us Carl was having an affair," Willards insisted. "It goes to motive for much of what's occurred."

Penny said, "Adel should have told you too."

"She should have," Willards admitted. "But we've

learned a lot about Adel, as you know. Most everything she's ever told us was a lie."

# # #

Outside the police station, Penny asked Michael how the girls were doing.

"Hanging in there. I think their time with my folks has helped a little. I was just falling apart inside, couldn't hold on much longer, needed some time." Penny patted his arm, pulled him close.

He said into her shoulder, "I want you to know, I loved Rebecca. Even after hearing all of this, I still love her. Things just…got away from us. I blame myself for not trying harder. I really do. She…"

"You don't need to say any of this," Penny whispered with tears in her eyes.

"But I do. I don't want you to think that it didn't matter. Our time together…our years with one another, having the girls, a family, it did matter. I loved her. She loved me. I feel so guilty for all of this. If I had—"

"Michael, please."

"—set aside my own anger, made an effort to reach out to her, she might not have gone after someone else, wouldn't have spent time with Carl. Never would have been seen by Adel. God, of all the people to have gotten involved with…"

Penny hugged him tighter. "It's not your fault. *None of this is your fault.*"

He didn't believe her. He heard the words, but he knew otherwise. He released her, said he should get home, asked what her plans were.

She nodded toward Sid, who always was nearby. "Sid's walking me home. We'll meet Ben at the school. And then I'll do what I've been doing for the past few weeks. Sit and wait for whatever happens next."

# # #

Sid and the police escort that was with Ben at school all day followed Penny and her son into their building. Sid and the other officer were chatting in the lobby when Ben pushed the button.

"Be right up," Sid said.

In the elevator, Ben excitedly told his mom about his day at school, then stopped himself. "Mommy, you forgot to get the mail!" He knew there had been some photos of his father sent in the mail weeks earlier, so it had become his duty to check the mailbox every day, just in case. Penny hadn't told him that the police were checking her mail before it was delivered; they'd have any correspondence from the kidnapper. But Ben insisted.

When they reached their floor, Penny said, "Okay, I'll let you in so you can watch your cartoons. I'll go back down and get the mail. I'll be right back."

Once Ben was safely in the apartment and the door closed, Penny returned to the elevator, pushed the button. When it arrived, she hit the lobby button. The doors closed. The elevator started its descent. The movement seemed unsteady. Each floor passed slowly. The doors opened on the third floor. Two laughing, college-age women stepped into the car. The door hesitated before closing.

The doors opened into the lobby. Sid and the policeman and the doorman were all chatting. Sid raised his eyes when he saw her.

"Forgot the mail," she explained.

"Where's Ben?" Sid asked.

"In the apartment."

"Alone?"

"But I—"

Sid ran to the empty elevator car and pushed the button to her floor before she could move. The doors closed. She watched the lights blink as the car ascended. Once it stopped on her floor, she hurried away, collected the mail. The Con Ed bill. That was all. Her heart pounding, she hurried back over to the elevator.

"Everything all right?" the police officer asked.

She nodded. *Hurry, hurry, hurry*, she begged the elevator. The ping sounded, announcing the car was there. It sounded like a timer, something was now all prepared or almost finished. The doors opened slowly. In her eagerness, Penny banged her shoulder painfully against them. She pushed the button, hit Door Close several times, heard the police man in the lobby get a call, take it, say "What?!" just as the doors finally shut.

The elevator lumbered up to her floor. Her hands were now sweaty with apprehension. Sid was with Ben now, it was all okay, but what *had* she been thinking, leaving Ben alone, even for just a few minutes?

"Come on! Come *on*!" she muttered under her breath, her teeth clenched.

The doors opened on her floor. She sprinted out into the hallway. Sid was standing by her opened apartment door, talking into his phone. He turned when he heard her. She saw the pained expression on his face. He spoke into his phone, ended the call.

His eyes, shocked, hollow. Just minutes before, he had been laughing downstairs with the other police officer and the doorman. "Penny..." He took a step toward her.

In slow motion, she felt her legs turn to sand as she crossed the last few feet to her door.

"Penny," Sid said as she collapsed. Falling into the

darkness, the last thing she heard was, "Ben's gone…"

# # #

Penny opened her eyes. Flat on her back. On the sofa. Horrible thoughts and images fled from her mind. Graham had been kidnapped, Rebecca was dead, someone had taken Ben. Such nightmares. She was glad to wake from them. She heard someone in the kitchen. A conversation. She managed to raise herself up.

"Hello?"

Sid in the kitchen. It all came crashing back on her. Graham was gone. Rebecca was gone. Ben was gone. She cried out, screamed. Sid hurried over. She noticed then that the front door to the apartment was open, the policeman from downstairs was there.

Penny struggled against Sid, crying, shrieking, calling out for Ben as the officer tried to calm her. He held her hands away from his face or she would have clawed him. She wanted to see blood, pain, remorse from him. How could he have let this happen? Over and over, she screamed Ben's name. She choked on her tears, caught her breath, finally was able to form words. "What happened? Where is he?"

Sid said, "The door was open when I arrived. He must have let someone in, he wasn't here."

"No! I told him not to open the door! He knew that! He knew better! How could he just vanish like this?"

"We're checking the other apartments, but no one has responded. Most of the people are probably still at work. The super's going to open the doors for us."

"Where is Ben? Where is my son!?"

Sid said, "The front desk isn't letting anyone leave, I've called Willards, the team is on their way."

Not hearing him, only the hollow shrieking in her

mind, Penny called out, "Where is my son? Sid, where is Ben? Oh, my God, where is my son?!"

# # #

Five minutes later, a half dozen police officers were on site, along with three members of the FBI task force and Willards. All the exits to the apartment building were secured, no one could enter or leave. The neighborhood was closed off. Each apartment on Penny's floor was being opened, access provided by the building superintendent, rooms were searched. The same was occurring on the floors above and below. Stairwells was searched, security camera footage was being reviewed.

Penny grabbed Willards arms. "It was Adel, wasn't it? She took him, didn't she?" For the first time, she saw actual pain and remorse in his eyes, real-life terror that this had happened. A child had been taken and the hopelessness and shock in his expression told her that she was correct.

I'll come back to get you.

Adel had finally taken a child.

Willards had to assume it was Adel. There were simply no other suspects. He was bothered at how quickly she had done it. Ben had been had been left alone just by chance, for precious minutes. It's like Adel had been waiting, was right *there*, ready to snatch him.

Penny stared off into space. She started to tremble. A high-pitched wail followed, the forlorn, desperate cry so disturbing that Willards was chilled. Penny was now rocking back and forth on the sofa, the terrible, awful keening coming from deep inside of her. One of the policemen stepped in from the hallway to see what was making such an unsettling sound.

Willards touched Penny's shoulder. She snapped her mouth closed, looked at him, her eyes black with raw, bottomless grief. "Addy's taken *everything* from me. She came back and took *everything*..."

From deep within her, a moan issued forth, filled the room, turned into a scream of anguish that spread quickly into the borders of madness.

# # #

After Penny was sedated and removed by ambulance to the hospital for evaluation, Willards briefed the other officers. It didn't take long.

Two people at home on Penny's floor hadn't heard anything out of the ordinary. Same with those on the floors above and below. Ben was not found in any of the apartments. The officers who had fanned out in a five-block radius also had no sightings of a child matching Ben's description, nor of anyone resembling Adel. Fingerprints were being checked in Penny's apartment, but it was thought that Ben had simply been tricked to open the door as soon as his mother had left the floor in the elevator to get the mail.

"So, how'd Adel get in and out of the building with no one noticing?" one of the officer's asked.

"One of two ways," Willards answered. "There's the back entrance, which leads to the basement. From there, you take the elevator or the stairwell to any floor you want. And there's the side entrance by the mail area in the lobby, but the doorman would see you, so I'm guessing she came in the back way. Remember, Adel lives in a similar building, they have the same general entrances and exits. She only had maybe five minutes to get out once we knew Ben was missing."

Tony added, "She probably did the same thing when

she invited Rebecca over to her apartment, used the service elevator late at night, dumped the body in the laundry room, bypassing the doorman all together."

The others nodded. Sid asked, "How'd she keep Ben quiet? Wouldn't he be screaming once she grabbed him?"

Willards looked around at the other men. They had all read the updated reports, knew Adel's past, what she had done, what she had been suspected of doing. "She subdued him, somehow. We all know what she's capable of."

"What about the security cameras?" a task force member asked.

"The one at the back entrance had something obscuring the view. Looks like it had been spray painted with something."

After the meeting ended, Sid approached Willards, quietly asked if the medical team had said anything to him about Penny's condition.

"Nothing yet, they are still checking her out. Did you hear the screams coming from her? I've never heard such…grief, desperation. It's like Adel managed to scratch out the very soul of Penny. I don't know how she's going to recover from this is we don't get her son back."

"And her husband," Sid said, "I got to say, I feel responsible. I should have stayed with them both, all the time. But I thought she was taking him up to stay with him, and I wanted to compare notes with Stan in case he had any insights to what was going on. We're all spread so thin. But before I knew it, she was back down here, with Ben left up here all alone."

"Don't beat yourself up about it. You did a fine job all the time she was out and about. We had no idea she'd leave Ben alone up there or that Adel was lurking around the building, watching and waiting."

"I should have gone up in the elevator with them. I always did before. I always checked the apartment before they went inside. *Always.* If I had done it this time…"

"Stop. It's no good, Sid. You'll paint yourself into a corner, never get out. I could easily join you there, too. Trust me. I've missed a lot in the past few weeks, believed what were lies, didn't dig deep enough. Plenty of blame and excuses to go around. We have to put all our energy and frustration into finding Ben. We *have* to find him."

# # #

Two days later, another Polaroid was received, but it was only a portion of the image.

After being scanned and checked for fibers and fingerprints, an envelope was delivered to Willards. It contained a piece of a photograph, no words from the game. The image on the Polaroid had one word: *Son.* He looked closer. There was a small *s* before the word *Son.*

He immediately called Tony, scanned the strip of photo into the case file folder, updated the information on the computer. Then, he called Gail.

"I got another photo. Actually, just part of one. It was just uploaded to the file. It's the missing section from the last one we received." He fingered the half inch edge of the image, the portion that had been snipped off of the previous photo. Then he looked closer. "I'll be damned! She tricked us! The last photograph had the sign on the chair that read *Reserved for Penny*, and Adel snipped off the right edge of the photo, right after the Y in Penny's name."

Gail said. "I'm looking at it now."

"See? The word *Son* with the small *s* next to it? She cut off part of the sign, it never read *Reserved for Penny*. The complete statement, when you add the missing section, reads *Reserved for Penny's Son*."

Gail thought for a moment, staring at the computer image. "This package is different from the other ones since it has the second of a two-part message to you. Any deviation from the regular pattern means she is rapidly undergoing some sort of change. She didn't even included words from the game, which is significant."

Willards wasn't following, waited for her to continue.

"Think about it, Steve. Adel sounds like an enraged child when she calls, right? You mentioned that, so did Penny. An angry child. And now she's actually played a little trick on us with the snipped photo, the revealed message. We already know that she herself was tricked or fooled many times as a child and it really impacted her. With this two-part, trick message, it's obvious she's zeroed in on Penny for some reason. I'm sensing a real rage behind this threat, one directed at Penny."

"Do you think Ben is okay?"

"I have no idea. Adel took him, but so far we have no evidence she's harmed anyone she's kidnapped, but her mental state is rapidly deteriorating…"

"And why hasn't she sent any pictures in weeks?"

"That might just be her regressive nature taking over," Gail explained. "As an adult, it was important to her, but once she disassociated herself—sending the hoax photo of the adult Adel being abducted—I wouldn't be surprised if we don't receive any more photos of anyone."

They went silent for a moment.

"We have to continue based on some suppositions," Gail continued. "For instance, either her confidence is growing or waning."

"I'm thinking if she can snatch Ben away from us, she's feeling pretty embolden!"

"But at the same time, imagine the stress she is under," Gail said. "She's still got to care for Carl, Graham, and now Ben."

"If they are all still alive," he said. "We now know she was aware of Carl's unfaithfulness to her—"

"—a trigger of betrayal, abandonment," Gail said.

"Then why kidnap Graham?" he asked.

"A way to get back at Penny, I suppose. Obviously, they had some significant run-ins as children."

"Bad enough for Adel to remember for all these decades and plot all of this?"

Gail said, "Yes, because childhood traumas stay with us all of our lives. They are the longest memories we have. I think whatever Penny and her classmates did to Addy scarred her for the rest of her life."

Again, a thick silence rose between them as they each mulled their thoughts.

Gail finally broke through his pondering. "Any word on how Penny is doing?"

"Not good. The hospital says she's now catatonic. Very subdued, disoriented. She doesn't seem to recognize anyone visiting her, not even her parents. She had no idea who her brother-in-law was. Didn't recognize a photo of her son or an adult photo of her sister, but her parents had some pictures of Penny and Rebecca as children. She responded to those."

Gail said, "Sometimes…actually, lots of times, when people are in stressful situations or in shock, they find a safe place to go until they are able to deal with what's going on. Children of divorced parents usually revert to memories of the pre-divorced age when adulthood gets to be too much."

"But Penny said her childhood was pretty hellish,"

Willards said, "told us she and Rebecca leaned on one another during the dark times. Her parents fought a lot. All she had was her sister."

"That explains why, in her mind, she went back there. She could recognize and identify the two of them at a safer time and when they had each other. No matter how bad things became in their home life, Rebecca was there, Penny felt safe. But we need to focus on Adel now, especially since she has Ben. I'm concerned that she will probably transfer all the rage she had as a child against him."

Speaking rapidly, Gail said, "All of Adel's psychosis is rooted in childhood abandonment. If you take that deep-seeded, overpowering fear and mix it in with the very real possibility of an inherited homicidal bent, it means that she's probably already in a psychopathic regressive mode, which is basically the breaking point for any neurosis."

Willards asked, "What does all that mean?"

"There's a certain time where the strain of the psychotic tendencies reaches saturation; the brain is in overload and simply can't take any more. That's the point where homicidal fantasies and rage kick into gear. It's like a pressure value needs to be opened, released. All these years, I think Adel has walked a tightrope, mentally. The strain of that balancing act must have been torturous. She's buried her past, changed her name, her identity, but she's probably always had the past tugging away at her, trying to resurface…"

"How do you mean?"

Gail said, "Her ideal mother, for example, the one she desired, Olivia Nelson. I think Adel *was* and is schizophrenic; she was and is hearing from her mother, hearing other voices too. Otherwise, she would have acknowledged Olivia was dead, shut off that valve to the past. Instead, she kept her shut away in a made-up dementia ward, so she could hear from her if needed. And I bet when Adel found out about Carl's unfaithfulness and his relationship with Rebecca, it not only triggered the fear of abandonment, I would think mother's voice would speak up even louder and more frequently. Think about it: all the kids at school had abandoned her when they played the game, and now her husband had betrayed her for another woman. She only had the illusion of her false mother left."

Willards sighed. "This…is so complicated."

"And sad," Gail quickly said. "It's tragic. I think Adel probably heard her mother's voice all her life when she needed to. Sometimes it was Merrill. Sometimes it was Olivia. Maybe it was a Good Mother and Bad Mother, a back and forth conversation with her. It probably helped Adel, kept her sane in its own fashion, kept her rage contained."

"But once she was aware of Carl and Rebecca—"

"—all her childhood pain resurfaced, almost taunting her with the title of that game. And, of course, the trigger of Scotty turning seven, the same age when she experienced her greatest abandonment, and her homicidal rage."

"'I'll come back to get you?" Willards said. "It's like her past was saying that it would never abandon her, it would always be with her, even if she wanted to forget it."

"And it can only be fulfilled with a child. That's why Adel took Ben. He will represent the child but this time, he won't be abandoned like Addy was. She wants to fix this issue in her life and will use Ben to make it happen."

Willards asked, "How will she do that?"

"Most likely, Adel is going to be the perfect mother,

the one who *won't* abandon her child. She wants to change the experience she had when she was a little girl."

"Which mother will she be? Olivia or Merrill?"

Gail said, "That's what we don't know. She has the perfect choice to make, Olivia the good mother, or Merrill the bad mother. Regardless of what she decides, I think Adel is going to choose to fully inhabit the role."

"What do you mean?"

"I think she will be certain history repeats itself," Gail said. "Just like Merrill and Olivia, Adel will be sure she doesn't make it out of this alive."

"What does this mean for Ben?"

# # #

Willards hurried down the hallway of the hospital to room 304 where Penny Spencer was being kept under observation. He flashed his badge at the officer guarding the door in the same way he had shown it to the front desk and the on-call physician. It was like an all access pass to anywhere he wanted to go in the city.

The room was empty of visitors. Penny was supposed to be resting. She was pale, seemed lost in her hospital bed, and appeared smaller than he remembered. Her eyes were large, round, and dilated due to the drugs. Watchful eyes, mistrustful eyes, no ability to see the reality around her. Her body was restrained to the bed with thick brown straps; a second set were attached to her wrists.

It wasn't until Willards settled next to her bed in a chair that he heard her softly singing.

"One, two, don't be blue, I'll come back to get you..."

She continued to sing the rhyme, doubling back to

the beginning.

"Penny? Hi. Remember me?"

"Three, four, watch the door, I'll come back, with one more." She turned, looked right through him. It gave him the willies, like he was invisible.

"Penny?"

No response at all this time. He wasn't even there. Neither was she.

"One, two, don't be blue…" She continued in her sing-song lilt, a grown woman sounding like a child. Helplessly, Willards watched her and waited for an idea that would help both of them.

"Penny?" A little louder this time. She turned to him, looked past him, but he was ready this time, immediately asked, "Penny, who is Addy Burk?"

She blinked. Continued to stare at the wall behind Willards.

"Penny, who is Addy Burk?"

"She's mean," Penny finally said, her pouty voice that of a young child. "She's a mean girl." She spoke to the ceiling. Her fingers began to snap and fidget as if electrical charges were surging though them. Willards was glad her hands were restrained.

"Why is she a mean girl?"

"*Stay away from her.*" A warning.

"Why?"

Penny let out an exasperated sigh. Her fingers continued to flick and bicker with one another. *A very agitated little girl or an extremely terrified woman,* Willards thought. *Or both, as her worlds merge.* She closed her eyes, started to take deep breaths. The fingers slowed down, ceased their snapping and began rubbing against one another. The sound of skin against skin was like the whispering of secrets. Then, she began to speak in a high pitched, childish voice.

"Addy started the game, she came to school with it, you know. Did you know that? She was new. She wanted us to like her. At first, she was a bit of a show off, wanted the attention. Said she had this game, a counting game, a mix of hide and seek and tag. It was brand new. Said it was fun and she'd teach it to us." Penny's fingers continued to rub, scratching against each other, making a gritting, shushing sound. It reminded Willards of the hush, hush, hush of time passing or a muffled, ticking bomb. Any second now.

"Why do you call her a mean girl?" he asked.

"Because she could be mean! You didn't want to get her mad. I did, when it happened… she'd hold her breath or have an attack, turn blue. We'd watch." Penny smiled, closed her eyes. "I'll come back to get you." Penny squirmed against the restraints, exhaled loudly, exasperated. She opened her eyes. Spoke to the ceiling. "Rebecca told me what her mother was. A witch. And what she did all the time with men…"

Dirty mother, dirty daughter, Penny recalled the chant she and Rebecca had created. How the kids loved to scream it at Addy. *Don't tell him about that. No one needs to hear how bad it got.*

"That's what we said, why we ran from Addy, wouldn't play with her much. We didn't chase her or didn't come back to get her, never returned to the circle, hid from her. Broke the rules, her rules. But she went after *them*. She'd find them, make them play the game again. Made them! Made them promise to come back to get her."

"And did they?"

Penny nodded, closed her eyes, grimaced as if she was watching an unpleasant memory. "Three did. Two girls and a boy, Tommy King. She fooled them. Tricked them."

Willards jotted down the name Tommy King. Penny began panting on the bed, thrashing about as if she was having a fit. She pulled against the straps. Her eyes remained tightly squeezed closed. She twisted her head back and forth as if she didn't want to see what was clearly in front of her.

Several seconds passed. He could see she was wearing herself out. He waited a bit longer until she was calmer. "Who were the two girls? What were their names?"

Penny shrugged. Opened her eyes. "I forget. They died, though."

Ice cream and berries, she thought. *Ice cream and berries.*

"And Tommy King," she said. "Fell down the stairs." She took several deep breaths. "And… Addy said that anyone who left her behind would get the same as Tommy King."

"Why was the game so important to Addy? Why did she insist you all play it with her?"

"Because she had no one else to play with. At home, it was just her dolls and sometimes, her mother. But she hated to play with her mother."

"Why was that?"

Penny relaxed into the bed, almost appeared to doze off.

"Penny?" Willards asked softly. "Why did Addy hate to play the game with her mother?'

She opened her eyes, focused on him. He knew she could see him now, very much in the moment. There were tears trickling down her cheeks.

"She told me once. It was a secret, but I told Rebecca. Soon, everyone knew. Addy said … Addy said her mother would sing to her, sing about how she'd come back to get her. But Addy kept running away from home. Her mother didn't know why, so she had to tie Addy up at night so she couldn't go anywhere, would stop running away..."

Willards stared into the face of Penny Spencer who seemed seven years old again; she was repeating a story told to her by another child of the same age.

"One night, Addy's mother didn't come back to get her." Penny's voice was a sad whisper, lost, empty. Her eyes welled up with more tears. "Addy warned us, said it would never happen to her again, that she'd never be fooled like that again. *Never*. Of course, we did it to her many times. I started it, telling everyone to hide from the dirty girl..." She closed her eyes, her chest rising, falling in a steady pattern. "Ice cream and berries," she murmured. Then, exhausted, she slept.

Willards backed away from the bed, shut his notebook, shaken at what he had heard, what he had written. He thought about it on the way back to the station, replayed it over and over. *Addy warned us, said it would never happen to her again, that she'd never be fooled like that again. Never.* So, that's why she had killed her mother and Nick. Merrill must have been out working the streets or off with Nick somewhere. She had left her seven-year-old daughter tied up alone all night to stop her from running away from her hellish home life. Something had snapped in Addy's mind, something that had been growing there for years. Whatever it was, that terrifying night of abandonment had triggered something in Addy. Either she had freed herself of the restraints and surprised Merrill and Nick when they arrived home, or they had released her, not aware of her pent-up anger. Regardless, she butchered them in a furious rage in the summer of 1994. When the bodies of Merrill and Nick were discovered, Addy Burk was taken away, never to be seen or heard from again, later to reappear as Adel Daniels.

But before that, while in the first grade, two little girls and Tommy King made the mistake of playing a trick on Addy, one suggested by Penny. They never realized that it was Addy's game, Addy's rules. They didn't come back to get her, didn't chase her down or didn't return to the circle when tapped by Addy.

Addy said that Tommy King never knew what hit him.

Willards winced. It would be easy enough to identify and confirm the deaths of the two girls and Tommy King, find out how they had died.

Ice cream and berries...

# # #

Tony burst into Willards' office, carrying a yellow evidence bag.

"What is it?"

"A birthday card for Adel's son, Scotty. It was addressed to you, just got it handed to me."

"Oh, shit! That's right, he turned seven a couple days ago." The card was of a race car with a *Happy 7th Birthday!* emblazed on its side. Inside was a Polaroid of Penny's son, Ben, sitting in a chair, his hands over his eyes. The words **I'LL COME BACK TO GET YOU!** were written on the bottom of the picture. On the back, etched in the black gloss was the name SCOTTY.

"A threat to get Scotty next," Tony said.

Willards nodded. "But he's well protected at the foster home, but alert them to this, emphasize that he can *never* be left alone." Tony nodded. Willards then told him all he had learned from his visit with Penny.

When he finished, Tony asked, "So what we had listed as deaths in her first-grade class were actually homicides? Adel not only killed her mother and Nick, she also murdered three classmates?"

"Three that we know of," Willards said. "And it seems that this rage came over her in response to the way Penny made her feel about herself and how she isolated Addy from the rest of her classmates."

# # #

On Monday morning, Tony and Willards were in the police station's conference room, studying the four walls. They had tacked up all the photographs received over the past month-and-a-half. On the floor in neat stacks sat piles of case notes. Tony obtained old school records and police reports that revealed Tommy King's cause of death was ruled accidental: a fall down a stairwell at school. His skull had been crushed. The photo they had of him showed a boy with thick glasses, slightly crossed eyes and a thick scar, which was the result of a badly repaired hair lip.

The two girls—Jada Emery and Tiana Smith—were both dark skinned. Jada had a friendly, round face but it was clear she was obese. Tiana had a long, narrow face, a mouth with too many teeth. Tony and Willards agreed that the appearance of the children would make them easy targets of bullies and they would probably have gravitated to Addy if she had shown them any warmth since she too was an outcast from the other classmates.

The deaths of Jada and Tiana were attributed to accidental ingestion of the poison belladonna.

"It was somewhat rare but did grow wild in the area. Somehow the girls got hold of it," Tony said. "They look just like blackberries. I read that ten to twenty belladonna berries are lethal for adults. Only two or three are needed to kill a child

Willards shook his head. "No, maybe that's what

they thought back then, that it was a tragic accident. Tell me you know how Addy get ahold of belladonna."

Tony smiled grimly. "I checked into her health records. Guess what chronic condition she had?"

"Surprise me."

"Asthma."

"And?"

"Belladonna is used for a lot of different medical conditions. Headaches, stomach ulcers, and asthma."

"But it's a poison. Isn't it illegal? How'd she get it?"

"It's poisonous only in high concentrations," Tony said. "And it's legal to grow in New York. Three or four drops made from the juice of the leaves is recommended for asthma. But it's the berries that Addy probably somehow tricked the girls into eating..."

Ice cream and berries, Willards mused, then asked, "Why didn't Addy use an inhaler or medicine like other kids?"

Tony said, "I'm guessing because Addy's general health and regular doctor visit were not a priority in her home. Besides, if her mother really believed in the power of the herbs she was growing, she probably assumed that was the right way to go."

"What a horrible woman," Willards said, "having no concern whatsoever for her own daughter's health. And it wasn't like they lacked money to get her medicine. I'm sure Nick was getting plenty from Olivia."

"Yeah, but that was *all* for Nick," Tony said. "Didn't sound like anything was shared with Merrill or Addy. They were on their own. Even whatever Merrill earned, most of it probably went to Nick. That was why she was always getting in trouble for petty crime. No wonder Addy's rage seemed to simmer all those years until it exploded."

"That poor, sick kid," Willards murmured, thinking

of his own kids, missing them suddenly, reminding himself to arrange to get with them soon.

Tony said, "Anyway, Addy probably just gave some of the sweet belladonna berries to her schoolmates. They are plump and shiny, very juicy, slightly sweet. The girls never knew she was poisoning them."

"Ice cream and berries," Willards said. "I hate to ask, but what happens when someone takes belladonna?"

"Depends on the dose and form or concentration. When dispensed over time as liquid distilled from the leaves, it affects eyesight, causing blurry vision, sensitivity to light, which can lead to headaches and vertigo. Higher doses, like when it's ingested as a berry, can result in coma, convulsions, respiratory or heart failure. Ultimately, death. It only took a few hours for the girls to die."

"Olivia Nelson died of a heart attack, didn't she?" Willards said.

Tony nodded. "You're thinking…"

"Why not? You said belladonna can cause heart failure. What if Addy somehow got the poison to Olivia?"

"Why would she want to kill her perfect mother?"

Willards shrugged. "Maybe she and Olivia really did meet face-to-face once and Olivia disappointed Addy or they had a falling out? She was the girl's last hope of an ideal mother, so…"

"Let me get the autopsy report, see if a medical examiner thinks the results could point toward poison," Tony said.

Willards looked at the timeline, realized that Addy's kill spree had been escalating at the time. Tommy, Jada and Tiana had been killed at the end of the first grade school year, right before summer break. Olivia Nelson died of a heart attack—or poison—on June 16, 1994 while riding the Metro-North train into the city. Addy's mother and Nick had been stabbed to death a few weeks later on July 7, 1994. She was locked up in White Stone where she spent the next eleven years thinking, reinventing herself, trying to suppress the rage she had felt at her schoolmates and her mother for betraying her. *But why kill Olivia?* he wondered. *How had*

Olivia abandoned Addy, or was that just a slight imagined by her?

"And why does Addy hold a grudge for such a long, long time?" he asked the empty room.

His phone chimed. It was Gail. "Hey! How are you?"

"I'm good. I'm actually going to be in New York this weekend but haven't had any luck finding a place to stay. Any suggestions?"

# # #

Gail arrived Saturday morning. Willard's plan was for them to hole up in his apartment, order in, never leave the bed or one another's side the entire time she was in town. But he knew that was a pipe dream, as did she.

The case had put tremendous pressure on everyone. The mayor and the local papers and cable news were all talking non-stop about it, with headlines asking where The Comeback Kidnapper was hiding Adel, Carl, Graham, and Ben. What were the police doing? The police department had managed to keep their suspicions about Adel out of the stories. As far as the media and public knew, Adel was just one of four kidnapped victims. Penny was under police protection and Adel's son, Scotty, was hidden away at a foster home.

Willards had to leave the apartment for a meeting with the mayor.

"Doesn't he know I'm in town?" Gail asked as she watched Willards get dressed.

"I told him, and he promised to keep the meeting short. We have these gatherings every day, just to keep him appraised of all that is going on."

"Which is nothing, right?" she said.

He nodded. "Just information. We now have so much information, so many motives and suspicious, but everything seems to be locked in place, no movement."

"At least Penny and Scotty are safe."

"Scotty is anyway. Mentally, Penny is in a bad place." He kissed her goodbye. "Here's my key in case you want to go out. I should be gone a couple hours unless something happens. Feel free to snoop."

"No secrets?"

She locked the door behind him, gave his apartment a more leisurely once over. It was rather sparse, a few books on the shelves; mostly stacks of files, magazines, and newspapers. Pictures of his kids. A few faintly green plants scattered about. She could tell he was obsessed with the case, his job. The space around her was just that, a space, a place to sleep, to eat, to shower, then back to the job. She was the same way and was glad they were alike in their approach to work. She knew she had been incredibly presumptive, inviting herself to stay with him, but between the phone calls and texts, it was clear they were attracted to one another. She knew he'd never get to Virginia with the case so red hot, so she had taken the leap of faith and he had caught her.

The bed was a tangled mess. As she made it, she thought of the lyric from that old Elton John song, "Wrecking the sheets real fine." Oh, they had done that all morning and up until they had showered together. He had pulled some breakfast together, they ordered up sandwiches so she cleaned up the few dishes they had used, found where they went, put them away. She poured herself a glass of tonic water and settled on the couch with the mystery she was reading. It had been a great companion on the plane but now she was restless, didn't really care who had done it. The escapades of the characters were not at all as compelling as the real-life case they were working on.

She stretched, smiled, thinking of Willards, how satisfying the sex was with him, how great it was to be touched again. It had been awhile. Neither of them really had the time or interest to date, no one understood the long, brutal and all-consuming hours their jobs demanded. The fact that they had crashed into one another working on this case was a big surprise for both of them. They appreciated one another's skills and their growing friendship had quickly turned into a real desire to see one another.

"And here I am," she said, realizing she missed him. Closing the door on him as he had left for his meeting had been so abrupt after the morning and early afternoon together. It was like the silence when music ceased; it was jarring, it took a moment for her to become used to the solitude.

"But only for a couple of hours," she announced, liking the sound of her voice in his apartment. It felt good to miss him, silly and very much like a schoolgirl crush, but she liked the way her heart fluttered when she thought about him.

She checked her phone. Nothing to respond to. She sipped her drink. He promised her dinner at his favorite local Italian restaurant that night. Then back home, where they'd spend their first full night together. Something else to look forward to. She felt cozy, drowsy, sank a little deeper into the sofa. It felt comfortable being in his apartment, his environment.

She could see herself staying there when she was in town, and he staying with her when he visited Virginia.

"Don't project, you just met—"

A knock at the door startled her.

She peered through the peephole. "Yes?"

"Laundry pick-up for Mr. Willards."

Gail opened the door.

# # #

The meeting with the mayor went long. It was the usual food chain nightmare. The governor and the press were riding his ass, so he was going to ride theirs long and hard. Inside the closed-door session, blame and expletives were flung about like blood splatter, and Willards only stood there, mute, waiting like a good soldier to respond. The chance never came. More accusations of incompetence were raised, flares against the black picture that was being painted of the New York Police Department. City officials chimed in, fingers were pointed, threats were made, an election was coming up—wasn't it always?—what was being done to rescue these people, find Adel Daniels? A headache had taken up residence in Willards skull, he felt ill, forced himself to think of Gail, which made him feel immediately better.

When it was finally over, he and Tony gathered up their papers, their unread statements, left the stale smelling room.

"TV and papers outside," one officer warned.

"So is fresh air," Tony said.

The press had been tipped off to the assembly, so they were waiting for statements. They wanted updates. They wanted reasons why Adel and Carl Daniels, Graham Spencer and his son, Ben, had not been located yet. Where were they being kept? Had there been more photographs received? Any evidence they were still alive? Who else was at risk of being kidnapped? Any updates on the I'll come back to get you rhyme and its meaning?

"No comment," was repeated over and over by Willards and others that had followed him into the chaos. The early evening air was cool, helped to revive the beleaguered cops. With nothing to feed on, the gaggle eventually dispersed.

"Now what?" Tony asked.

"Italian dinner with Gail. My phone's on. I'm at everyone's beck and call."

# # #

Gail had his only key. He had texted, then called her that he was on his way home, but there was no response. Hopefully she hadn't gone out since he was starving. He was ready to eat, then get back to bed with her.

Willards didn't live in a doorman building. Outside, he pushed the intercom button for his apartment. He was all set to say, "Honey, I'm home!" into the speaker when Gail answered, buzzed him up, but there was no response. He texted again. Buzzed again.

Was she in the shower?

After pushing several buttons, someone finally buzzed him in, the oldest and most dangerous and easiest way to enter a building in Manhattan. But it always worked. The elevator was slow to arrive. The doors hesitated before opening. Then, once he was inside, they sluggishly closed. He called, texted again. No response. A flutter of unease brushed past him. Had the elevator always been so lethargic? It began its slow ascent; the lighted display showed each floor as it inched pass. The mechanism creaked, groaned, no interest in making haste. A slight bump, then a pause on his floor. The doors remained closed. He was preparing to tear them away with his bare hands when they clicked, yawned open.

He had a second key to his apartment tucked under the carpet of a neighbor's door. He'd never needed it, hoped it was still there. He jogged down the hallway, reached under the carpet, then hurried to his door. He tried the handle, was surprised it wasn't locked.

Once inside, he called out, "Gail?" Listened for the shower. It wasn't on. He said her name again. Everything was wrong. The air was wrong; it was coiled, tense, like the atmosphere before a storm. His heart was now tight, hammering hard and fast. He looked over the living room, kitchen. Dishes not in the sink. She'd cleaned them, put them away. He hurried down the hallway. Looked in the bathroom. Empty. No steam on the mirror, she hadn't taken a shower. Then why hadn't she answered any of his calls or texts? Where was she, why'd she leave the door unlocked?

The bedroom. Bed made, place had been tidied up.

"Gail?"

He retraced his steps, didn't take long in a one-bedroom apartment. Her suitcase and clothes were still there, toiletries still in the bathroom.

Everything was where it belonged, except the front door hadn't been locked, and Gail was gone.

Willards couldn't move, couldn't create a thought. This had to be a terrible dream. *Gail was gone.* He stared at her belongings, items she had casually left about his apartment, breadcrumbs that led nowhere. He picked up her hairbrush, stroked the bristles. They had showered together early that afternoon. He had to get cleaned up for the meeting with the mayor, needed to shave but mainly needed to wash the scent of sex off of him. Didn't want to, but others would know. Tony, who knew him so well, would know. He had washed Gail's hair, his fingers going deep into her hair, massaging her scalp while she oohed and aahed! in great pleasure.

In the closet hung the dress she had planned to wear that evening. He fingered the material. Smooth, delicate, like Gail. Still trying to get some momentum going, had to decide what to do next. He paced. Where could she have gone? And why? She would have left a note, would have answered her phone, would have responded to the texts he'd sent. He called again, heard a sound from the living room. Her phone? He followed the chime, found her phone on the sofa, ringing. He ended his call. Her phone went silent.

He looked out the window. The setting sun glowed bright against the dark sky. He'd have to call Tony, tell him Gail was missing.

From the bedroom, a sound. He turned, wondering what he had heard. Then, a hard thud on the floor. Again, from the bedroom. He stood in the doorway, waited, strained to hear.

A muffled sound. Willards pulled his Glock 22 out, stepped closer to the bed. Where was it coming from? For a second, he thought he saw the mattress quiver just a bit. A squeak as if...

He dropped to his knees, lifted the bedspread.

"Gail! Oh, my God!"

He lifted the bed frame, gently helped her out. Her hands were tied in front of her, a thick piece of tape had been placed over her mouth, her ankles were tightly bound. Only by straining against the heavy mattress frame and stomping her heel against the carpeting under the bed was she able to make a sound, indicate where she was.

Once he had removed the restraints, she fell into his arms and wept. It took her a moment to catch her breath. Willards looked nervously around the room; he was glad he had checked everywhere. No one else was in the apartment. "Who did this?" he asked.

"A woman." She buried her head back into his shoulder. "It happened so fast, she said she was here to pick up your laundry."

"I don't send out my laundry."

Gail looked at him. "Well, obviously! I know that *now*." She almost laughed, winced, felt the back of her head. "I opened the door, she came in and before I knew it, she bashed me over the head with something. That's all I remember…"

He gingerly felt the back of her head. She gasped in pain. It was crusty with dried blood, a lump had formed. "It's not bleeding now, which is good, but we'll get it checked out."

"I came to under the bed. I heard you calling out, but I could barely move around."

"It was Adel, right?"

"It happened so fast. I couldn't say for sure, but who else could it be? This woman had a scarf over her head, I remember that. Multicolored scarf. She wore glasses, had on a big, baggy t-shirt."

He helped her up, they walked slowly toward the front of the apartment. Glancing around, Willards said, "I don't think she took anything. Nothing seems to be missing." Gail leaned heavily on him, still dizzy. He made her an ice pack, settled her on the sofa while he looked more thoroughly around the apartment.

When he returned, she asked, "Nothing missing?"

He shook his head. "No, not that I can tell. Not that I have anything of great value but nothing in the drawers has been disturbed, no cabinets opened, nothing looks like it was touched."

Gail winced, moved the ice pack to a different section of her head. "Maybe she didn't come to take anything, maybe to *leave* something?"

"You think she knew you were going to be here or were you a surprise to her?"

"From what we know about her, she's a planner. She knew I was here," Gail said, "and she knew you had left the building."

"How are you feeling?" he asked.

"I want to get checked out but give me a couple minutes to rest. And I still think you should look to see if she left you anything. She came here for a reason; I was just in the way."

"But where would she leave me something?"

"The bedroom area, I would think," Gail said, closing her eyes. "Start there. She could have just tied me up and left me out in the open, but for some reason, she wanted me confined under the bed."

Willards returned to the bedroom. The bed was off-centered, disheveled. He got down on his knees again, looked around slowly. On the far side of the bed he saw a white piece of paper. He retrieved it. It was a Polaroid. He turned it over.

He returned to Gail, looked at her.

"What?" she asked. "What is it?"

He handed her the photo. It was a picture of her, unconscious, flat on her back on Willards' bed. Her hands were tied and loosely placed over her face in a hide and seek position. At the bottom of the white border that surrounded the image, the words **I'LL COME BACK TO GET YOU** were written. She dropped the photo onto her lap, her hands trembling. She sat back, disturbed at the image. The bump on the back of her head began to throb painfully as her heart beat faster.

"I don't know, but I don't think you were her target," Willards said slowly. "Not based on everything we know." He flipped the photo over, squinted at the glossy darkness. "And there's no name written on the back."

"She was following *you*, Steve. She knew you had left, knew I was here. Why would she do this, act so reckless?"

Willards shrugged. "Is it reckless, or daring?"

Gail winced as she sat up. "Think about it. It really is like lashing out, right? Going after the person who is most likely to expose her, wanting to hurt someone close to him."

"That's you," he said.

She grinned. "Yes, that's me. Adel's behavior is that of someone who is quickly unraveling, doesn't care what the stakes are, lashes out at the people most likely to expose her. Come on, get me to the hospital. I want to know what kind of damage she's done to me."

# # #

Fortunately, Willards knew the Lennox Hill emergency room physician on duty and it wasn't a busy time. Gail was examined within thirty minutes and it was determined she hadn't been seriously injured.

While they were there, they decided to check on Penny Spencer. She was watching TV when he and Gail entered her private room after nodding at the cop posted outside her door. By the shimmering glow of the screen, Penny's face was slack, dark shadows lined her face. She listlessly recognized the detective, acknowledged the introduction to the profiler, and stared at the bandage on Gail's head but didn't ask about it. Gail and Willards pulled up chairs close to the bed. Willards didn't know how to begin but was relieved that Penny seemed to be in the present, wasn't caught up in her past any more. The restraints were gone too.

"Watching TV is pointless," Penny finally said. "Isn't it?"

"What do you mean?" Gail asked.

"Because all you do is *watch*. You have no control over the events. Like everything that's happened to me, I only watched it occur. Addy Burk has come back out of the past. She's killed my sister, taken my husband and my son." Her voice caught itself, held for an instant, then cracked. Penny turned away from them.

"Penny?" Willards said. "Listen to me. Why do you think Adel has targeted you? What happened between the two of you in first grade that she never forgot?"

Penny looked at them, her eyes deep, black pools of dread.

"It's my fault, isn't it," she finally said. "This is all happening because of what I did."

"What did you do?" Gail asked. "What did you do to her?"

Penny finally told them everything.

# # #

Tony met Gail and Willards at the hospital cafeteria just before it closed.

"I figured we'd just meet here since we might have to talk to Penny again," Willards said as the three of them set their trays down at one of the tables. "For Adel to have orchestrated all of this, she had to go about her everyday life without raising suspicion yet also make time to take the photos of Carl and Graham, feed and care for them."

Tony nodded. "Incredible to think she did this all

alone. It seems so complicated. So many moving parts."

"Remember," Gail said, "as a child, she was forced to be independent, was left on her own most of the time, and developed a tremendously powerful fantasy life. Just had three dolls to play with at home. At school, she was abandoned by all her classmates because of the horrible things Penny said about her, so she surrounded herself with three other misfits, Tommy, Jada, and Tiana. She treated them like her dolls, didn't even think of them as human, just figures to play with, to keep her company. All by herself, she survived."

Willards said, "But at some point, even her three playmates at school must have rejected her or not done as she wanted, so she lashed out at them."

"And was left alone again," Tony finished.

"She was never a joiner," Gail said. "She kept herself to herself, and we know from the school records and the detention facility that she never mixed with the other kids. She tried at school with Tommy, Jada and Tiana. She was the leader of the outcasts in first grade. Once she had disposed of them, I think it made her feel powerful, special, maybe even able to better cope with the pain and isolation in her life, both at school and at home. To successfully kill three children when you're seven years old must have been a huge turning point for her. But once she was put away, she kept to herself."

Gail turned to Tony. "So, I think she was more than capable at planning something so complex as kidnapping Carl, Graham, and Ben. All it took was discovering Carl's betrayal along with the trigger of Scotty turning seven, and I think the plan came together quickly, probably without her consciously even being aware of it."

Willards asked, "You mean she really did believe Carl was kidnapped by someone else?"

Gail nodded, pulled out her phone, sorted through the photos, showed them the pictures of Carl, Graham, Adel, and Ben. "One thing I keep forgetting to mention. See how they are tied up? It's the same in each instance and I think that's how Addy remembers being tied up. The hands over the face are just part of the game, but the way they are bound, that's probably exactly how Addy experienced it."

Willards asked Tony, "Any new thoughts or leads about where she's keeping them?"

"We still think it's got to be in Brooklyn, near where she worked. It goes back to what you were saying about her need to keep her daily routine the same so no one would catch on to her."

"That's what I keep going over and over in my head, trying to figure it out. She sets up that bogus estate sale at a Brooklyn address, knocks Carl out, ties him up, transports him somewhere, takes his photo, mails it to herself, then goes home, receives the Polaroid a couple days later, and calls us to put the game in motion." Willards looked at Gail and Tony, who both nodded.

"Except," Gail said, one finger up on caution, "to Adel, it's not a game. She hasn't regressed to Addy Burk yet, so to her, it's really happening."

Tony said, "So when she was insistent that she return to work every day, she wanted to keep her usual routine and didn't want to sit at home, that was all because she had to be near Carl when she took her breaks from work. That's when she went to look after Carl and later, Graham."

"Same with all the times she told us she was aimlessly driving around, looking for Carl's work van and posting missing fliers about him," Willards said. "She was actually feeding and caring for Carl, then Graham."

"And now, hopefully, she's still looking after both of them and little Ben," Gail said.

"Let's talk to Adel's boss again," Willards said. "We need to see if she can correlate what times Adel took breaks or lunches, if she left the store, how long she was gone, then search locations within that timeframe."

"We should also check with Adel's neighbor, Sally," Tony said, "see if we can match the times she looked after Scotty against when Adel was away."

"And *find* her," Gail urged both men. "We have to find Adel and locate where she is keeping Carl, Graham and Ben."

# # #

Nedra Whyler glanced at her watch, answered the phone at Second Hand Rose. It was after six, she was technically closed, was prepared to leave, but business was bad and any call could be a sale.

"Second Hand Rose," she said, surprised to hear Detective Willards on the phone. She hadn't spoken to him in weeks. When Adel had first been abducted, the police and newspapers and television reporters had swarmed all over, *like bees to honey* as her mother used to say. And all the attention had stung and filled her shop with customers who just looked, didn't buy. Sales fell off, and she was still recovering.

"Yes, she took a couple breaks a day, detective," she said in answer to his questions.

"Usually an early lunch, around 11:30, and then a short break in the afternoon."

"She stay in or go out to eat?"

"She'd go out."

"Anywhere in particular?"

"Not that I know of. There are diners and fast food

joints all over. She only had 30 minutes so it couldn't be anything fancy or too far away."

The questions continued. Nedra answered as best as she could, realizing she had never paid that much attention to Adel or how she spent her time. She had only been employed a little more than six months. She'd always been a good worker: usually prompt, good with the customers, familiar with the items in the store, had a smart sense when to lower the price to close a sale. At his request, she told the detective again about when she had first met Adel Daniels.

"You sure you want to come out here every day?" she had asked. "There's no place in the city you'd prefer to work?"

Adel had smiled, explained that she wanted some time *out* of the city. "With my son at school, I'm free most of the day. And I love that ten percent of your profits are donated to Nelson's Most Needy orphan outreach."

Nedra had beamed at that. "Yes, a member of my church—now deceased—knew Mrs. Nelson. She lived in Westchester, had formed the charity there and a branch here in the city. You know, people forget that Brooklyn still has some rough areas—Bed-Stuy, Brownsville—with a lot of children raised by their aunts, uncles, grandparents."

"Their parents have died?" Adel had asked.

"In some cases, or just abandoned their kids for drugs or just ran off. Anyway, I'm glad to do what I can for them."

"I've always felt so drawn to children who had been left behind," Adel had said. "I would love to work here, help increase the amount of your charitable donation."

Nedra had been touched that this kind-hearted, capable woman would be willing to accept minimum wage and drive thirty minutes each way to help sort through castoff clothes, books, furniture, records, CDs, and a myriad of other items. All to help give a portion of the funds raised to orphaned children.

"I'm sorry, what was the question?" Nedra asked, pulled back from her recollections. "Strange or strained behavior? Um, no, nothing like that at all. She was always very pleasant to work with."

"What about before she went on her break or lunch or when she returned?" Willards asked. "Did she ever seem especially anxious or nervous?"

Nedra thought about it. "Well, she was ready to take her break or lunch when the time arrived. I mean, she was out the door, no hesitation. Which was fine. I mean, she was a good worker but a few times we had several customers in here but she insisted she had to leave the store."

"When she left for her break or lunch, did you by any chance notice which direction she went? Was it the same every day or—"

"Funny you mention it. That I *do* recall. You see, the shops and food places are all to the left of the store when you leave, you'd think she'd head that way. But the few times I noticed, she went off the opposite direction."

"To the right?"

"Yes, to the right. Come to think of it, that doesn't make a lot of sense, does it? We're at the end of the block as you know. There's nothing in that direction for a lunch break. There's the subway station, and then just an overgrown section, high weeds, trees, some old storage units and an abandoned warehouse."

"But she always went that way when she left the store, right?" Willards asked, knowing the answer.

# # #

"She's probably got them in some storage unit or in some part of that old warehouse," he told Tony, Gail and the task force after he immediately called a meeting. "There are a lot of derelict buildings there. She was only away from the store for thirty minutes, so she has to have them in the immediate vicinity."

Tony said, "We think she checked on them twice a day while she was in Brooklyn, to feed them, give them water, care for them, take a picture—"

Willards nodded. "Then she made certain she was home by 3:30 to pick her son up from school."

"What about the weekends?" someone called out. "She didn't work Saturday or Sunday."

Gail said, "I bet the babysitter was asked to watch Scotty in the morning and afternoon so Adel could go to Brooklyn. Let's check to see about a timeline."

"And remember, she said that she would drive around, day after day, looking for the van, posting fliers about Carl, always feeling the need to do something," Tony reminded everyone.

"That sounded crazy back then," Willards admitted. "If we only knew…"

June 11, 1994

Dear Diary,

These damn headaches! If it's not my eyes, it's the vertigo I've been experiencing at times or the pounding in my head that forces me back to bed with the shades pulled. In silent darkness, I pray the pain passes but it seems to only slowly tick by. What is wrong with me?

Billy insists I see the doctor. I will, I tell him. Deena's party is just five days away. I just need rest. After Deena's party, he can summon the doctor. If there is bad news for me, it can wait just a bit longer. If what I have is serious, what difference can a few days make?

I had to send the angel away yesterday soon after she arrived, wasn't feeling well. She was furious with me, didn't understand. I sometimes forget how awful she can be at times. Billy came to my room, drawn by her shouts. He gently led her away but the looks she gave me were troubling. Such rage from one so young.

<u>The Final Week</u>
Addy

Adel had been surprised when Rebecca Roberts had called her at work three weeks ago, just after Graham had been taken. Even Mama hadn't known it was going to happen.

"Hello, is Ms. Daniels there?"

"Yes, speaking. Who's this?"

"My name is Rebecca Roberts. My sister is Penny Spencer. I saw you at the police station briefly last week."

"You did?"

"Yes, you arrived just as I was leaving Detective Willard's office. Remember?"

"Oh, yes. Of course, Ms. Roberts. I do remember. Is there any word about your brother-in-law?"

"No…nothing yet. Anything about…your husband?"

"No…," Adel said. The conversation was awkward. What was Rebecca up to? More lying, more deceitful behavior? Or did she have more lies to tell about Mama being a witch or what a dirty girl she was? Adel heard Rebecca clear her throat.

"This is such a terrible thing. Penny is having an

awful time about it, as am I. When the detective was speaking with us, he mentioned you had no family and…I was wondering if I could possibly come to see you some time. To talk about all of this."

Adel didn't know how to respond. Her face had tightened into a disbelieving grin. *Was this really happening?* she wondered. *This stupid, stupid woman who had an affair with my husband, enticed him to betray me, now wants to meet because this is all so "terrible?"* Her thoughts ran red. How long had she been silent? She needed to say something. "Ms. Roberts?"

"Yes?"

"I'm so sorry. I'm just…scattered. Your call—and your suggestion—caught me off guard, I guess…"

"I apologize. This is so abrupt. We all feel so helpless. I'm sorry to have intruded."

"No, it's fine, actually. Really, very kind of you, in fact. And you're right, I have no family. Our friends have been supportive, but no one really understands what this is like unless you're living through it. As you and Penny are. Thank you for reaching out to me. It's so kind. I *would* like to talk with you. When would you like to get together?"

"Actually, I could be there today, if you're available. I was planning to be in the city, but I could meet you in Brooklyn where you work."

Adel had said, "Just a moment, Rebecca." She muted the phone, told Nedra she wasn't feeling very well, hadn't felt herself all morning, could she leave early? Once it was settled, Adel said, "I'm planning to leave early today, why don't we meet at my apartment?"

Adel provided the address, ended the call. She thought about her schedule for that day, figured how to rearrange her plans. Everything would be doable. Some things just might have to wait a bit. First things first. When she returned home, she realized her hands were shaking with anger as she emptied the dishwasher, the plates sharply clacking as she put them away on the shelves. Couldn't quite believe the cunt had called her at work, so innocent but so sly. Just wants to know if I have any information about Carl that hasn't been on the news. Wait until Mama hears about this!

On cue, her phone rang. She dried her hands.

"Hello, my bell."

"Guess who called me?" Adel said breathlessly. "That woman! The one you told me about! The one who called you a witch, said I was a dirty girl, the one who has been fucking Carl!"

Mama was silent. Adel could sense the rage over the phone.

"What did the bitch want?"

"To see me! To *visit* with me! To *console* me!"

"Does she suspect? Do you think she knows that I told you about seeing them together?"

Adel shrugged. "No, she didn't sound like it. She sounded…"

"What? She sounded like what?"

"Curious, I guess."

"Oh, she misses her Carl I suppose," Mama purred.

Adel gripped the phone so tightly, her hand started to go numb. She easily recalled the day when Mama had phoned, said she was out doing errands, and who had she seen? Carl and some woman going into a hotel. "What were you doing in the city that day, Mama? Why didn't you tell me?"

"I don't tell you everything, my bell," she had said slyly.

"Adel?" Mama's voice on the phone snapped her back from the troubling memory. "What do you plan to do with her?"

"I'm not sure yet. I've been thinking…"

"I have an idea, my bell," Mama said, then began whispering furiously.

#

"Thank you for seeing me on such short notice," Rebecca said, removing her coat.

"Not at all. I appreciate you thinking of me and coming over. Would you like something to drink?"

"Yes, a diet anything would be fine if you have it."

Adel returned with two drinks. They settled across from one another in the living room. Scotty was still at school for another couple of hours. The apartment was quiet.

Rebecca sipped her Diet Coke. "I'm not really sure what to say. I have spent so much time with Penny in the past week, can't imagine not having someone to talk with."

"Yes, it must be a comfort to have someone to turn to," Adel said, trying to tap down the rage that was simmering. "Have you always been close?"

"Yes. I'm the big sister, always protected her, looked out for her. But now—"

Adel murmured, nodded her head. "I never had a sister. It was always just me. And my dolls." She let the sentence settle hard in the room.

"I can't imagine how terrible this must be for you," Rebecca finally said.

"It's been three weeks since Carl was taken," Adel said quietly. She watched Rebecca flinch slightly at the mention of her husband. Then she added, "I love my husband so much, it's so terrible that he was taken from me." It was sweet to use the word terrible—Rebecca's word—once again. *Use her words against her*, Adel heard Mama say.

Rebecca said, "After Penny received the photo of her husband and Carl, I couldn't help thinking of you—"

"Really? Why me?"

"Well, like you said, you're all alone," Rebecca stammered. "No sister or family. And I've seen how hard it's been on Penny. I wanted to reach out."

Adel watched her, simply waited. *She has no idea who I am*, she marveled. *I'm the dirty girl you made fun of, but who's the filthy whore now?*

Rebecca said, "The most recent photo you had of Carl. He seemed all right, didn't he?"

Such a fool, my bell! Mama cackled. *Doesn't even mention her brother-in-law, only concerned about the man who abandoned you for another woman.*

"Yes, he looked all right. But as you probably know, we've received no word from the kidnapper. No ransom, no calls. Just the photos. Both men seemed all right. Penny and you must take comfort in that."

Silence as thick and deep as the sofa cushion settled in between them. Rebecca kept nervously taking gulps of her drink. *Good,* Adel thought. *Drink it to the dregs!* She stared at Rebecca, speculating: Had Carl pursued her or had she gone after him?

The woman broke into Adel's thoughts. "How is your son handling all of this?"

"He's all right. He's almost seven, the magic age, getting to be a big boy."

Children are strong, resilient, Mama cooed. *They can handle more than you think they can. Right, my angel?*

Not really, Adel thought back. *We aren't made of stone. What happens leaves scars, rough patches. You should know that, Mama...*

Rebecca yawned, wide and deep and hard. "Excuse

me," she said, covering her mouth. Adel watched an image of Carl's tongue in that mouth, exploring it, owning it, enjoying it. His body on hers.

"I have two little girls and have learned that what's a crisis one day is forgotten the next. Not that what has happened isn't horrible," Rebecca added quickly. "I don't mean it's not terribly difficult for everyone…" She yawned again.

"You seem tired," Adel said with sympathy. "Would you like to lay down?"

"Oh, no. No, I'm fine. Excuse me!" she exclaimed as another yawn overpowered her. "May I have another drink, though? For some reason, I'm really thirsty."

"Of course."

Adel took Rebecca's glass into the kitchen, glanced at the grainy residue in the bottom of the tumbler. It looked like undissolved sugar. Adel smiled. This was so much easier than belladonna. No need to extract the fluid from the leaves to add to tea or fake-eat the berries. With the back of a spoon, she crushed three more Ambien tablets until they were a powder, then emptied them into the glass. She poured in the soda, vigorously stirred the mixture. The doctor had given her a prescription for the sleeping pills weeks earlier to help her deal with the stress of Carl's abduction. He had told her to take half a tablet at first to see how she would respond. Mama had suggested she get another prescription, said she'd need more, so Adel had called the doctor's office, told them she'd accidently knocked the bottle of pills into the toilet. He gladly wrote her a new prescription, grateful to help the woman who was going through so much.

By the time Rebecca finished her second glass of soda, she would have ingested six tablets.

"Here you are," Adel said, handing the glass to

Rebecca.

"Maybe I'm coming down with something," she said, yawning again, not even bothering to conceal it. She took a big swig of the drink.

"Maybe you're coming down with a guilty conscious?" Adel suggested pleasantly.

Now bleary-eyed, Rebecca peered at her. "Excuse me?"

She looks so stupid, Adel thought, *with her mouth open, her eyes dull. A dullard, that was the word.*

Adel cleared her throat. Rebecca looked at her closely, tried to focus.

"Do you remember who I am? You used to call my mother a witch. Told all the other kids in class that she would cast a spell on them, said she made evil potions in her garden. Also said she was a whore, slept with all the men in town but she had to pay *them* because she was so ugly. She was a dirty woman, and I was her dirty child. *On her back and on her knees!* Remember now?"

Rebecca only stared at Adel, unable to fashion a response. Her mind was shutting down on her, a fuzzy coating had thickened her tongue. She tried to speak. "What? Who are you talking about?"

"Mama saw you, told me about you and Carl. You're the whore, the dirty girl, not me! You tried to take him away from me."

Rebecca dropped the glass. It thumped, bounced on the rug under the coffee table. The soda spilled, pooling for an instant on the carpet, then sank in, leaving a brown, foamy stain.

"I saw you myself," Adel said. "Even followed you. Sometimes, not every time. I like to know what's going on around me."

Then, Rebecca remembered. All at once, a pinpoint of clarity. Her words slurred, slow and thick, she said,

"Addy…Burk. Right? Oh, my God. Addy Burk." More recollections surfaced. "I'm so sorry."

"Sorry? For what? Spilling your drink? Trying to steal my husband? You and your sister tormenting me in school?"

"I'm sorry. We were just kids. So long ago…"

Adel leaned closer. "For you, maybe. For me, it *never* went away. It came back to me over and over again. It was never far away."

"What's…wrong with me?" Rebecca put her hands over her face as if she was trying to keep it from falling off. "I…feel…sick…"

Adel pushed her face nearer, spat the words at her. "You *are* sick! Trying to rip my family apart, take my husband from me, then you'd go after Scotty, right? Your two girls and my son! Take it all away from me, leave me alone, abandoned again, with no one for *me*!"

Rebecca slouched over the couch, her body unbalanced, turning to mush. She groaned, her motor functions unable to work as the medication pulled her under.

"—made my husband forsake his wedding vows and *me*!" Adel was saying. She licked her lips, squeezed her hands into fists, watched as Rebecca lost consciousness. Mama had been correct, six pills worked perfectly.

Between clenched teeth, Adel said, "Carl swore he'd *never* leave me!" She grabbed the throw pillow, settled herself next to Rebecca. She placed the pillow over Rebecca's face, pushed down, hard. Really leaned into it.

When Rebecca was still, Adel pulled the thick sheets of plastic out of the closet. Once Rebecca was positioned in the middle of one and the surrounding area had been covered, Adel grabbed the butcher knife from the kitchen and went to work.

She panted three words over and over and over again: "Never! Never! *Never!*"

#

Willards continued speaking to the task force. "We're searching that old warehouse and those old storage units in Brooklyn near the shop where Adel worked."

Tony said. "At this time, we're assuming she drugged them or knocked them out, got them into her car, drove them to wherever she's keeping them, secured them, took the photos, then left, only to return to feed and care for them a couple times a day."

"All by herself?" a task force member asked skeptically.

Willards nodded wearily. "Yeah, we know it is a challenge to hold all this together, but based on the history of this woman, the strong homicidal bent she exhibited as a child, we believe she is more than capable to carry this out."

"What drives her to do this?" the same person asked.

"Fear," Gail said. "An all-consuming fear of abandonment. It is a core symptom of borderline personality disorder. She is also schizophrenic."

Willards said to her, "Why don't you talk about that a bit, just so they know what we're dealing with."

"Sure. People with borderline personality disorder will find that their whole being is given over—consciously or unconsciously—to inflicting hurtful revenge on the world around them for neglecting their emotional and physical needs, for leaving them helpless. This rage is often expressed in a dramatic attempt at seeking revenge on those perceived to have abandoned the person."

Willards said, "In this instance, Adel—who now

thinks of herself as seven-year-old Addy Burk—has entered a regressive state where she is replaying in her mind, over and over, this game that left such a scar of abandonment. The game promised that those who left you would always come back to get you. However, the kids in her first-grade class tore apart what little family identify she had, calling her mother a witch and a whore, saying she was as filthy and unwanted as her mother was. She was abused and left alone at home and at school. No one ever came back to get Addy Burk."

Gail said, "And so by kidnapping Carl, Graham, and Ben, she has literally taken captive three people who cannot abandon her, who won't be able to leave her. We know that when she was a little girl, she mentioned to Penny Spencer, a school mate who was also the focus of the bullying, that she had three dolls she cared for at home; and we think that subconsciously, that's another reason why she wanted to capture three people to keep as her own, to have total control."

There was silence in the room as the men and women tried to process all that was being said. Willards gave them a moment, then said, "Look, I know this doesn't all make sense to us. Adel's motives are so foreign, but all that matters now is locating the three people she has kidnapped. We have officers already searching the storage units and the warehouse. We'll join them but at the same time, I want us to find Adel Daniels."

A woman called out, "What's her state of mind right now?"

Gail said, "Disturbed, paranoid, delusional. Maybe even suicidal. Somewhere inside of her is a terrified, seven-year-old who may be thinking, 'I'll show them! When I'm dead, then they'll know how awful they treated me.'"

"And she's dangerous," Willards added. "She killed

as a child and most recently, she murdered Rebecca Roberts. We don't know the state of Carl, Graham, or Ben, so we need to find her immediately before she does anything to them."

# # #

Five hours earlier, before the sun had set, before the police had lit up the area searching for her, before dogs had been employed to locate Carl, Graham, and Ben and sniff out crime scene evidence, Addy Burk had meandered past Second Hand Rose. Her head was turned slightly, straining to hear whatever Mama said. Turn right? Left? Straight ahead? Take a left at the corner?

The voice was more of a clattering mutter, like water echoing and gurgling away twenty feet under a bridge. It wasn't the harsh whisper it used to be. The intense temperament was gone, the insistence that it be heard. Now it was up to Addy to make the effort to hear; Mama wasn't going to shout. This required that she move slower and hesitate more often. It felt a little like she was blind, fumbling about without a white cane. Sometimes she was called bell, sometimes angel.

Even though the voice seemed fragile or coming from a great distance, Mama always came through. So, Addy waited, standing still, alert. Finally, she heard, nodded to acknowledge she had received the information. Her head felt heavy; her mind buzzed with emptiness. She started for the storage unit, pushing her way through the mass of trees and overgrowth as she had dozens of times in the past six weeks.

Once inside the stuffy darkness, the stench rose up to greet her. It was overwhelming, a disgusting stew of shit, urine, sweat, spoiled food, fear. It repulsed her. She closed, latched the heavy door behind her, switched on the flashlight she kept inside the space.

She had thought at first the dolls would keep themselves clean. She kept their senses dulled with the Ambien tablets she crumbled and snuck into their water and food. They were always half asleep or barely shifting about when she arrived to care for them.

"They are your best friends, they'll never leave you," Mama had constantly reminded her. "Take good care of them, my angel."

Addy always made certain they were tied tightly to their chairs so they wouldn't fall down or hurt themselves. They were so floppy, like Raggedy Andy dolls. She fed them each in turn, one at a time like a mother bird with her chicks. Sometimes they peed themselves or couldn't wait for her to loosen the ropes just a bit so they could squat over the bucket. She cleaned them up, took care of them like any good mother would…

She heard a stirring, shuffling. The sound of bound feet shushing across the floor? Were they lose? Or could it be the rats again? The dolls had complained about them, she had to get traps. Addy moved the thick, heavy flashlight beam over the two big dolls. They groaned, moved a bit as if twitching in a dream, then were still. The little doll at the end, her favorite, a boy doll, was slumped over. Without seeing his face, his body reminded her of another doll, a little girl figure who was tied up in the same way. She hated to remember what that had been like.…

The flashlight showed the last chair was empty, the ropes scattered on the floor. Directly across from it was the tripod, the silver legs flashing abruptly when the beam of light rode over them. The Polaroid was still attached on top. The automatic timer had worked perfectly. Addy had only needed to use it once to take a photo of Adel Daniels. Addy made certain the woman looked like a doll, too, and placed her hands over her eyes. That had been Mama's idea, back when her voice was louder, harder, easier to ear. The photo had fooled everyone, given Addy time to think after she had burned Rebecca in the dryer.

"They burned witches," she had muttered as she shoved the corpse into the machine. She closed the door, added hours to the cycle, set the temperature to high, then pushed start. "My Mama was never a witch, but you are. Or you were. You and your sister. Mean witches…"

"One, two, don't be blue, I'll come back to get you," Addy sang to herself so she wouldn't feel so all alone in the dark place. Again, she thought she heard the dolls stirring, but it was only her imagination. She liked them to be still when she cared for them. They knew that by now.

She began to shovel the food into the hungry doll that sat bound before her. By the light of the flashlight, she'd see the mouth would open, she'd poke in a spoonful of rice and chicken she had obtained from the fast food restaurant. The mouth eagerly chomped at the meal. She fed it some more, then tilted the water bottle in so the figurine would be hydrated and subdued with the Ambien. The lips violently moved about as they sucked in the water.

"Easy, easy," Addy said, smiling to herself. More food, then more water, on and on until it was time to check on the next, bigger doll. First, she confirmed the ropes were secure, cleaned up the piss and shit that may have accumulated. Then it was food and water, then on to the third and final doll. It was all so automatic to her that she was able to complete the process while her mind went elsewhere, went to thoughts of her mother.

So much seemed to be changing.

For years, Mama had comforted Addy, her soothing tone like a lullaby for her angel. She'd help Addy sleep through the long, black nights at the White Stone facility. Mama was always there, she hadn't abandoned her, hadn't turned red and silent the way Addy had last remembered her, back when Mama called Addy her bell...

But lately, in the past few days, her voice wasn't as loud as it once was, nor did it speak so frequently. It left Addy with a lot to figure out on her own...

After the third doll was fed, watered, and cleaned, Addy double checked to make certain they were all secure in their chairs. Then, she waited in the darkness for Mama to speak, to know what to do next, where to go.

Silence.

Addy had never spoken aloud in the room before. Mama had warned her to always keep the room dark, to never speak. She strained to hear her mother.

A groan. A chair squeaked. A child's cry.

"Quiet!" she said before she could help herself. "I can't hear Mama!"

More rustling and shuffling of chair legs scrapped against the floor.

"Shhh! All of you. Be quiet!"

A tired voice, a male voice: "Who's...there?"

Addy flinched in surprise. She thought she had heard a man's voice. The dolls should be asleep. She swallowed, hot and sweaty in the closed-up room. Strained to hear Mama.

"Help us."

Not Mama's voice.

A weary voice pleaded, "Can you help us?"

A second: "Who are you?"

Crying, sniffling from the smallest doll continued.

They *were* talking to her, but they couldn't be, they were asleep. Her dolls didn't speak.

"I'm not hearing you!" she shouted. "You can't be speaking to me. You've been fed and watered. Now sleep!" She expected that to end it.

Instead, most frightening: "Adel?"

The name meant nothing to her other than it was similar to her own. She flicked on the flashlight, aimed it at the doll that had been there the longest.

"Adel? My God, are you in here too?"

That wasn't her name, but it was close, so close that she had almost answered. *My name is Addy Burk*, she told herself. *Addy Burk, Addy Burk. Alone in the dark with my dolls.*

"Adel? Honey, it's Carl. Are you okay?"

Addy switched off the light. It was better in the dark, clearer for some reason. Her thoughts were mixed up, a snow globe of ideas all shaken up, all swirling around. They weren't settling down. She knew she shouldn't speak, but it dawned on her maybe it was Mama just playing with her.

"Mama? Are you there?"

The hush in the cramped, smelly space was thick, held no promise of a reply. Addy sensed she should leave but really wanted to know what Mama thought, wanted to be told what to do next. She whispered, "Mama? Where are you?"

"Adel? What's going on? Are you able to untie me? Where are you?"

Addy ignored the voice; it wasn't Mama, it didn't matter. Time to leave. She turned on the flashlight, followed the beam to the locked door, pulled out the key, let herself out, slammed and secured the door behind her. The cool, late afternoon air revived her. Maybe now she could hear Mama without all those awful smells to deal with. She leaned against the old, wooden door, heard nothing behind it. The cement storage area was a world of its own, a keeper of her dolls. Even if they were speaking to her, no one would hear them outside. She pulled the dead shrubs over so they provided some camouflage, hiding the door, the structure, its contents.

"Hurry, my bell!"

She turned when she heard her mother's voice, started down the street.

Police cars and officers were arriving, darting about so Addy kept to the emerging shadows. No one paid any notice to a seven-year-old girl in the deepening twilight. She was used to that, wasn't surprised.

At the subway station, she swiped her card through the turnstile, scurried forward as the train pulled in. She knew Adel's car had been left behind, a few streets away from the Second Hand Rose. The police would find it soon enough, but that didn't matter. She was just a kid. She giggled at the thought of trying to drive a car like an adult.

The subway ride from Brooklyn to Manhattan took less than twenty minutes. None of the passengers paid any attention to a child riding alone. Addy ignored them too. She stared off into the middle distance just like everyone around her. The train rumbled along. Mama would whisper to her, nudge her to make certain she was paying attention. She was.

Once she exited in Manhattan, she was immediately engulfed in the above ground traffic leaving the 68th Street station. Students from Hunter Collage were streaming into the subway. They bumped, jostled her as if she wasn't even there.

On Lexington Avenue, she trudged along, passed a liquor store, a book store, a dry cleaner, a shoe repair shop, a deli, a stationary store. One by one they slowly passed her as if she was a piece of merchandise on a conveyer belt.

Mama suggested something. Addy nodded. When she reached the building, she entered by the garage, walked to the basement, summoned the service elevator so the doorman wouldn't see her. She hoped it would arrive empty. The lights above the steel double doors counted down until finally the B light was illuminated. The doors slid open, she stepped into the vacant space, pushed the button for the floor Mama whispered.

Slowly and smoothly she rose, no stops along the way.

"You're lucky, my angel" Mama said.

Addy nodded. She was.

The doors slid upon with a *ping!* Addy darted out onto the floor like a startled deer. The hallway was empty. She hurried to unlock the door, slipped into the apartment, closed the door quietly behind her. Something was wrong with the room. It wasn't the filthy old White Plains home she had grown up in with her mother's ramshackle garden in the back. This was much nicer. And so clean! She sniffed the air. It smelled good. Panicking, she wondered if she was lost. She was not in the right place!

She hurried into the living room where she saw a stack of mail on the coffee table. Looked at the address label on an envelope. It had been sent to Carl and Adel Daniels. *Who are they?* she wondered. *Where am I?*

Her voice quivering, trying not to cry, she looked slowly around the room, whispered, "Mama? Help me..."

The voice was now so low, she had to hold her breath

to hear it. But she understood what her mother said to her, nodded to herself. It all made sense now. Breathing heavily with renewed excitement, she gave herself a moment to settle down, hugged herself, listening all the while as Mama continued to murmur in her ear, her voice low, the words running together.

"Slow down!" she finally said. "I can't understand what you're saying." Mama went silent, pouting. Addy used the break to visit the bathroom. She washed her face, hands, brushed her hair. She felt more confident, apologized to her mother, asked her to continue, nodded as the voice patiently began explaining what to do next.

Addy went to the refrigerator, pulled out a plastic bottle of Poland Spring water. She returned to the bathroom, took down the bottle of Ambien. "Yes, Mama," she said, even as her mind went elsewhere and she thought about how things had once been, when her mother worked hard for Nick, when she was always tired. Sometimes she called her my bell, but lately she called her angel. Nick never called her by any name.

"Leave your mother alone," he would say, moving in too close to Addy. She could smell the stale cigarette smoke and musky residue of something dangerous that seemed to hover about him like a mist. "She needs her rest so she can get back to work this evening."

Addy couldn't help it. She pouted. "She was *supposed* to play with me. She said…she'd come and play with me. She promised…" Couldn't help it, her voice wavered, she began to weep.

"Come here," Nick said, gesturing to her. She shook her head. Looked at her mother, snoring softly on the bed. She was exhausted, had nodded off as soon as she had laid down.

"*Now*," Nick said, that whispery, excited edge to his voice. He left the bedroom, headed to the guest room.

"Addy?" he called out.

Nervous, her throat still tight with tears, she rubbed her wrists where the ropes always held her tight. He was careful to always put some padding around first so the ropes would never leave burn or gash marks. It was as if whatever happened between them never really happened because she never had any proof. With Mama working all night, sleeping most of the day, it was usually just she and Nick when she arrived home after school. He was usually waiting for her.

"Come on, Addy. *Now*. I don't have time for this shit."

She looked at her mother, wanted to wake her up, but knew she'd get in trouble. From the other room, Nick called her again…

Addy trembled at the old memory. *Hadn't thought of that in a long, long time,* she realized.

"My bell, get to doing what I told you!"

Startled at the harsh tone, Addy nodded, grateful that her mother's voice had returned louder and much stronger. Pushing away from the old, dark memories, she got to work, crushing the tablets, adding them to the plastic bottle, and shaking it up. She put one Ambien in her mouth and washed it down. Mama sent Addy to the bedroom and showed her a purse she could use. Addy dumped the contents on the bed, put the water bottle into the purse.

"Now, look around, Addy," Mama said, a smile in her voice. "I have something for you, my angel"

The room was strangely familiar, as if she had been there once before. On top of the dresser were her three dolls, much smaller than the ones she had been caring for. It would have been nice to play with them, but Mama told her not to. Instead, she opened the dresser drawer. Inside, Addy found a woman's undergarments.

A guilty thought fled past. *Should I be doing this? Looking at these things? Touching them?*

"I told you to," Mama's voice insisted. "It's always okay to do something if I tell you to, my bell."

Addy pushed aside the clothing, felt a hard object nestled amongst the items, pulled out a jewelry box. She carried it over to the bed, sat down, opened it. Why would Mama want her to have jewelry? Inside was a tray of earrings, bracelets, some rings. Addy, compelled now by her mother's insistent voice, lifted the tray as directed. A flat, faded book took up all the space in the bottom section of the box.

"You remember what it is?" Mama asked gruffly. "Put the box back where you found it, take the diary with you." Addy remembered reading the diary years ago, taking it from a secret, hidden place. She had read the pages many times, learning the hurtful things the woman had really thought of her.

"What do you think of this 'mother' now, my bell?" Mama had asked.

Addy had watched that night when the woman left, dressed so beautifully. Then Addy had snuck back into the house when the lady was gone, took the diary from the secret place, kept the contents hidden from everyone all these years...

Next thing Addy knew, she was out of the apartment. She locked the door, sprinted to the service elevator, pushed the button, and the doors opened immediately. Again, she was in luck, the elevator had never left the floor. She grinned as she descended, her heart pounding with excitement even as she felt the first gentle blanket of slumber began to settle over her. The sleeping pill was beginning to shut down her system, she needed to hurry.

She rushed down the street toward the subway, her

body feeling like it was disengaging from itself as her eyes felt gritty. Slumber pulled at her.

"Hurry, my bell!"

"I…am, Mama." People glanced at her when she spoke, but they quickly turned away. She joined the crowd that was pushing, forcing itself down into the subway, fighting against those attempting to make their way up the staircase. For a few seconds, Abby just let the mass of people around her carry her down.

The cement smacked her, hard. She had fallen. One young man paused and asked if she was okay, but he moved on before Addy could answer. Once she had stood up, she almost collapsed again. She managed to make her way out of the pack of people to lean against the wall for a few seconds, clutching her purse in a panic. After the crowd had thinned out, she ventured to the turnstile, feeling as if the floor was swaying under her feet.

She leaned against the dirty, tiled subway wall. The train arrived. She staggered inside and fell into a seat, so grateful to sit. The doors closed. With a screech, the subway car roared off downtown. Soon it eased to a stop at Grand Central. Addy hobbled out of the car, all the time listening, listening, listening to each and every word her mother spoke to her.

Addy made the transaction with the ticket machine to be on the 11:40 p.m. Metro-North train to White Plains.

"Home, my angel," Mama whispered. "You're going home, my bell."

# # #

By nine p.m., the police were half-way through their search of the warehouse and storage spaces that were within a short walking distance from Second Hand

Rose. The dogs were sniffing, the officers were calling out to one another, walkie-talkies were keeping everyone informed as each section of the warehouse was broken into, explored, and then labeled all clear. Two news trucks had set up their satellites; three more joined them soon after. The area was ablaze with lights, armed police officers, and neighbors gathering around the cordoned off areas buzzing about what was going on, what had happened.

The storage unit they were looking for was at the far end of their spectrum, three blocks over. It stood on a tax-delinquent area that dated back to the 1960s. It quickly became an overgrown, abandoned, and forgotten space. Made of coagulated iron, the unit was one of four that had remained standing for decades in the empty lot. It was surrounded by the trees common to Brooklyn, each of them present as if wanting to guard the old structures or were curious to see what happened when this day arrived. London planetrees, Norway maples, honey locusts, pin oaks, and Callery pear trees all crammed in and around the area like too many guests at a cocktail party. Over the years, they all had grown wild and unruly. Since it was an empty lot with nothing but decrepit buildings, it had never been a priority to trim back the robust foliage. The units and the warehouse were hidden away, not seen, out of sight, out of mind.

Under the glow of the moonlight, the police officers divided into four groups. There was a hushed silence. At Willards' word, each unit had its heavy front door battered open. Soon, shouts of all clear were heard. First one, a second, then a third.

Finally: "Over here! Over here! We found them!"

# # #

Addy Burk sat in the waiting area of Grand Central Station, listening to her mother, whose voice was now much easier to hear. She didn't know if she was awake or asleep, nor did it really make a difference anymore. Her head kept jerking about. She was dizzy, exhausted, and finding it difficult to breathe. She wanted to sleep but felt so awful. All she did was yawn before finding herself staring with blurry vision at the space around her. Time jumped ahead, then stood still. It was 10 p.m. then 10:35 p.m.

All that mattered was that she was going home. Addy hugged the purse tighter. The diary fell out. She picked it up, but her tired eyes burned when she tried to read. She put it back in the bag.

She was going home to be with Mama.

She dozed, then jerked awake when her train was called.

"Hurry, my angel!"

Addy climbed onto the train and put her ticket under the clip so the collector wouldn't have to wake her. Mama kept reminding her to shake the bottle of water and drink from it.

With each stop north, the late-night Metro-North train emptied out, few boarded. By midnight, Addy—in the third car from the front—was slumped over the seat. At some point, just after the train pulled out of Scarsdale, she vomited. Mama quickly woke her.

"Drink a little more, my bell. Go ahead, my angel. A little more water. Finish it all now. Go on."

Smiling weakly, Addy Burk did as her mother said.

# # #

By the time the train reached White Plains, the third car from the front had only one passenger.

Adel Daniels, her face flushed a bright, burning red, lay dead on the seat, her mouth slightly agape. In her hands, she held the purse that contained the diary of Olivia Nelson.

And in the center of Adel's crimson left cheek blazed a faint, pale spot that looked exactly like a tiny, white bell.

# # #

Willards and Gail fell into his bed. It was after two in the morning. Exhausted, they laid together in silence.

He held her while she stroked his chest. Too tired to make love, they were more than content to just hold one another.

"I'll never get over the sight of them in that storage unit," Gail said. "In all the years I've been doing this, all I've seen, to see Ben, only a child…"

Willard pulled her closer, wanted the images to go away. He kissed her forehead. "I know. But the medical team said all three should be okay. Much of their appearance was due to dehydration and the horrible conditions they were in."

Gail said, "I know, but for them to have had to go through so much…"

They listened to their breathing.

"And it was so odd about Adel," Gail said. "To die on the train, just like Olivia Nelson had, with her diary in her possession. Even in her last moments, I guess she wanted Olivia to be her mother, was probably thinking she was returning home to her."

"I remember you said something about history repeating itself. Like her two mother figures, Adel was certain to be sure that she didn't make it out of this alive." Willards paused for a moment, then added, "And now that we have the diary, we see how Addy actually did meet her ideal mother, spent weeks visiting with her. I guess that for a short time, Olivia and Addy really needed one another."

"Until Olivia made the mistake of angering Addy…"

They resettled themselves on the bed.

"How does Carl ever recover from this?" Willards asked. "Where does he even start? He has Scotty, but knowing all that Adel did because of his affair, how can he make sense of his life?"

Gail murmured something, said, "At least Graham and Penny have each other and Ben. Penny has a long road of healing ahead, but she has her husband and son. Ben's the one I'm most concerned about. A six-year-old recovering from that kind of trauma…"

After a few moments, Willards asked, "Do you think, ultimately, this was all cause and effect?"

"What do you mean?"

Willards said, "Did Carl having the affair—and Adel finding out—cause her to respond this way?"

"Oh. Well, that's impossible to say, isn't it? It could be that but you also have Adel dealing with the trigger of Scotty turning seven and all that that stirred up in her."

"Do you think…" he started to ask, sitting up in bed.

"What?"

"That gene, the one that may have been passed down to Adel from Clay and Nick. Do you think maybe Scotty has it?"

She turned, faced him. "Where do you come up with these questions?"

"I'm just asking your professional opinion."

"Like I've always said about your theory, I can't say for certain. We'd need DNA samples of everyone involved. But based on everything that has happened, I think Scotty—and probably his dad—will be in therapy off and on for much of their lives. I'm sure their therapists will be on top of any suspicious behaviors that Scotty exhibits that are out of the norm. Does that settle it?"

"Yes. It does. For now." He snuggled in closer. "You know, there is only one good thing that came out of this case."

"What was that?"

"Meeting you."

She kissed him. "Yes, detective. I've enjoyed working with you these past few weeks too."

"Is that all it's been, a few weeks?" He sighed again. Then: "Do you see a partnership forming?"

"I thought Tony was your partner?" she teased.

"Answer the question."

And, smiling, she did.

June 16, 1994

Dear Diary,

Instead of tea, she brought over a handful of fresh berries, insisted I eat them with a little cream.

I did as she asked, wanting to keep the peace. I've found if I don't do as she asks, her anger flares up, but I've had enough. No longer shall I see her after what just occurred. My hand still trembles.

It was all so strange. She pointed out some birthmark on her cheek that I really couldn't see, explained that when she has one of her asthma attacks and her face goes red, the mark looks like a little bell. She asked that I no longer call her an angel but instead call her, "My bell." When I demurred, she became enraged, demanding that I use the phrase. I couldn't fathom where this passion was coming from, why was it so important to her?

She looked at me so strangely, such confusion in her eyes. She simply said, "Because you're my mother, and you've always called me that."

I finally had to summon Billy, as if he wasn't already on his way! That a seven-year-old could behave in so ghastly a manner! Such screaming. After he had secured her from the house, Billy returned to check on me, implored me (again) not to attend Deena's event this evening due to my health concerns. But now more than ever I plan to go. I want to be out among the people tonight, put distance, noise and much fun between this room, this journal, and most of all, this dark angel.

I ponder the fact that both my "children"—one by birth, one by recent acquaintance—have turned so harshly against me. I am a terrible mother. The despicable threats my son makes, the demands for money, the promise to tell the world who he really is and who his daughter—my granddaughter—is, if I don't continue to meet his demands. He exhausts me.

As if I didn't know this girl, Addy Burk, my angel, is my granddaughter.

There it is, written down here for the first time. A fact. A secret no more. It took a little digging but the truth is never buried that deep. But there is no one to tell the facts to except these pages. I'd go mad without them.

Perhaps for the brief time I've let Addy Burk into my life, I've pretended that I've been able to atone somewhat for the destructive force of Nick that was unleashed on this world. He's like a whirlwind of evil, very much his father's seed, tearing up everyone in his path, even his mother, even his daughter. Thank goodness Reggie never knew any of this! His heart could never bear it.

I've decided to stop bankrolling Nick. He can say what he wants about who he is and who I am. It will only darken my name since it was before I ever knew Reggie. Addy has a mother, that I have confirmed, so she can look to that woman for what she needs in life. She was my angel, but no more. She should only answer to her birth mother. Let that woman call her "my bell," which is Addy's desire.

Enough! My train leaves in an hour. I must dress. I'm so looking forward to this evening.

END

ABOUT YOUR AUTHOR

Jeff C. Stevenson is a professional member of Pen America, an active member of the Horror Writers Association, and a finalist for the Best Published Midsouth Science Fiction and Fantasy Darrell Award. Jeff has published more than two dozen dark fiction stories and has been included in anthologies alongside Clive Barker, Ramsey Campbell, Richard Chizmar, Jack Ketchum, Brian Lumley, Adam Nevill, Graham Masterton, Edgar Allan Poe and Algernon Blackwood. Jeff is the author of the Amazon #1 bestselling *FORTNEY ROAD*: The True Story of Life, Death, and Deception in a Christian Cult. HellBound Books published his supernatural thriller based upon the Fox Sisters in early 2018. Jeff also writes mainstream fiction under the pen name of Mary Saliger.

Author profile: http://goo.gl/dWEA8N

Twitter:
https://twitter.com/JeffCStevenson

OTHER HELLBOUND BOOKS
WWW.HELLBOUNDBOOKSPUBLISHING.COM

The Children of Hydesville

When the malevolent entity that Maggie and Katie Fox unleashed in Hydesville in 1848 returns in 2018, it must be stopped - at all costs.

Manhattanites Derek David and his wife Edith receive an invitation to visit the Keilgarden Colony, a secluded community located five hours north of the city in the village of Hydesville. Dedicated to nurturing children with psychic abilities, the colony was built in 1948 on land that includes the cottage where Maggie and Katie Fox first heard the ghostly rappings in 1848 - which started the Spiritualist movement.

But what begins as a late-summer respite swiftly turns into a confusing and terrifying ordeal as Derek and Edith experience increasingly bizarre and disturbing events, which drives Derek to set fire to the Fox house.

Months later, New York Times reporter Sheila Irving and her boyfriend, Kevin Jackson, visit Hydesville to investigate Derek's motivation. If those gathered in the village succumb to the powerful entity that controls the area, they will partake in the creation of union children - psychically gifted offspring whose malevolent powers will reach far beyond the confines of the small township.

The Synagogue Horror

Rabbi Avrum Steinberg is so much more than just a horror movie loving rabbi of a small, run-down synagogue on New York City's Lower East Side - he is also a small time private eye, albeit with cases no more exhilarating than locating debtors and errant, deadbeat husbands. Following the bizarre murder of a young woman in his synagogue, Steinberg begins to suspect that a vampire may be loose in New York, and before long, his suspicions are proven true. It takes the help of Wilomena - a young, mysterious, African-American minister - to help the rabbi hunt down the infamous Count Dracula himself, who is holed up in an abandoned subway tunnel beneath the City's bustling sidewalks. In their perilous and terrifying journey, the rabbi and Wilomina are joined by a band of elderly Kabbalists and Steinberg's son, and along the way the vampire hunters encounter zombies, fallen angels, some familiar vampires, and even a ghost or two. This unique urban vampire story pits the powers of faith against an ancient, dark power of evil - proving once again, that dispatching the master vampire is by far no easy task.

Shopping List 3

By popular demand, the third volume in our bestselling anthology series, twenty-one spine-chilling, terrifyingly creepy tales of terror by a bunch of the best independent horror authors writing today!

Featuring horror stories - and shopping lists - from: Richard Raven, Dhinoj Dings, Jeremy Thompson, Jeremy Wagner, Nick Manzolillo, Steve Stark, Jeff C. Stevenson, Kevin McHugh, James Watts, Don Jones, Nick Swain, Mark Thomas, Brian McGowan, Jason Gelehrt, Mark Deloy, Richard Barber, Sergio Palumbo, Megan E. Morales, Angela Thornton, JN Cameron, and David Simon

Made in Britain

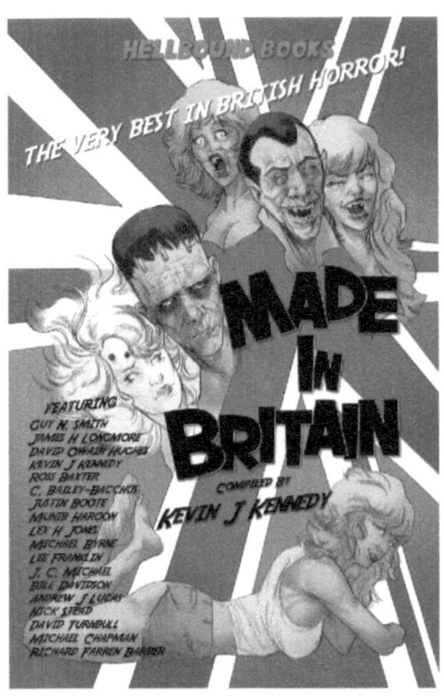

There is something quite special about this fine collection of tales of terror from the Sceptered Isle, each and every one crafted in the dead of the night by twisted, fevered minds, who have brought crawling and slithering to life the darkest denizens of the blackest shadows to terrify those brave souls amongst you who are brave enough to read...

For your delectation, Dear Reader, we have assembled together between these illustrious covers an array of the finest British authors writing today:

Guy N. Smith, James H Longmore, David Owain Hughes, Kevin J Kennedy, Ross Baxter, C. Bailey-Bacchus, Justin Boote, Munib Haroon, Lex H Jones, Michael Byrne, Lee Franklin, J. C. Michael, Bill Davidson, Andrew J Lucas, Nick Stead, David Turnbull, Michael Chapman, Richard Farren Barber

Mother Legs

A giant, telepathic spider befriends a small boy, seeing the world through his eyes, with murderous intent... When Blake Turner's addict mother disappears in rural Canada, he assumes she's simply relapsed. But, when his search for her uncovers evidence of a terrifying monster and the sinister conspiracy to hide its existence, he must decide just how far he is willing to go to protect his loved ones. With only a depressed park ranger and a local reporter to aid him, Blake delves deeper into the mystery to discover what the creature is, and why it wants to start a family.

Take Me

An intense, steamy thriller set in the brutal world of human trafficking

Adriana Santos, a fearless, idealistic young police officer on beach patrol, interrupts the sale of a young Mexican girl into slavery.

Adriana goes undercover to break up the human trafficking ring, a mission complicated by a the vicious serial killer 'Juan the Ripper'" who stalks the streets of central Texas and brutally murders young Mexican prostitutes.

In Corpus Christi, Adriana is kidnapped, her partner left for dead. She struggles to establish a relationship her captor, both feeling a strong mutual attraction. In her quest to help the girls that are held captive, Adriana causes trouble with her captor's ruthless boss, and despite their disagreements, she and her captor must learn to work together to survive.

Twerk

Desire, a spark, a decision made too fast (in haste), and a Las Vegas stripper is plunged into the depraved world of a psychopath. But is she the only target of his twisted desires?

A regular Sunday night in a Las Vegas strip club is rocked when a local oddball dies mysteriously, during a private dance. Amber falls immediately in lust with the hot paramedic who arrives, and follows him outside, anticipating sizzling romance. But, her casual encounter quickly descends into a terrifying, twisted nightmare from which she is unable to escape.

Five days later, and it's Lana's next shift at the club; she's a fly-in-fly-out stripper paying her way through law school - she's also Amber's best friend.

Where is Amber? And what about the dead client? Was it an accident? Suicide? Or murder?

Finding neither the police, nor the club are taking much interest, Lana conducts her own inquiries, even though she finds herself the victim of a social-media hate campaign, and an ex-boyfriend who is sending her death threats. She's desperate to uncover the truth about the death, but the person she most needs to speak to is Amber, who has failed to show up for her shift yet again...Lana is thrust into a web of lies and deceptions she is determined to unravel, in which everyone is a suspect.

An addictively dark, psychological thriller laced with steamy romance, mystery, action and suspense; Twerk exposes the working lives of Las Vegas strippers behind the glamor - the challenges, the rewards, and the deadly risks.

**A HellBound Books LLC
Publication**

http://www.hellboundbookspublishing.com

Printed in the United States of America